PINE MANOR COLLEGE

ANNENBERG LIBRARY
AND
COMMUNICATIONS
CENTER

A Gift of
The Raymond and Adelaide
McCracken '44 Wean, Jr. Fund

Dracula's Crypt

Bram Stoker, 1906 (Bram Stoker, *Personal Reminiscences of Henry Irving* [New York: Macmillan, 1906], 1:321).

Dracula's Crypt

Bram Stoker, Irishness, and the Question of Blood

JOSEPH VALENTE

UNIVERSITY OF ILLINOIS PRESS
Urbana and Chicago

Library of Congress Cataloging-in-Publication Data
Valente, Joseph.
Dracula's crypt : Bram Stoker, Irishness, and the question of
blood / Joseph Valente.
p. cm.
Includes bibliographical references (p.) and index.
ISBN 0-252-02696-9 (cloth : alk. paper)
1. Stoker, Bram, 1847–1912. Dracula. 2. Stoker, Bram,
1847–1912—Knowledge—Ireland. 3. National characteris-
tics, Irish, in literature. 4. Horror tales, English—History and
criticism. 5. Dracula, Count (Fictitious character).
6. Ireland—In literature. 7. Vampires in literature. 8. Blood in
literature. I. Title.
PR6037.T617D7894   2002
823'.8—dc21   2001001897

For my son, Matthew,
during whose young life this book took shape

Contents

Acknowledgments   ix
Abbreviations   xi

Introduction: More Irish Than the Irish *Dracula*   1

1. Double Born   15
2. "The Dualitists": Prelude to *Dracula*   42
3. The Metrocolonial Vampire   51
4. Double Agents   84
5. Beyond Blood: Defeating the Inner Vampire   121

Notes   145
Index   165

Acknowledgments

My greatest debt, as always, is to my wife, Joanne Slutsky, for her intellectual and emotional support and her editorial and technical assistance.

A close second is the debt owed my mother, who instilled in me the desire to read, and my father, who instilled in me the discipline needed to write.

I am particularly grateful to my colleagues Amanda Anderson and Stephanie Foote for their intellectual generosity, displayed yet again in their astute and encouraging commentary on this work while it was in progress.

A special thanks to John Paul Ricquelme for his extensive and invaluable editorial and critical suggestions.

I am also deeply indebted to Molly Anne Rothenberg for her psychoanalytic insight, which had a shaping influence over certain aspects of this study.

I am likewise indebted to Vicki Mahaffey, who taught me most of what I know about Irishness.

Special thanks, finally, to Marjorie Howes.

My work has also benefited beyond measure from intellectual exchange on various topics with Celeste Langan, Marjorie Levenson, Athena Vrettos, Cheryl Herr, Colleen Lamos, Jean-Michel Rabate, Tim Dean, Derek Attridge, John Bishop, Christine Van-Boheeman, Robert Spoo, Brandon Kershner, Garry Leonard, Chris Lane, Jim Hurt, Bill Maxwell, Julia Walker, Mark Wollaeger, David Lloyd, Jed Esty, Janet Lyon, Gregory Castle, Anne Fogarty, and Geoff Harpham.

For his encouragement of the project, I would like to thank Willis Regier.

For research suggestions, I thank August Gering, William Brockman, Simon Joyce, and Zohreh Sullivan.

I would also like to thank the Newberry Library in Chicago for a Mellon Fellowship that gave me access not only to some important research materials but also to the bracing and truly delightful intellectual company of the year 2000 seminar fellows.

Finally, heartfelt gratitude and appreciation to the late Ted Irving, my honors English professor, without whom I might well be doing something less interesting.

Abbreviations

D   Bram Stoker, *Dracula,* ed. Nina Auerbach and David Skal, Norton Critical Edition (New York: Norton, 1997).

ED   Bram Stoker, *The Essential Dracula: The Definitive Annotated Edition of Bram Stoker's Classic Novel,* ed. Leonard Wolf (New York: Penguin, 1993).

NPH   Bram Stoker, "The Necessity for Political Honesty," auditor's *Address to the Trinity College Historical Society,* first meeting, twenty-eighth session, November 13, 1872.

Dracula's Crypt

Introduction:
More Irish Than the Irish *Dracula*

The decade of the Irish *Dracula* ended in 2000. After a spate of historical exegesis, in which Bram Stoker's masterwork emerged as an all-purpose allegory for a series of distinct contemporary discourses on the state of the British people and society (degeneration theory, reverse colonialism, criminal anthropology, inversion theory, and the like), attention has increasingly focused upon the specific relevance of Stoker's homeland to his most famous literary creation—partly in the hope of finding a framework within which these disparate glosses might finally coalesce. Biographical tomes such as Barbara Belford's *Bram Stoker* (1996) and Peter Haining and Peter Tremayne's *The Un-Dead* (1997) have exhumed and autopsied the Irish ancestors of the vampire legends resurrected in Stoker's fiction.[1] New editions of *Dracula*, such as *The Essential Dracula* (*ED*; 1993) and the Norton Critical Edition (*D*; 1997) turn the implicit Irish dimension of the text into an explicit if desultory theme of the textual apparatus. Meanwhile, literary scholars have begun to develop the novel's seemingly lateral Irish references along the lines of racial and national allegory. Beginning with Stephen D. Arata's postcolonial tour de force, "The Occidental Tourist: Stoker and Reverse Colonization" (1990), and continuing with articles by Cannon Schmitt (1994), Chris Morash (1995), David Glover (1995), Seamus Deane (1997), and Michael Valdez Moses (1997), *Dracula* has been wrested from its anomalous place in the margins of the English canon and certified to be Hibernian in its roots, its rhetoric, and, less systematically, its referents.[2]

While promising an "epistemological break" in *Dracula* scholarship, however, the Irish approach has remained heavily mortgaged to the British historicist model that preceded it. On the one hand, the cited essays display a shared confidence in the underlying assumption that despite Stoker's avowed, though unorthodox, Irish nationalism, his racial politics were finally essentialistic and Anglo-supremacist, consistent with the "racial science" of his time and committed to conserving the racial stock responsible for Britain's cultural advancement and political dominance. As Jeffrey Richards puts it, in an ambiguously blunt formulation, "Stoker's romances are finally set in a context of belief in and support for the British empire and the Anglo-Saxon race."[3] On the other hand, following in the wake of so many "regional" constructions of *Dracula,* in which synecdoches of the novel parade as similes (*Dracula* as . . . urban Gothic, queer drama, Oedipal myth, capitalist allegory, reform novel, etc.),[4] these essays betray a shared insecurity over the potential reductiveness of their own symbolic grids and translations—or the Irish "line" generally—for some hypothetically totalized reading of the text.

David Glover articulates most precisely this tension between settled premise and uncertain consequence: "Though shot through with Irish references, *Dracula*'s horror ultimately eludes the deftness of allegory, spilling out in too many directions to be contained by any single racial logic. Indeed . . . the novel reveals the multiplicity of forms that the ideology of degeneration could take."[5] Glover begins by conceding the irreducibility of *Dracula*'s textual excess and the "horror" it portrays to any "single racial logic" only to turn around and fold the novel's "multiplicity of forms" back into the "single racial logic" that has haunted most of the Hibernian allegories of *Dracula,* the elite, fin de siècle obsession with "degeneration."[6] That is to say, Glover presumes that *Dracula* allegorizes the perceived late-imperial menace to existing demarcations of racial superiority and subalternity, he situates the Irish subtext of the novel as a medium for delimiting and negotiating that menace, and he openly questions the capacity of his own Irish analogy to comprehend that menace in its various ramifications. Much influenced by Glover's approach, Michael Valdez Moses's dense reading of *Dracula* against the backdrop of contemporary Anglo-Irish politics is informed by the same mode of critical disavowal: he repeatedly identifies Count Dracula with a particular national figure (Charles Stewart Parnell), a broader ethnic and class grouping (his violent Celtic-Catholic minions), and a specific political ideology (physical force Irish nationalism), only to admit that the vampire's "composite" construction and "polymorphous" capacities exceed these identifications, which he nonetheless continues to advance.[7] With this type of gesture, the Irish *Dracula* school pays its debt to the critical heritage at large in legitimate doubts about its own sufficiency, without finally theorizing those doubts or incorporating them into a more historically capacious account.

My contention, in contrast, is that the same sociopolitical context that warrants an Irish take on *Dracula* demands a more decisive break from the inherited paradigms of the novel and, in turn, some radically different deductions about its racial and national politics. This new departure does not entail treating *Dracula* as more authentically Irish in any traditional nationalist sense: that is, as a Celtic- (or Gaelic-) identified rather than an Anglo-Saxonist text, as a subaltern rather than a creole text, as a text of colonial resistance and self-invention rather than one of imperial adventure or settler anxiety.[8] Such an inversion of existing practice would only restore, on other terms, the unilateral racial logic that the Irish school has rightly suspected in itself. Instead, the Irishness of *Dracula* should be read and understood in light of what I call its *metrocolonial conditions of production,* which function at both the collective level, shaping the cultural and political identity of the Irish people, and at the individual level, giving a peculiar slant to the psychic terrain of Stoker himself.

For centuries, the Anglo-Protestant settlers of Ireland, unlike their peers in India, Jamaica, or Hong Kong, identified themselves as national subjects of their adopted homeland, as the Irish, in short. By the late eighteenth century, however, the bulk of this population, unlike their Anglo peers in America and Australia, elected to sue not for separation from but for reintegration with the metropolitan state of Great Britain. And with the Act of Union in 1800, it succeeded. Ireland ceased to be a distinct if colonized geopolitical entity and assumed the unique and contradictory position of a domestic or "metropolitan" colony, at once a prized if troublesome colonial possession and a despised but active constituent of the greatest metropole on earth, the United Kingdom. From that point in time until the founding of the Free State (1922), the Irish people at large found themselves at once agents and objects, participant-victims as it were, of Britain's far-flung imperial mission—in short, a "metrocolonial people."[9]

The self-division thus inflicted upon the collective identity of the Irish people roughly corresponded to the ethnic division of status and authority that already existed within Ireland. Members of the Anglo-Protestant minority, their self-identification as Irish notwithstanding, mainly participated and profited in the administration of empire, both at "home" and

abroad, while members of the Gaelic or Celtic majority suffered their connection to the British empire as a bitter subjugation, notwithstanding their
participation in many British cultural and political institutions, customs,
and practices. In Stoker's case, however, even this deeply compromised line
of ethno-national division was effaced. For Stoker was not a standard issue middle-class Anglo-Irish Protestant, as has been almost universally
imagined, but an interethnic Anglo-Celt and hence a member of a conquering and a conquered race, a ruling and a subject people, an imperial and
an occupied nation.[10] As these items suggest, the metrocolonial condition,
of which Stoker's subject position was an extreme and therefore exemplary case, names an uneasy social and psychic space between authority, agency, and legitimacy on one side and abjection, heteronomy, and hybridity
on the other. Accordingly, it conditions a peculiar economy of desire wherein individual subjects are defined, in analogous but often divergent ways,
by the simultaneous enactment and betrayal of their conflicting cultural
identifications. If, as George Stocking Jr. has convincingly argued, "there
was a close articulation, both experiential and ideological, between the
domestic and the colonial spheres of otherness," the formations of a domestic or a metropolitan colony, both experiential and ideological, were
inevitably caught in the netting.[11]

Because the generative matrix of Stoker's literary authorship was thus
doubly inscribed and doubly motivated (both and neither metropolitan/
colonial, imperialist/irredentist, etc.), the veiled symbolic references to this
condition in *Dracula,* its en-crypted Irishness, amounts to something *crucially different* than just another unitary allegorical framework baffled by
the textual excess of the novel. *Dracula*'s Irishness functions instead as the
privileged vehicle of that excess, a point of reference that is always other
than itself; continually remarked as such, it necessarily breaks the frame
of allegory or, to be more precise, it constitutes an always already effract-
ed allegory. Instead of a coherent design that shades into multiple inde-
terminacies, as Moses suggests,[12] the Irish *Dracula* represents something
like a *coherent indeterminacy,* a semiotic space doubling and dividing
against itself, obeying what Jacques Lacan calls the logic of the *vel,* "more
than one and not quite two."[13] As detailed analysis bears out, every prominent Irish motif in *Dracula* splits internally along the metrocolonial fault
lines surveyed herein and shivers into opposed yet overlapping ethnic
significations, class associations, partisan connotations, and sectarian resonances. The writing of Ireland, *Dracula* attests, is in itself a writing across
or between—not within—distinct racial and even political logics. To read

Dracula, accordingly, is to read across or between, to inter-view, these manifold logics.

My revisionist Hibernian reading takes a still more decisive swerve from the established courses of *Dracula* scholarship than do its predecessors. For it implies that the specifically Irish elements in the novel—far from simply voicing or reaffirming the pervasive late Victorian/Edwardian panic at the prospect of racial degeneration, atavism, and intermixing—serve to modulate *Dracula's* central metaphorics of blood into a spectacular if less than fully systematic critique of this racialist logic and its attendant illogic, racialist paranoia. Whereas the prevailing "Irish" reading has been that "the spectre of bad blood and degeneration evoked in *Dracula's* imaginary terrains and sinister inhabitants always refers back to an anxiety about the health and vigor of the race," a more nuanced explication of Stoker's Irishness helps to identify the real "spectre" or threat delineated in *Dracula* as racialized anxiety itself.[14]

In making this case, my interpretive premises diverge in a number of significant respects from those shared by the main exponents of the Irish (and the English) *Dracula.* For one thing, I break with the custom of taking the novel's point of view as substantially identified with or sympathetic to its vampire-busting protagonists. I see the men neither as "heroes" nor as "righteous voices" combating a virulent evil by which they are sometimes, and adventitiously, corrupted.[15] To my mind, the cleverness of Stoker's narrative method consists in striking an unstably ironic attitude toward his characters' moral and political assumptions, sentiments, and dispositions, even while maintaining a certain patina of the righteous and the heroic about them. To sift the nuances of this posture, behind the first person accounts, I extend full credit and patient attention to the ambivalent effects of the novel's subtly calibrated narrative and symbolic arrangement. Whereas previous criticism has discovered in *Dracula* a more or less univocally conservative racial politics, blunted and blurred by stylistic and structural incoherence, I find a carefully wrought stylistic and structural complexity that enacts a more tentative and progressive ideology.

This is in part to say that I read *Dracula* by the lights of the "high" literary culture to which Stoker aspired rather than the codes of the popular fiction to which his work has largely been relegated. I see *Dracula* as consciously adopting the kind of sophisticated, post-impressionistic strategies of representation that have signaled, for generations of readers, the aesthetically serious complexity of early modernist artists such as Ford, Conrad, and the young James Joyce and have distinguished them from the practitioners of popular fiction, including Stoker himself.[16] At their heart, such strategies generally comprise a taut, ironic oscillation between discrepant levels and modes of being in the world: an intensively subjective or privatized immediacy of experience aligned with unreliable hero-narrators (Stephen Dedalus, Marlowe, John Dowell) and a more distanced critical reflection, implicit in the narrative structure itself, on the phantasmatic roots and distorting ideological conditions of that immediate experience.

In his prefatory note to *Dracula,* Stoker announces his contribution to this literary hermeneutics of suspicion and does so in just the stylistic register, muted irony, that his modernist successors would come to privilege. What is introduced, of course, is a strange tale mainly drawn from the personal diary and journal entries of several parties to the vampiric ordeal and from private correspondence confiding the romantic sentiments and amorous experiences of Dracula's two female victims. The propagating of such an improbable, yet elemental, narrative out of personal impressions recorded in peculiarly intimate or interiorized scenes of writing indexes the decisive importance of unconscious desire and fantasy in the story's construction and calls its evidentiary status into question. When Mina Harker wonders, "Did [her husband] get his brain fever, and then write all these things down or had he some cause for it all" (*D* 161), she poses an unanswerable question ("I shall never know"; 161) that could easily be adapted to every one of the accounts, including her own, and is seconded late in the novel by Jack Seward: "I sometimes think we must all be mad and that we shall wake to sanity in strait-waistcoats" (240). Stoker's opening note is, in rhetorical form, an assurance of the tale's clear-eyed veracity, which he predicates directly upon the proximity of the documentation presented and the events reported: "All needless matters have been eliminated, so that a history almost at variance with the possibilities of later-day belief may stand forth as simple fact. There is throughout no statement of past things wherein memory may err, for all the records chosen are exactly contemporary" (5). But Stoker immediately proceeds to tease out a logical corollary of this state of affairs, which is bound to consume all assurance: "given from the standpoints and within the range of knowledge of those who made them" (5). Stoker here invokes a well-established literary convention for authorizing narrative fictions as historical facts, the so-called "found document," only to turn it to diametrically opposed ends, casting doubts upon the reliability of such documents, even while affirming their authenticity. To avoid risking the errors of memory, Stoker implies, is to leave in place other no less weighty sources of error: the bias of the eyewitnesses' "standpoints" and the limits of their "range of knowledge"—it is to avoid the *corrective* of precisely that "later-day belief" to which Stoker slyly pitches his appeal. Understood in these terms, the opening note carries a legible admonition *against* conferring undue authority on the hero-narrators of the novel, that is, against confusing or conflating their perspective with that of the author. Moreover, the poker-faced reference to the editorial collation and selection of the records is plainly designed to reinforce this warning by directing the reader's consideration to possibilities of narrative intervention that could only make a difference owing to the *structural divergence* of the act of telling from the acts told, and hence to the absence of anything like "simple fact."

This last point is especially important inasmuch as the Irish school critics of *Dracula* have reposed their faith in the vampire fighters' viewpoint on structural rather than personal grounds. That is to say, they have not generally found Seward, Jonathan Harker, Professor Van Helsing, and the others to possess practical acumen, analytical skill, political sensitivity, or ethical integrity worthy of admiration. To the contrary, these critics have generally treated Stoker's band of heroes as fairly typical middle-class metropolitan elites suffering the erosion of the Victorian domestic and imperialist order at the fin de siècle and responding with a powerful, often bizarre mixture of social assertion and anxiety, fantasy and phobia, played out in the overlapping registers of class, gender, and ethnicity, or "blood." But they have also taken Stoker to occupy a subject position similar to that of his heroes, to possess a like economy of self-interest and self-estimation, to share their ideological propensities and pathologies, and to identify with them strongly as a result.[17] The effect of this presupposition, tenaciously held, is to filter out the text's ironies as incidental to its conservative, even "pre-fascist" reflection of the late Victorian Anglo-professional Imaginary. In short, the presumed continuity of Stoker's viewpoint with that of his characters is but a particular version of the assumed continuity of Stoker's writerly mindset and sensibility with a certain social and discursive context. To put the matter less charitably, the allegorical force of Stoker's heroes has often been determined by turning Stoker himself into an allegory, a type of his age and his society.[18]

Under this set of cultural studies premises, *Dracula* itself comes to stand as a collective mode of symbolic enunciation, to constitute a vehicle of racial and cultural identity politics *avant le lettre*. The critics of the Irish *Dracula* have all but acknowledged as much, treating the novel not just as popular literature—literature for a mass audience—but as popular fantasy as well, the dreamwork of an entire community with whom Stoker has been identified. Thus, Cannon Schmitt analyzes the Gothic thriller as a collective creole nightmare of racial immersion, that is, as a text that registers the apocalyptic anxieties of embattled Anglo-Irish subjectivity *as such*.[19] Michael Valdez Moses and Bruce Stewart likewise construe the vampire narrative as a collective Anglo-Irish "dream" brooding upon the specter of nationalist violence and the Ascendancy's resulting loss of place (standing/land).[20] Despite his awareness of Stoker's "split identification," Stephen D. Arata takes the novel to voice a collective metropolitan fantasy of "reverse colonialism," the infiltration of the British homeland, the corruption of British culture, and the resulting subversion of British rule by supposedly inferior, subdominant peoples.[21]

David Glover once again summarizes the general thrust of this body of scholarship in a statement of his critical method: to unpack the novel's symbolic treasure trove according to the Freudian logic of a dream or fantasy, while eschewing the long dominant "psychobiographical" approach to *Dracula* in favor of a broader social analysis.[22] Stoker's novels, Glover asserts, offer themselves as "public and primarily conscious fantasies."[23] This formula bears at least two correlative significations: they are fantasies consciously arranged by Stoker for public (largely British) consumption and they encode the fantasies emerging from British public consciousness. True to his announced conception, Glover in *Vampires, Mummies, and Liberals* not only regards *Dracula* in the light of contemporary sociopolitical obsessions and the discourses that articulated them, a germinal and useful project, but he also actually cedes center stage to these tributary discourses (particularly tracts on the dangers of racialized degeneration and criminality to British dominance), which the symbolic framework of *Dracula* is seen to draw upon and integrate, rather than to engage, undermine, or resist. Taking the characteristic principles of Irish *Dracula* studies to their logical extreme, Glover treats the "characteristic forms and devices" of the novel exclusively as "evidence of the deadlock and unresolved problems of the society in which [Stoker] lived." By insisting on what Stoker importantly rejects, a decidable relation between aesthetic representations and their surrounding contexts, Glover underestimates the opportunities such contradictory circumstances afford a text like *Dracula* to "write back" against the ideological regime on which it nonetheless continues to rely.[24]

Two problems with the cultural studies itinerary in Irish *Dracula* scholarship stand out, one historical and one theoretical, and together they help me to specify further, *via negativa,* the terms and stakes of my dissent. The historical problem centers on the question of Stoker's subject position and its implications in establishing the constituency whose sociocultural fantasies might be articulated in his novel. The Hibernian school of criticism has displayed some confidence that *Dracula* can be housed within the Anglo-Protestant Gothic tradition exemplified by Sheridan Le Fanu and given scholarly currency by Victor Sage.[25] The consensus upon which the so-called Irish *Dracula* has largely been constructed is that the novel's dense and sometimes unruly allegorical dynamics express the concerns, register the anxieties, and even mythologize the struggle of an increasingly beleaguered hegemonic group, the Anglo-Protestant garrison, whose members were vainly striving to secure the borders of their collective identity against the nightmare of political violence and abandonment, the terror of racial absorption, and that "spectre of bad blood and degeneration." In this family of readings, the encrypted Irish references of the novel are disposed, with sophistication and frequent qualification, into bipolar constellations of resilient heroic *virtu* and uncanny occult power, each carrying distinct ethnic and sectarian associations.

As I elaborate in chapter 1, Stoker qualifies neither as a proper Anglo-Irishman nor as a slightly compromised metropolitan elite. His ambiguous class station growing up—middle-class respectability without middle-class affluence—combined with his doubly hybrid or "immixed" ethno-national status—what I have called Anglo-Celtic—made Stoker a highly improbable conduit for the cultural fantasies of the ruling groups cited, according to the criteria of the very identity politics that would underwrite such an analysis. In fact, given his interlineal identity, at home neither in the cultural center nor in the cultural margins, Stoker cannot be said to have met those criteria with respect to *any* clearly and closely demarcated social constituency of his time. *Dracula* is Stoker's greatest work in part because it registers this undecidability in a structural ambivalence, even skepticism, toward the racial distinctions, social hierarchies, and political assumptions that inform the Anglo-Irish literary heritage to which it is so often annexed. Rather than simply adopting the characteristic generic template of that heritage, the Gothic, Stoker extends the duality endemic to that form from the level of the motif or symbolic element, where binary oppositions take hold, to the level of the narrative and symbolic logic itself. He thereby succeeds in troubling such binaries and the ideological attitudes they support.

With the interrogation of these attitudes, however, an entirely different and still wider form of representativeness ultimately accrues to Stoker's writing, one that espouses no ethos or politics of identity, but rather one of doubleness or alterity: the undecidable otherness of *every* single person to the particular collective(s) and context(s) in which they nevertheless belong. Stoker was, if you like, quintessentially Irish in the metrocolonial sense: his was, in Luce Irigaray's terminology, "an identity which is not one," that does not conform to the logic of identity itself. Yet, for that very reason, it afforded him expressive access to a generally representative form of *social* identity as such.

Owing to the ambiguity of his ethnic, class, and national status, and the corresponding ambivalence of what the Lacanians would call his "symbolic mandate," Stoker had difficulty forgetting a lesson that contemporary cultural/Irish studies badly needs to remember: whatever one's identity formation, there is always something left over, an alterity that exceeds and resists the sum of the positive social determinations of one's being. To be sure, this residuum is itself socially inflected in its excess and resistance, but exceed and resist it does nonetheless, and in so doing, it marks the difference between static classifiable identity and dynamic human subjectivity. At the same time, it renders such subjectivity finally illegible from within as well as without, so that we remain, in Julia Kristeva's phrase, "strangers to ourselves."[26] The psychobiographical name or locus of this residuum is, of course, the unconscious, and inasmuch as any fantasy, including Stoker's Irish fantasy, presupposes a subjectivity so defined, Glover's notion of fully public, primarily conscious fantasies amounts to a contradiction in terms. It is in the very nature of fantasy to move along culturally scripted paths, allowing its subject to occupy different social roles and positions, and yet to remain finally bound by the singular psychic history and economy from which it proceeds. As such, the movement of the phantasmatic exemplifies the kind of undecidable relationship that *Dracula* thematizes between psychic apprehensions, including self-apprehensions, and their potentiating contexts.

To treat *Dracula* as a fantasy on its own terms, then, one must fashion a necessarily abrasive and unstable synthesis of psychobiographical and cultural studies approaches to the novel. This will be the methodological aim of my study. Conjoining these differing modes and levels of assessment will extend the historical relocation project undertaken by the Irish *Dracula* school from the novel's objects of reference to its strategy of representation and from the cultural universe the novel encounters to the nature of the engagement. Most importantly, this strategy involves interpreting

Dracula not as a symptomatic reflex of its social and discursive milieu but as a *peculiarly situated and motivated response* to that milieu, an exteriorization of Stoker's residual, partly efficacious, often unconscious resistance to his own sociocultural determination.

Now as Slavoj Žižek has emphasized, from a psychoanalytic point of view this exteriorization of significant resistance, what he calls "the meaning" of the dream or fantasy, inheres not in its content, manifest *or* latent, but in its syntax, its peculiar narrative and symbolic disposition, precisely the aspect of Stoker's Gothic fantasy that has been given short shrift.[27] Instead of focusing primarily on how the cultural context of *Dracula* shaped its content, broadly construed, I pay equal attention to how the novel's layered structure, its peculiar textual circuitry, resists and reworks that cultural context. Instead of assuming that a phantasmagoric vampire tale heavily freighted with class and racial anxieties automatically carries and transmits the contemporary preoccupation with blood as a signifier of identity, I will examine where and how the arrangement of this freight functions to subvert the (ideo)logic of that contagion (not only with reference to the Irish other but, perhaps more surprisingly, with reference to the Jewish other as well).

By thus reading *Dracula* against the grain of its time and the criticism of today—in part by returning intensively to the textual specifics of *Dracula*—we will discover in Stoker's manipulation of the Ireland-Transylvania analogy a paradoxically noble, *socially minded* gesture of *personal* wish fulfillment: an effort to break with the pervasive blood consciousness of fin de siècle Britain as a means of allaying the status anxiety he had long suffered on its account. So concerted is this effort in *Dracula*, in fact, that it harbors an implicit critique of the racial ideology underpinning the larger imperialist project that Stoker endorses elsewhere. Conversely, keeping Stoker's status anxiety in mind will enable us to read in his narrative engagements with current racial thought and classification something other than the familiar mix of fascination and loathing of the exotic stranger: the sense that our response to the alien involves a tortuous attempt to discharge or reconcile the otherness within ourselves. Finally, by crediting *Dracula* with the sort of motivated aesthetic distance typically reserved for supposedly "serious" literary efforts, we will discover a burden unsuspected and even actively excluded by the Irish school: that *blood does not matter at all,* and to think otherwise is to think like a vampire.

One final note on the structure of this revisionist account. Certain critics who have spotted the Irishness of *Dracula* have elected to analyze the novel in the light of Stoker's earlier and more explicitly Irish novel, *The Snake's Pass*, on the grounds of their common frame of historical reference.[28] I have elected instead to examine *Dracula* in the light of other works— specifically his first piece of longer fiction, *The Primrose Path*, his most complexly elaborated shorter fiction, "The Dualitists; or, The Death Doom of the Double Born," his manifestic autobiographical vignette, "The Voice of England," and his spectacular intellectual debut, "The Necessity for Political Honesty" (his 1872 *Address to the Historical Society of Trinity College*)—all of which not only share *Dracula*'s Irish frame of reference but also anticipate in some measure the recursive logic that *Dracula* deploys and the problem of Irishness demands. As with my methodological tactics, I again propose to reverse the curious privilege that content has enjoyed in *Dracula* criticism over matters of rhetorical and aesthetic technique.

But there is an additional issue at stake. *The Snake's Pass* substantially adheres to the generic conventions of the "metropolitan marriage," an Anglocentric framework for projecting gendered, hierarchically disposed stereotypes of Englishness and Irishness under the sign of a harmonious reconciliation of the two lands and peoples. While Stoker's use of this framework necessarily amounted to an ideological gesture, with unmistakably racialist/Celticist implications, it was *primarily* an act of literary apprenticeship. By transposing what had become a popular stage form, which Stoker witnessed as both drama critic and theater manager, into a map for charting the narrative course of a first novel, Stoker was less intent upon encoding a political message than establishing that basic formal mastery necessary to any future innovation.[29] It is worth noting in this regard that the stage-minded Stoker regularly took up the works of Dion Boucicault, Anglo-Ireland's most successful playwright, as sources for his Irish fiction. "The Dualitists" riffs on *The Corsican Brothers*, which Stoker had helped to produce five years earlier. Boucicault's *The Phantom* supplied the subject matter of *Dracula*, which Stoker desperately petitioned Henry Irving to put on the boards. And *The Snake's Pass* closely derives its allegorical plotline from Boucicault's most famous and formulaic Irish offerings, *The Colleen Bawn* and *The Shaughraun*, particularly the latter, which could, with certain details altered, easily stand as a stage version of Stoker's novel.[30]

Precisely owing to the conventional limits that *The Snake's Pass* derives from its Boucicaultian models, it turns out to be a less useful and reliable guide to the sophisticated representational strategies of *Dracula* than the less programmatically determined Irish pieces that I emphasize in my commentary. And because these borrowed limits were coextensive with an equally conventional deployment of English and Irish types, *The Snake's Pass* also proves a less useful and reliable gloss on the politics of blood in *Dracula* than those other works, each of which anticipates, in some measure, that novel's underlying antiessentialism, its vision of Irishness as a fundamentally mixed and mobile identity formation.[31]

This crucial ideological divergence leaves its imprint not just on the content of the respective bodies of work but also on their basic narrative orientation and trajectory. The metropolitan marriage comedy sees an English soldier (*The Shaughraun*), settler (*The Colleen Bawn*), or tourist (*The Snake's Pass*) engage a native, exoticized Irish girl on her home turf, her stationary life-posture standing for her relatively unitary and organic, because premodern, ethno-national identity. My alternative genealogy of *Dracula*, like the novel itself, sets the Irish or Irish-identified figures themselves in transit, whether by way of incursion ("The Dualitists"), social-climbing emigration (*The Primrose Path*), or both ("The Voice of England," *Dracula*), the movement correlating in each case with the itinerant and transferential nature of an identity demarcated along and across metrocolonial lines. Given how far Stoker's own immixed ethnic origins, restless parvenu ambition, and immigration to London combined to mold his self-conception, we should not be surprised to find his engagement with the question of Irishness in particular and blood in general to be registered most acutely and profoundly in this less domesticated line of Hibernian narrative.[32]

I

Double Born

The Anglo-Celt

My reassessment of *Dracula's* Irishness must begin with a recalibration of Stoker's authorial subject position. For his ethnic, sectarian, and class status, or the predominant construction thereof, has typically been invoked to anchor the thesis that the novel expresses, entertains, and finally works to contain fears over the decline or disturbance of Anglo-Saxon hegemony. In order to perform this function, however, the reigning profile of Stoker has tended to flatten the contours of his Irishness. Stoker has generally been regarded as a member in good standing of the creole Anglo-Protestant garrison class in Ireland: a man of English ancestry on both sides of his family whose social intimacies, cultural sympathies, preferred creative genres, and institutional affiliations linked him closely with the Ascendancy.[1] In this light, his permanent residency among London society would likely seem both an active assertion and a practical index of his aggressively Anglo-Saxon (though not necessarily English) self-conception. Such an identification would have necessarily involved a disassociation from the imperialist stereotype of the native Celt or "mere" Irish as brutish, wild, backward, improvident, childish, indolent, feminine, lawless, and violent.

In fact, Stoker's ethnic origins and social inscription were a good deal more complicated than this portrait of West Britonism suggests. Because they were stoutly Church of Ireland, Stoker and his family were eligible for a wide range of sectarian advantages, but they were by no means members of the Ascendancy, or even of the true bourgeoisie, to whom their professional-managerial aspirations must have seemed decidedly arriviste.

Moreover, only Stoker's father, a hapless functionary in Dublin Castle, could claim strictly Anglo-Saxon, or even British, descent. Stoker's mother grew up in the rural west of Ireland and hailed from the Galway Blakes on her distaff side—not, however, from the famous Norman Caddel family, renamed La Blaca and then Blake, but from *a native Irish family* whose original Connacht moniker was O Blathnhaic.[2] That Stoker himself came partly from Celtic stock, that he was an Anglo-Celtic rather than a traditionally Anglo-Irish subject, surely undercuts the popular position that Stoker substantially shared the anxiety of Anglo-Irish intellectuals like W. H. Lecky or imperialist politicians like Lord Salisbury at the prospect of Celtic racial pollution, atavism, or degeneration.[3] He was, after all, a stealth version of the sort of racial immixing that made such men uneasy. Moreover, that Stoker derived his Celtic blood from his mother casts serious doubt on Cannon Schmitt's argument that Count Dracula's maternal inversions are designed to register this particular anxiety—or at least places these inversions in a far more ambiguous psychosocial perspective.[4]

Using the very narrative means that would eventually earn Stoker accolades, his parents combined to transmit a sense of their subtle ethnic difference to their youngest son and thus to convert hybrid racial status into a dual cultural inheritance. During his long childhood convalescence from a mysterious and paralyzing ailment, Stoker's Anglo identifications and accompanying sense of racial entitlement were fostered on his father's heroic tales of the Williamite invasion of Ireland, which was thought to have first brought the Stokers across St. George's Channel in the person of a regimental officer.[5] During the same convalescence, his "so Irish" mother nurtured Stoker's nativist adherences on all manner of Irish myth, on Celtic folklore, and, most conspicuously, on macabre accounts of the Great Famine just passed, her experience of the 1832 cholera epidemic, including the flight of her family from Sligo, and the horrors of the Banshee, whose wail supposedly accompanied, among other things, the death of her Celtic mother.[6] Stoker's transferential identification with his mother's life history was probably heightened, retroactively, by the belief that his disabling childhood illness had resulted from contagion following in the potato famine's wake. In any event, the story form established itself from the outset of Stoker's conscious life as a *fundamental yet fundamentally indecisive* instrument of ethnic and cultural interpellation, a means of delimiting social identity and accommodating social difference simultaneously. His later creative efforts, accordingly, may well be seen to revisit the unresolved ambiguities haunting his ethno-national identity, especially since his generic preferences, heroic romance and Gothic macabre, so closely tracked those of his parents.[7]

His parents' narratives not only helped to quicken the ethnic uncertainty to which Bram Stoker was born but also impelled him to translate it as gender instability, in accordance with the imperialist sexual ethnology that came to maturity with him.[8] His father's tales specifically celebrated the ambition, adventurousness, and martial valor of Stoker's English forbears, their enactment of an aggressive, disciplined, and dominating ideal of masculinity, which was just then being consecrated, in a range of nascent academic fields (ethnography, anthropology, sexology, poetics, evolutionary history), as a characteristic racial inheritance of the Anglo-Saxons.[9] The influence and currency of that ideal can later be discerned both in Stoker's daily life, where his heroic exploits earned him the designation "muscular Christian" in a well-known London gossip column,[10] and in his greatest work, wherein every male protagonist, Dracula included, expressly subscribes to the "muscular" ethos of manhood and repeatedly measures himself and others by it. The tales of his mother, conversely, commemorated the domestic suffering and passive endurance of her Irish peasant compeers, their conformity with a patient and subservient ideal associated with femininity, a gender estate that was just then being posited, in the same academic disciplines, as a defining property of the native Irish.[11] The influence and currency of this feminine ideal can be discerned in Stoker's portrayal of his preeminent heroine, Mina Murray Harker, whose birth surname just happens to be of distinctively Irish origin.[12] These parental narratives thus expressed the subtle ethnic differences within the Stoker family in a starkly gendered division of virtue consonant with the long-standing allegory of the "metropolitan marriage"—between a manly John Bull and a hyperfeminine Erin—that had by midcentury begun to function as the symbolic frosting on the "scientific" cake.[13] Against this discursive background, the splitting of Stoker's identification between dissonant racial and cultural legacies could not but acquire considerable sexual energy and assume greater unconscious power on that basis.

Here we have the primal (discursive) scene, wherein the ethnic, historical, cultural, and psychosexual strains of Stoker's family romance intertwine and knot together a subject position of remarkable complexity and profound ambivalence. His parents' ancestral narratives provided an early private script of Stoker's origins, social station, and prospective course of development, which both straddled and encompassed the main racial categories of Hibernian life and, with them, different ranks of cultural and political distinction. Stoker was not interpellated to what Homi Bhabha has designated "colonial hybridity," a *borderline* condition of almost assimilable yet always radical otherness to the metropolitan norms it helps to secure.[14] He was rather interpellated to a still more compromised, more conflicted, and yet, for that very reason, less conspicuous and less pathologized cognate that I call metrocolonial immixture, an *agonistic* condition in which his affinity with the metropolitan (Anglo) center was assumed and even assured, but was at the same time shadowed (both troubled and exaggerated) by his continued connection with the colonial (Celtic) fringe.

Under these singular circumstances, a subject like Stoker is constrained to disavow (in the Freudian sense) a strain of his ethno-national heritage. He comes to regard that element of his ego formation as simultaneously an object of shame and an object of desire, but an object of danger in any case, menacing the subject from within. This psychosocial condition, the relationship of the subject with his own immixed otherness, closely resembles the vampiric condition in *Dracula*, the relationship of subject-victims with their undead emanation or doppelgänger. More than simply Irish, Dracula can be seen as the objectification of Stoker's own eccentric (peculiar/decentered) Irishness, a form of identity that both lacks and exceeds coherence or closure and so perpetually both desires and threatens itself.

This historical and biographical framework illuminates the relevance to *Dracula* of Slavoj Žižek's intuitively just analogy of the undead to the unconscious.[15] According to Žižek, both the undead and the unconscious bear the function of an intimate estrangement, mobilizing "species" of desire so proximate to their "author" that they cannot be contemplated save as alien forms of danger. What species of desire could be more proximate and more estranging than a desire that attaches to one's identity and thereby testifies to its lack or default? Not coincidentally, the feature of Stoker's narrative most amenable to Žižek's psychoanalytic analogy, the much discussed crossing of gender boundaries effected by Dracula's predations, also bears most heavily upon the ethno-national immixture of the Anglo-Celtic subject.[16]

Successively developed by such influential thinkers as Thomas Carlyle, Matthew Arnold, Charles Kingsley, and Thomas Hughes, the dominant late-Victorian conception of manhood hinged upon and honored the capacity to sustain the sovereign, autonomous, self-contained ego formation against all possible incursions or admixtures, endogenous or exogenous, on and across several ontological levels: the integrity of the body needed to be secured against its own passions and others' penetrations, and the stylizing of the male anatomy as a hard muscular bulwark symbolized and affirmed this imperative; the psyche must be secured against its own affective excesses and the emotional manipulation of others, and the ethos of hard-headed rational self-interest advanced this imperative; finally, the social group must be secured against its own corruption and the specter of alien infiltration or invasion, and the imagination of such a community as bound by shared self-discipline, troped in terms of manly leadership or even a collective "cultural" manhood, helped to shore up this imperative.[17] Indeed, the specifically psychoanalytic construct of the phallus, whose masculinist origins are roughly coeval with *Dracula*, speaks precisely to the fantasy of such perfectly achieved self-possession. In an age of imperialist triumphalism, doubt, and incipient decline, however, the specifically *racial* constitution of the individual or collective subject was seen either to enhance or vitiate this self-enclosing capacity, depending upon its own putatively masculine or feminine properties. Insofar as colonial hybridity is always, in the words of Robert J. C. Young, about "making sameness into difference" and "turning difference into sameness," it inevitably breaks the containment model of masculinity, particularly when the hybridized elements bear opposed gender affiliations (Anglo-masculine, Celtic-feminine).[18]

The same held true, *mutatis mutandis,* for Stoker's less conspicuous yet more conflicted brand of metrocolonial immixture, whose sexual aspect was correspondingly more occulted and therefore more anxiety inducing. Stoker's performance of his strong Anglo identification in terms of manly athleticism (he was a walking champion), heroic courage, and self-composure (he risked his life to save a drowning man)[19] was forever haunted by the remembered strains of a feminized Celtic legacy, replete with hysterical Banshees, that his mother rehearsed during his bout with childhood paralysis.[20] As a result, Stoker suffered with unusual, largely unconscious intensity the interanimation of the narcissism of masculine display, or *parade virile,* and the thrilling dread, the *frisson,* of feminization. Such dread acquires a positive cathexis, becomes a species of *frisson,* in part because it certifies that the cherished property, in this case manhood, is currently under threat and so is still in existence: the aversive surge of anxiety always carries an intoxicating sense that all is not lost.

It is this conflictual desire, not an "inverted" homoerotic impulse per se, that seizes Jonathan Harker in the famous seduction scene at Castle Dracula.[21] Remember, before Harker submits, with flirtatious half-closed eyes, to the phallic bite of the vampiress, he has already come to embrace a complexly sexualized yet sanitized image of his domestic confinement. In manly defiance of the Count's wishes, he relocates to "the portion of the Castle occupied [by women] in bygone days" (*D* 40), remarking appreciatively its pastel charms. He likens his diary keeping to the "love-letter" writing of "some fair lady" seated at the same "oak table" (40). Finally, in a covert transference with his fiancée, he again defies Dracula's warning manfully and sleeps "where of old ladies had sat and sung and lived sweet lives whilst their gentle breasts were sad for their menfolk away in the midst of remorseless wars" (41).

Just such an eroticized interdependency of virile display and (self-fulfilling) fears of feminization characterizes Jonathan Harker and his circle (Jack Seward, Professor Van Helsing, Lord Godalming, Quincy Morris) in their own "remorseless wars" with Dracula. On the one hand, the blood warriors invariably frame their pact and their struggle to rid the world of vampiric monstrosity as the very mark and test of their manhood. And in providing the real motive force for their apparent "self-devotion to a cause" (199), this narcissistic dedication to their own phallic authority and imperialist potency drives the group to display an indefatigable fortitude.

> "Your courage is your best help. . . . You are a man, and it is a man we want." (113)

> "A brave man's blood is the best thing on this earth when a woman is in trouble. You're a man, and no mistake. Well, the devil may war against us for all he's worth, but God sends us men when we want them." (136)

> He bore himself through it like a moral Viking. If America can go on breeding men like that, she will be a power in the world indeed. (156)

> That going down to the vault a second time was a remarkable piece of daring. . . . I was prepared to meet a good specimen of manhood. (199)

> "Brave boy. Quincy is all man and God bless him for it." (201)

> "We men are determined—nay are we not pledged?—to destroy this monster; but it is no part for a woman." (207)

> A brave man's hand can speak for itself. (210)

On the other hand, such obsessive concern with asserting and demonstrating their collective masculinity in the muscular mode betrays a deep-seated anxiety or want of self-confidence that is unmanly on its own terms and repeatedly issues in that most unmanly spectacle, the nervous or hysterical paroxysm. Upon finding the garlic flowers removed from Lucy Westenra's room, the group's leader, Van Helsing, "break[s] down" in a fit of "loud, dry sobs that seemed to come from the very racking of his heart" (123). Once again, upon Lucy's death, Van Helsing gives way to "a regular fit of hysterics," causing his lieutenant, Seward, "to be stern with him, as one is to a woman under the circumstances" (157). Subsequently, Lucy's fiancé, Lord Godalming, "grew quite hysterical" in "a perfect agony of grief" (203).

The heroism affected by these men always turns out to be fundamentally hysterical, then, while the hysteria affecting them always proves a spur to still greater heroism. Indeed, the highly volatile mixture of hysterical heroism and heroic hysteria forms the very essence of the masculine personality in *Dracula*. That is to say, Harker and his comrades neither fail nor succeed in compassing the manly norms or ideals of their age. Rather their *successful* performance of these mandates begins with and proceeds through an alienation in the feminine, which leaves the impress of *failure*; while their anxiety over being feminized, in announcing that their collective manhood is in danger and so not yet destroyed, stakes the possibility of recovery and ultimate success on the next heroic geste, the next act of splendid self-assertion.

The matrix for this dialectical contradiction, in which manhood is sustained in and through the feminization that undercuts it, lies precisely in Stoker's experience of a hyperbolic ethnic immixture allegorized chiefly along crossed gender lines. Far from simply affirming or apologizing for the femininity of his own Irishness, as Glover contends, Stoker's writing unfolds the gendered conflicts implicit in that distinctive Irishness, that amalgam of Anglo and Celtic adherences, and, in consequence, winds up troubling the normative disjunction of masculinity and femininity far more dramatically than the standard colonial inversion or exaggeration of these categories generally permits.[22] In fact, the reception of *Dracula*'s sexual politics, no less than its racial politics, stands in need of correction, and along substantially the same lines: the misogyny of Stoker's heroes, like their blood consciousness, does not simply relay the sentiments of a like-minded author, but focuses the ambivalence and elicits the irony of a man whose otherwise wholehearted embrace of conventional gender types and hierarchies was complicated by their metrocolonial application.

Domestic Cosmopolitanism

As Stoker graduated from the strictly private sphere of the family romance into the public romance of national politics, the limited visibility characteristic of metrocolonial immixture allowed him to consolidate a relatively elite Anglo-Irish niche for himself via a series of strategic institutional affiliations (Trinity College, its Historical Society and Philosophical Society, Dublin Castle, the *Dublin Evening Mail,* etc.). But Dublin's enclaves of Anglo-Irish privilege often served to catalyze rather than contain Stoker's ingrained sense and symptomatic expression of the other(ed) side of Irishness.

A popular student at the Anglo-Protestant bastion of Trinity College, Stoker seems to have made numerous friendships and contacts among the relatively small population interested in the various strands of Irish nationalism: he socialized with Isaac Butt, the notable lawyer and nationalist politician; he was solicited to join the Irish party by J. G. Smith MacNall; and he befriended Standish O'Grady, the father of the Irish cultural revival, who counseled Stoker to submit his collection of Irish short stories to Sampson Low.[23] A prominent member and officer in Trinity's most prestigious intellectual clubs, Stoker used these elect forums to voice not only a love of England and empire that was to last a lifetime but also the early stirrings of an Irish irredentism that was to crystallize in an equally enduring commitment to Home Rule.[24] In Historical Society debates, Stoker repeatedly voted against the dissolution and even the devolution of British imperial rule.[25] Yet he also repeatedly voted and spoke in approbation of the career of Daniel O'Connell, which having compassed the enfranchisement of Catholic Ireland, culminated in the struggle to repeal the Union.[26] Further, and perhaps more tellingly, he argued and voted for abolition of the Irish viceroyalty.[27]

However contradictory it may appear to support both British imperial designs and Home Rule, this solution to the Irish Question seemed perfectly consistent to its proponents, who were, it should be noted, virtually coextensive with the early Home Rule movement itself, as crafted and led by Stoker's acquaintance Isaac Butt. In fact, this sort of metrocolonial exceptionalism, involving a liberated Ireland in the administration and the rewards of Britain's global conquests, receives direct expression in *The Proceedings of the Home Rule Conference,* in which Butt asserts: "Many of these possessions have been acquired during the period of our disastrous partnership. . . . Heaven knows we have paid dearly enough for them. We are entitled to them."[28] The language of Butt's claim here indicates how Ireland's dual status as partner in and victim of British colonial oppression served to produce the most flagrant political oxymorons, like imperialist Home Rule, as straightforward common sense. The historian R. F. Foster notes, "The Irish were more politically conservative and imperialist than a people supposedly breaking the bonds of colonialism had any right to be"; and Stoker himself was not immune to this form of mystification.[29]

For Stoker, however, such ideological disavowals of the metrocolonial condition invariably returned as psychomachia. Thus, in the same series of Historical Society debates, Stoker voted against the proposition that India was currently being governed in the best interests of the native population, a remarkable stance for a man who would later celebrate the "wise kindliness" of English colonial governance generally and the "beneficent pioneering" of the imperialist adventurer Henry Stanley in particular.[30] More remarkable still was the manner in which Stoker internalized the imperialist/irredentist contradiction of Buttite Home Rule *within* the domestic space of Ireland. He voted once in favor and once against Pitt's Unionist policies in the same session,[31] and perhaps his most characteristic gesture in this forensic context was to seek a rewording of a question on unionism so that the policy might be affirmed outright and room still be left to entertain schemes for Irish autonomy.[32]

These collegiate efforts at political disavowal culminated in his auditor's *Address to the Historical Society,* "The Necessity for Political Honesty" (1872), wherein Stoker contrives simultaneously to presuppose and to undermine the radically sectarian view of Irish civilization institutionalized in and by the college itself. In the process, Stoker sublimates his own ethno-national ambivalence and begins to articulate a kind of *domestic cosmopolitanism,* whose unifying impetus embraced rather than erased social contradiction and complexity in Britain. His idea anticipates in an embryonic and idiosyncratic form the multicultural ethos of the present day.[33]

The most memorable portion of Stoker's *Address,* the peroration, draws upon contemporary notions of racial atavism and degeneration to situate the "Irish people" as both a prospective antidote to the effete decline of Western civilization and an instance of evolutionary arrest, hence a possible totem and agency of such decline. As an "old world people—seemingly half-barbarous amid a world of luxury" (NPH 29), Stoker's Irish are associated both with "lethargy" (28) and with "vital energy" (29), with a "new order" (30) of national culture and with a residual "chaos" of factional strife (30). Since Stoker so plainly relies upon primitivist typologies of subject peoples, it is hardly surprising, especially given the misconceptions about his ethnic pedigree, that most critics have taken these comments to reflect a predictable Anglo-Protestant uncertainty and anxiety at the anticipated rise of the "Celtic race." Chris Morash supplies an elucidation of this view: "For a member of Dublin's Protestant middle class in the 1870s, the prospect of a 'half-barbarous' Celtic race returning 'amid an age of luxury' to claim its position was a prospect to be viewed with mixed emotion."[34]

It is important to observe, however, that Stoker does not characterize the "Celtic race" as "seemingly half-barbarous," but the "people of Ireland" in toto (29), a referential distinction with a world of difference in an ethnically hybrid and divided metrocolonial space. Indeed, viewed in context, this passage juggles and confounds the terms of Irish reference in a manner calculated to *textualize* Stoker's social vision, to introduce domestic cosmopolitanism at the level of the name. Stoker will underline the paramount importance of this gesture years later by repeating it in the concluding note to *Dracula*, in which an intermixture of blood is sanctified and sublimated in a sequence of patronyms (*D* 326).

Stoker punctuates the main body of his *Address* by dismissing the "old errors" (NPH 25) of parochial nationalism and proclaiming a new "nationalism of humanity" (26) keyed by the belief that "what is best in the world is best for the nation" (25–26). Turning on this note to his own homeland, Stoker first designates Trinity College the present "intellectual centre" of "our race" and "our country" of Ireland (28). He then speaks of the economic and political future as belonging to the "Celtic race" (28), which he differentiates from the presumably Anglo-Protestant constituency of Trinity College, but does so along the permeable lines of class rather than the more naturalized and calcified lines of ethnicity. He goes on to conflate "our race" and the "Celtic race" under the corporate rubric of "the Irishmen" and "the Irish race," which he explicitly distinguishes from the "Anglo-Saxon race" (29), to which his critics typically, and erroneously, assign him. "The Irish race has all the elements of greatness," Stoker writes, while "the Anglo-Saxon race is dwindling" (29–30). This corporate Irishness gives way in turn to the still more inclusive "people of Ireland" (29), who bear the "seemingly half-barbarous" label cited above. But by this point, Stoker has so unsettled his own rhetoric of racial difference that this last, seemingly slanderous characterization applies across the board. And, in fact, Stoker concludes his sanguine account of Irish destiny by tacitly identifying his Trinity College interlocutors as a part, albeit the foremost part, of the advancing "Celtic race" (28). He urges them, as "the teachers of the [Celtic] people," to a new "patriotism" (28), combining "a love of our country and belief in the future of our race" (30).

With the latter ploy, a mutual interpenetration completes itself wherein each of the main ethnic lines of Ireland, Anglo and Celtic, remains visible even as each is assimilated to the other under the sign of Irishness. Instead of proposing a simple elimination or homogenization of ethnic status, Stoker looks for the Irish to transform their hybrid or double-born position from bane to boon. For he dimly sees in the imbrication of the island's racial and sectarian groupings the economic and cultural potential of the whole. In much the same way, he predicates the health of modern nation-states upon their immediate "consolidation in a common league" (25), the presumed site of Stoker's cherished paradox, "a nationalism of humanity" (26). In what would prove to be a staple tactic of his later writing, Stoker's speech negotiates profound metrocolonial contradictions by going with rather than against the grain, by intensifying rather than diffusing ambivalence, by exfoliating ethnic differences to the point at which they begin to destabilize the very hierarchies they appear to subtend.[35] Far from an underlying motive in Stoker's writing, as has been generally supposed, racialist ideology increasingly forms an object of suspicion, one that anticipates later critiques, post-structural, postmodern, and postcolonial.

The ethnological profile of Ireland in "The Necessity for Political Honesty" unmistakably recalls the hybrid ethnological vision of Great Britain that Matthew Arnold had set forth just five years earlier in *The Study of Celtic Literature*. As a consequence, Stoker's domestic racial politics have been likened to those of Arnold.[36] But this correlation elides much of the strategic nuance of Stoker's *Address*, contributing not only to the general overestimation of his Anglo allegiances but also to the general underestimation of his rhetorical skills. In "The Necessity for Political Honesty," Stoker deliberately evokes Arnold's already influential typology of Britishness in order to call attention to the subtle, yet decisive critique implicit in his own typology of Irishness.

As Robert J. C. Young has demonstrated, hybridity was hardly a univocal concept in late-Victorian racial science; it could be invoked to characterize varying types and degrees of ethnic fusion, integration or disjuncture, and to serve correspondingly disparate or conflicting political ends.[37] Arnold's *The Study of Celtic Literature* elaborates a "decomposition thesis" of hybridity, in which racial lines were seen to coalesce, only for the resulting issue to revert back to the stronger "parent type" or to remain dominated by that type.[38] The Celt and the Anglo-Saxon have come together for Arnold, but they have amalgamated "back" into Englishness, forming in effect a higher or greater breed of Anglo-Saxon, which remains the controlling element in the racial composite. Young takes this fundamental disequilibrium of Celt and Anglo-Saxon in Arnold's design to signify that he ultimately "does not advocate an amalgamation that results in emerging and fusion but rather an apartheid model of dialogic separation."[39] Yet given how Arnold's work, which was published in the year of the great Fenian Rising, assumes the Irish Question as its most salient political context, a more apposite model of Arnoldian hybridity would be the institution of marriage, metropolitan and otherwise, *under English common law*: husband (John Bull) and wife (Erin) become one person and that person, as William Blackstone said, is the husband.[40] Arnold specifically celebrated the imaginative emotionalism of the feminized Celt *insofar* as those qualities were available to be colonized by and integrated within the rationalistic hegemony of the masculine Anglo-Saxon intellect. His Celticism was a discourse of assimilative hierarchy rather than "dialogic separation," and as such it formed a precise ethnological correlative to the paternalistic unionism espoused in his later *Irish Essays*.[41]

Stoker's youthful manifesto counters Arnold's well-known account in several crucial respects. First, by supposing the same racial types, Celt and Anglo, to be compounded in "the Irish people" rather than in the English, he undercuts Arnold's quiet bionaturalization of imperialist hegemony, his assumption that the group who conquers and rules automatically bears the racial makeup that absorbs. Second, by the same gambit, Stoker de-essentializes the connection between race and nationality. Compounded of the same "parent types," Irishness and Englishness would come, on Stoker's account, to be defined by residence and fealty, along much the same lines proposed a quarter century earlier by Thomas Davis and Young Ireland.[42] Lastly, and most importantly, Stoker's rhetorical approach implicitly challenges the very idea of racial incorporation and appropriation, Arnold's particular variant of the decomposition thesis. The referential confusion in Stoker's *Address* of the Trinity Anglo elite with the Celtic people-nation points to their eventual interfusion, their common future of complete hybridization. Instead of either one serving as a supplement in the completed or sublimated version of the other, Anglo and Celt converge in an Irishness identical with neither group by itself, but an Irishness to which both have laid different sorts of approved historical claims. The theory of hybridity thus advanced would seem to be closest to what Young termed the "proximity thesis," which holds that nearly allied races may achieve complete intermixture though more distant ones could not, a credo perfectly accordant with the metrocolonial exceptionalism of the early Home Rule movement, which Stoker supported.[43]

Evidence of a linkage between Stoker's support of Irish Home Rule and his opposition to Arnold's incorporation model of hybridity invites a revisionist interpretation of the political impetus of *Dracula,* which ratifies this linkage in turn. For does not the vampire Count boast of the hybrid nature of his own race of origin ("We Szekelys have a right to be proud, for in our veins flows the blood of many brave races"; *D* 33)? And does not his vampirism involve and indeed allegorize racial "decomposition," absorbing all blood and incorporating all bloodlines into a single, endlessly reproducible "race apart"? "For centuries to come he might, amongst [London's] teeming millions, satiate his lust for blood, and create a new and ever-widening circle of semi-demons to batten on the helpless" (53–54). How, one might ask, could Stoker more persuasively denounce the Arnoldian ideal of metrocolonial assimilation than by representing its core thesis as a "nightmare vision" of uncontained vampirism? And, in this light, does not the driving of a stake through the heart of the vampire evoke and redound against Arnold's celebratory metaphor of trade and tourism serving as an "English wedge [pushing] further and further into the heart of the principality" of Ireland?[44]

The Primrose Path

Stoker's Trinity College pedigree assured him of a bureaucratic post in Dublin Castle, like his father before him, but he found himself far too alienated by administrative routine to feel like a member of the ruling apparatus, to identify with the interests of that political class, or, consequently, to embrace his father's Tory unionism. This was doubtless all the more inevitable since Stoker's alienation responded to the socioeconomic fate of his parents, which eerily carried forward and even encapsulated the contradictions attendant to his mixed racial heritage. His father's position as a functionary in the administration of empire gave the petit-bourgeois couple that sense of Anglo-Irish superiority that they enjoyed and then enhanced by sending their sons to Trinity College. But the low wages of the castle position combined with the high expenses of a Trinity education to drain their resources and produce a class demotion that smacked of an ethnic reversal: the established Anglo-Protestant Stokers underwent an ordeal typically reserved for youthful Celtic-Catholic peasants and proletarians, economic emigration. As a young adult, Bram Stoker stood on the quay and watched his parents quit Dublin, where they could no longer afford to live, for less expensive Swiss boardinghouses, where Stoker himself would remit part of his castle salary to supplement their dwindling retirement funds[45]—in a clear inversion of that Irish Catholic staple, the Christmas letter from America. By an uncanny logic, which Stoker exploits throughout *Dracula,* his parents' deliberate steps toward Ascendancy culture and society bore them ever closer to the sad plight of the Irish people-nation. By a reverse logic, Stoker himself would support the political aspirations of the Irish people-nation even as he sought to distance himself from them.

The expatriation of his parents was an ex-patriation for Stoker in another sense: it became a momentary disconnection from the settler heritage of security and privilege associated with his father's blood and a reconnection with the unsettled heritage of distress and flight associated with his mother's blood. His response to this in-Fringe-ment of the Celtic other can be understood as an impossibly ambivalent gesture of simultaneous affiliation and disaffiliation with that other. He attached himself to a journalistic pillar of Tory unionism, the *Dublin Evening Mail,* preparatory to extricating himself from the practical execution of such unionism as a castle employee and from the practical consequences that office held for his parents. Interrupted in this pursuit by an appointment as the inspector for the Court of Petty Sessions (and a raise in pay), Stoker's resulting travels through the Irish countryside only whetted his devolutionist impulses, exposing him to the cruelties, inequities, and inefficiencies of the landlord system, and whetted his impulse to leave.[46]

That impulse, while powerful, however, was by no means unalloyed. Stoker may indeed have regarded Ireland as a land of Philistinism, as Glover asserts; and on being offered the chance to leave, he did exultantly inscribe the words "London in view" in his journal,[47] a gesture often taken to summarize his feelings comprehensively. But Stoker's psychomachia at the prospect of seeking his fortune in England was sufficiently pronounced to supply much of the narrative and thematic inspiration for his first piece of longer fiction, the odd, amateurish, and little-read novella *The Primrose Path.*[48]

Published serially in the *Shamrock* in 1875, just three years prior to Stoker's departure for London, the novella possesses a no less Irish frame of reference than *The Snake's Pass,* his better-known novel of Irish life. *The Primrose Path* is a curious production, in fact, because it not only combines two genres of particular saliency in Stoker's homeland, the temperance tract and the emigration parable, but also endeavors to superimpose their divergent ideological itineraries directly onto one another. Of course, most if not all cautionary tales of emigration show their protagonist falling into unwonted habits of a vicious or criminal nature, such as drunkenness. But what makes the construction of *The Primrose Path* unusual and awkward is that the perilous vice in question is far more closely identified, by the text as well as its presumed audience, with the lost homeland than with the new frontier.[49] *The Primrose Path* is also a disappointing production owing to the same structural foible: by conflating the question of metropolitan emigration, to which Stoker brings a serious, and seriously conflicted, interest, with the issue of drink, to which he is indifferent enough to rely upon stock temperance movement rhetoric, Stoker fails of a full nuanced engagement with either one. In its outright clumsiness, however, this conflation prompts a search for authorial design, which yields some unsuspected insight into the linkage between Stoker's lived experience of Irish duality and the racial problematic animating his more celebrated emigration novel, *Dracula.* For this reason alone, *The Primrose Path* deserves the critical scrutiny it has not yet received.

The Primrose Path begins with a christening party, a significantly self-referential gesture for a first novel. Jerry O'Sullivan, a respectable and increasingly well-to-do carpenter, and his wife, Katey, an idealized type of maternal and wifely virtue, have invited family and friends to their house to receive their third child into the social world. Once refreshments of all kinds are served, one of the honored guests, the Anglo-Irish Mr. Parnell, a personal and professional mentor of the O'Sullivans, finds an opportunity to deliver a denunciation of alcohol as the single greatest evil known to man. His temperance evangel is met with resistance and ridicule by the other guest of honor, the whiskey-drinking Celt Mr. Muldoon, a rich collateral relative of the O'Sullivans, after whom the newborn has been named in the hope of future benefaction. The two men are soon at loggerheads, Parnell growing ever more zealous in his gospel, and Muldoon ever more malicious in his satire.

> Jerry felt that a gloom had fallen on the assemblage, and tried to lift it by starting a new topic.
>
> "Do you know," said he, "I had a letter from John Sebright the other day, and he tells me if you want to make money England's the place." (28)

"Going to England," it turns out, is an "old 'fad'" (28) of Jerry's and an
equally long-standing bête noire of his wife and his mother, who recruit
the prudent Mr. Parnell to assist them in dissuading Jerry from further
consideration of the move. Their unsuccessful effort to dispel Jerry's metro-
tropism provides the rather muddled moral crux of his decision.

To judge from Jerry's further consideration over the next few days, the
central question underlying his debate with his loved ones—and, ultimately,
with himself—is whether and to what extent deep-seated personal aspirations, suddenly answered by opportunities for advancement, should take
priority over other social adherences, public or private. At the party, Parnell opines that leaving Ireland "'to make a little more money'" is not
unlike selling out one's homeland, a suggestion at which Jerry bristles de-
fensively, while Katey simply bursts into tears at the prospect of uproot-
ing their "happy home" and spends the remainder of the affair "crying
quietly" (32). These are the arguments with which O'Sullivan must reckon when Sebright subsequently offers him the chance to become a "theatrical carpenter" at a "very liberal" salary (38, 39), a post that would simultaneously satisfy his childhood passion for the footlights and his mature
longings for social and economic ascent.

> The chance now offered of employment was indeed a temptation. If he
> should be able to adopt the new life he would have an opportunity of
> combining his romantic taste and his trade experience, and would be
> moreover in that wider field of exertion to which he had long looked for-
> ward.
>   And so he waited with what patience he could, and shut his eyes as close
> as possible to the growing miseries of his home. (39)

The reference to "that wider field of exertion to which he had long looked
forward" indicates that there is more at stake in Jerry's "fad" than a wish
for greater material prosperity or for the lost magic of a boyhood dream.
There is also a longing to escape the narrow margins of the United Kingdom and to take his place at its expansive metropolitan center. It is this
hope of social, implicitly ethnic promotion that determines him to shut his
eyes to his wife's reluctance.

One other, seemingly insubstantial objection to Jerry's dream is not only
raised but given great symbolic prominence at the party. Toward the end
of his impromptu, intermittent temperance lecture, Parnell produces "an
allegorical picture" entitled "Death and Devil" or "To and Fro" (30–31).
It depicts a man traveling on horseback through a bleak mountain pass

encumbered, piggyback, with a luridly garbed "demon," who "bore a basket full of bottles" and "laughed with glee" at the ruin his elixir has wrought (31). For Parnell, the contemporary significance of the image is clear, Muldoon's mockery notwithstanding: "'[Drink] is the curse of Ireland in our own time, . . . so surely as Irishmen will not use the wit and strength that God has given them, [it] will drag her from her throne'" (31–32). Logically, if unexpectedly, Jerry seizes upon the ethnic stereotype lodged in this commentary as partial vindication of his own beleaguered initiative to live abroad: "'One thing John Sebright tells me, that there is less drunkenness in England than here'" (31–32). To compensate for his strategic error, Parnell intimates, without any evidence, that Sebright is inviting Jerry to join and to subsidize his own degenerate pastimes, so that the danger of encountering or succumbing to drunkenness is, in this instance, even greater in London than on "the isle of dreadful thirst."[50] Then, with the party drawing to a close, he hands the memento mori to his protégé, saying, "'Jerry, old boy, if you ever do go, keep that in your purse, and if you ever go to pay for liquor for yourself or others, just think what it means'" (32). As the clumsily obvious repetition of the predicate *go* indicates, the Gothic picture is now more than an allegorical representation of alcoholic dependency; it is an allegorical map of a proposed synchrony between the dangers of inebriation and the dangers of expatriation.

More than that, the picture is what the sometimes Gothic movie director Alfred Hitchcock (*The Birds, Rebecca*) called a "maguffin," a diversionary motif that is not meaningful in its own right but is situated to configure and even determine the future course of the action. Jerry never looks at the picture or ponders the peril that it signifies as he makes his fateful decision. Nor is there any apparent reason for him to do so. Since he has never exhibited a particularly marked attachment to the culture of drink in a land where it is felt to be ubiquitous, it would be at least curious if not foolish for Jerry to allow the conjured specter of bibulous debauchery to influence significantly his choice of residence or career path. Once the die is cast, however, and the emigration proper has commenced, it suddenly becomes obvious that the temptation to such debauchery was the main factor to be weighed after all.

Jerry no sooner reports to the Stanley Theatre than he befriends an actor named Mons, who "was performing the part of Mephistopheles" (51). This is the very role he comes to play in Jerry's life, acquainting him first with life at the scruffy "local" and then with its malignant barkeep and proprietor, Grinnell, a hideous death figure who plots Jerry's downfall.

Although Jerry begins by imbibing with his accustomed moderation, he soon finds himself drinking more heavily than he should, and a series of events conspire with the sinister Grinnell to put Jerry out of regular work, out of money, in thrall to whiskey, and in debt to the man (Grinnell) willing to satisfy his habit.

Things go rapidly "down the hill" from there (83). Jerry descends from functional alcoholism, which leaves him perpetually "in a state of fuddle" (82), to frequent brawling, which lands him in the lockup, to the loss of all employment, which turns him against his sainted, long-suffering wife, to regular, violent domestic abuse, which responds to Katey's untiring attempts to save him. The slide culminates in complete devastation. After being taunted as a cuckolded, wife-beating "Irishman" (102), during a barroom fight with Grinnell's stooges, Jerry goes home in a drunken rage and bludgeons Katey to death with a hammer, one of the tools of his trade that she had somehow managed to keep out of hock. Recognizing the enormity of his deed, Jerry takes another of his as yet unpawned tools of advancement, a chisel, and cuts his throat. Before doing so, however, he offers a last testament, clearly designed to punctuate and to rivet the strained parallelism between the primrose path to England and the primrose path to insobriety: "'Katey, Katey, what have I done? Oh, God, what have I done? I have murdered her. Oh? the drink! The drink! Why didn't I stay at home and this wouldn't have happened'" (104).

Far from settling the issue, this mode of narrative closure reopens the question raised by the forced generic connection that the fiction as a whole attempts to sustain. In his introduction to the new edition of *The Primrose Path*, Richard Dalby calls it "an obvious tract on the degradation and evils of alcoholism" and cites Parnell's catch phrase "the curse of Ireland" (9). But that leaves one to wonder why Stoker's protagonist must go to London to fall under it. In the very next paragraph, Dalby writes, "Stoker appears to be urging his countrymen to be content with their happy, if poverty-stricken lot in Ireland . . . rather than succumbing to the devilish temptation of false riches and excesses of London" (9). But that leaves one to wonder why Jerry's experience in London replicates the alcoholic excesses common to Ireland instead of elaborating upon the frustrations specific to the worship of (English) mammon. In other words, *The Primrose Path* is less provocative in its formulaic message(s) than in what Freud would call its dream work, those breaks or peculiarities of form that register the pressure of the unsaid. Like *Dracula*, Stoker's first novella is most usefully read not as parable or as simple allegory but as fantasy, a species of text whose meaning inheres in its machinery of distortion. As previously suggested, the predominant mode of dream work in the novel is condensation, a fusion of different motifs or narratemes that act together to mask or redirect certain of their signifying possibilities. The predominant object of this dream work is the autobiographical germ of the story.

For this reason, the readiest starting point for unpacking Stoker's fantasy construction is with his overdetermined resemblance to its doomed protagonist. Stoker created Jerry O'Sullivan out of his own abiding but conflicted interest in heeding London's siren call. He even conferred upon O'Sullivan his own specific motive for moving: not the material necessity that impelled the bulk of Irish émigrés to urban England, but metropolitan ambitions, a restless urge to quit an already comfortable situation in Dublin on a search for the main chance, social and economic, that only a place like London could afford. Contra Dalby, the introductory portrait of the O'Sullivans is devoted in part to emphasizing their prosperous distance from the lot suffered by most of their compatriots—"so prosperous that the idea of failure in work seemed too far away to be easily realised" (34). The author's empathy with this sort of single-minded drive creeps at points into his otherwise skeptical representation of Jerry's self-centeredness: "Deep in the minds of most energetic persons lies some strong desire, some strong ambition, or some resolute hope, which unconsciously moulds, or, at least, influences their every act. No matter what their circumstances in life may be, or how much they yield to those circumstances for a time, the one idea remains ever the same. This is, in fact, one of the secrets of how individual force of character comes out at times" (33). Like Stoker, Jerry O'Sullivan is a "mick on the make," to use R. F. Foster's phrase, a willful ethnic parvenu, whose Irish identity is thrown into sharper relief by his ambitious relocation.[51] Lastly, Stoker rounds out O'Sullivan's relentless push with his own "romantic taste" for the theater. O'Sullivan's chosen occupation, theatrical carpenter, is a recognizable lower-caste displacement of Stoker's avocation at the time the story appeared, theater critic: the one attends to the physical structure of the stage; the other attends to the dramatic structure of its offerings.

In light of these multiple connections, Stoker may have hit upon alcohol as the motor of Jerry's demise because the irrelevance of that vice to Stoker's personal conduct helped to obscure the full extent of the novel's self-referentiality, which he would have found as embarrassing and even troubling as it was essential to the project. In a sense, self-reference proves the overriding purpose of *The Primrose Path*, which works through in story form the doubt, guilt, and apprehension of its author about his nonetheless "resolute hope" to move into metropolitan society. But such a working through, for Stoker, entailed assessing the hope itself and the possible consequences of its fulfillment in the harshest possible light, moral and prudential. The problem of drunkenness functioned within this economy as a site of compensatory disavowal (in the psychoanalytic sense of the term), a means whereby the author's most rigorous judgments upon his fictive surrogate might be discounted as not fully applicable to his own case.

Thus, on the moral side, Stoker ascribes Jerry's determination to pursue his London dream in the face of wifely opposition to "the power of evil" in his heart, as revealed in his newly expressed "cruelty" and "obstinacy" (35–36). But he represents these "evil qualities" as a direct outgrowth of Jerry's "sensual nature" (36), a character profile that speaks less to his present ambition than to his future appetite, or, rather, a profile that tends to tar the former with the latter, undermining O'Sullivan's credentials as an admirably "energetic" if rather blinkered personality. In other words, while Stoker fashions O'Sullivan as a vehicle to anatomize his own Faustian proclivities, he ultimately grounds O'Sullivan's self-destruction in a Falstaffian weakness that he himself did not share. Hence, Jerry's Mephistopheles, Mons, is only a play "actor," a drinking cadge and companion in the metaphorical guise of a demon.

On the practical side, Stoker likewise writes, as it were, with both hands. He so characterizes his protagonist as to allow for and explore the possibility that a most respectable Irish immigrant could court and meet with calamity in London; but the disreputable means and milieu of O'Sullivan's calamity serve rather to qualify than to corroborate that possibility. Along the same lines, Stoker registers his own trepidation at being subject to invidious Irish stereotypes in the reception that he arranges for his protagonist: everyone's initial assumption that O'Sullivan, being Irish, must like his grog, coupled with the ethnically tinged antagonism that his pubmates come to bear him, contributes measurably to his downfall. But here again, Stoker confronts the anticipated problem across a reassuring class abyss. The Stanley Theatre is situated in a grimy, impoverished section of London, and the men Jerry encounters seem but a social grade or so above the notorious urban "residuum," with no more claim to the status of entitled metropolitan subject than Jerry himself and much less than the respectable Stoker already enjoyed. The author thus objectifies and so to an extent exorcises his emigration anxieties in a social context sufficiently distant from his own sphere of aspiration as to leave their practical validity a conveniently open question.

At the same time, Stoker manages to transform his misgivings about laboring under ethnic preconceptions into a critical interrogation of the racial sensibilities of his social environs. He would come to execute this maneuver far more adroitly in *Dracula,* due in part to his intervening first-hand experience of being Irish in London, in part to his greater familiarity with the emergent racial sciences, and in part to his growth as a literary craftsman. *The Primrose Path* does, however, offer a working sense of his method under development. Stoker deploys stock racial images, properties, and associations in his Irish fiction, not with an eye to endorsing them, as many critics have inferred, but to shifting their point of reference from the ontology of the groups thus classified to the cultural psychology of racial classification itself. The authority of this classificatory sensibility, which I am calling blood consciousness, is accordingly unsettled if not debunked. By the time of *Dracula,* as we shall see, Stoker was capable of advancing this strategy through the sophisticated manipulation of generic, specifically Gothic conventions. But in *The Primrose Path,* where Stoker is still reliant upon a relatively untutored ingenuity, the strategy is bound up not with formal innovation but formal breakdown, precisely that genre abrasion we have been canvassing.

The temperance tract tends to locate the vulnerability to evil in the innate makeup of the delinquent and is therefore amenable to the moralizing racial essentialism of early ethnographical discourse. The emigration parable is almost by definition environmentalist in its etiology of vice, treating ethnically marked subjects as profoundly susceptible to social and cultural dislocation. Besides playing off the increasingly intense nature/nurture debate of the late Victorian era, the arrangement of these normative paradigms in *The Primrose Path* seems designed, however clumsily, to contest the essentialist with the environmentalist perspective, at least as far as Anglo-Irish differences are concerned. Parnell's temperance lecture sets the tone for the first movement of the novella, and it explicitly affirms the reigning stereotype of the Celtic-Irish as congenitally predisposed to dipsomania and unwilling "to use the wit and strength God has given them" to conquer this failing. And yet the fact that Jerry must immigrate to London before contracting this moral pathology, and only does so under the influence of English expectations to this effect, suggests that there is an element of self-fulfilling prophecy in the Anglo-Irishman's sermon and the racial typology upon which it draws. The supposedly innate infirmity of the Irish Celt is represented here as a consequence not only of environment but also of an alien environment, and not only of an alien environment but also of an alien environment informed, or deformed, in advance by the imperialist stereotype of Irish infirmity.

The same sort of double inscription can be discerned in Jerry's decisive encounter with Mons. Explicitly cast in the "role" of Mephistopheles, Mons can be understood as a doppelgänger figure embodying and eliciting the self-destructive desires harbored by his host. Such a function would be consistent with the temperance allegory of Parnell's Gothic picture and with the characterological bias of the temperance movement generally. But like Mephistopheles, Mons is also an independent agent seducing his victim to indulgences otherwise avoided—in short, an external factor consistent with the environmentalist impetus of the emigration tale. When Mons introduces Jerry to Grinnell, the bartender immediately remarks upon the ethnicity of "the stranger" and, taking it to augur a taste for whiskey, offers him a homemade "decoction" labeled "Gift" in the hope of bringing Jerry gradually under his spell (53). Jerry promptly attempts to refuse the beverage, but Mons interrupts to insist that he accept on pain of giving offense, grounds strictly extrinsic to the appetites he might be taken to incarnate and manipulate. In a clever twist, however, Mons's *external* influence on Jerry might well proceed from the assumption that he was merely encouraging Jerry on the path of his *inner* all-too-Irish desire for drink. That is to say, Mons might be understood to take the stereotypical Irishman for the real one and, aided by the stranger's ethnically marked eagerness for social acceptance (52–54), to conjure that stereotypical Irishman into existence. Not for the last time, an erroneous interpretation of Jerry's conduct, guided by preconceptions about the Irish character and finding acquiescence in his own zeal to belong, turn around and foster circumstances in Jerry's life under which he comes to vindicate those preconceptions.

As Jerry finishes sampling Grinnell's gift, he peers for the one and only time at Parnell's gift, the pictorial warning, and muses "that his new life was beginning but badly, drinking in the middle of the day" (53). Besides marking this incident as the pivotal point in O'Sullivan's downward career, the appearance of the drawing at this juncture momentarily reveals, beneath the jumbled interplay of temperance and emigration plotlines, the ironic counterpoint that Stoker was laboring to effect. Parnell proves irrefutably correct about the danger Jerry faces, but for substantially the

wrong reason. His protégé does not fall prey to his supposedly Irish proclivity for drunken excess *except* insofar as it is activated by conditions
resulting, at least in part, from the supposition itself. This recursive, con-
structivist logic, which Stoker will refine and recalibrate in *Dracula,* not
only carries the unrealized potential to reconcile the divergent generic
strains in *The Primrose Path* but also has the virtue of reconciling the
novel's broadly political and narrowly personal agendas in a single stroke.
The logic contests as illegitimate the crude moral classification of racial
makeup, while specifically conceding the power of such phantasmatic taxonomies to outstrip and supersede the reality they distort. As such, this
logic also vents an emigration anxiety more haunting than any Stoker
expressed and displaced in the horrific details of the story: that invidious
ethnic stereotypes have the power not just to traduce the Irish émigré but
to transform him into their image and alibi, to so saturate the social meaning of his every action as to compel him, *après coup,* to enact them. Despite his continued metropolitan longings and identifications, Stoker was
plainly attuned to the flip side of the self-styled imperialist mission of soul-
making, the colonial fear of being body-snatched by one's own "blood"
profile or type: a fear, by the way, that strongly resonates with the dynamics of vampirism in *Dracula.*

The Voice of Ireland

In his avocation as a drama critic, Stoker encountered the famous actor
Henry Irving, who nurtured Stoker's metropolitan longings in the most
potent conceivable manner. Beyond inviting Stoker to London on a permanent and well-remunerated basis, Irving introduced his new manager
into the society of such imperial notables as William Gladstone, Sir Richard Burton, and Sir Henry Stanley, inspiring and apparently justifying that
exultant note, "London in view."[52] And yet Stoker's eagerly anticipated
sojourn at the heart of English cultural identity only served to throw his
Irishness, like that of his lower-class alter ego, O'Sullivan, into sharp and
disorienting relief.

   As Laurence Irving's biography of his father attests, the actor's retinue
generally regarded Stoker through the darkening lens of their ethnic prej-
udices, wherein his marvelously efficient management of Irving's Lyceum
Theatre appeared at once self-serving and unreliable, a predictable outgrowth of Stoker's racially ingrained irresponsibility, his propensity for
"blarneying," and his parvenu status and ambitions.[53] Rivalries inevita-

bly emerged between Stoker and other members of the company (the sec-
retary, Louis F. Austin, and the stage manager, H. J. Loveday), in which
Stoker's weapons were regarded as typical of the colonial Irish arriviste.
In the words of Laurence Irving, "Stoker, inflated with literary and athletic pretensions, worshipped Irving with all the sentimental idolatry of which
an Irishman is capable, reveling in the opportunities to rub shoulders with
the great."[54] Painfully aware of his reception as an ethnic social climber,
Stoker in fact bore toward the imperious Henry Irving a deferential, de-
pendent, yet resentful posture that mirrored the colonial subjacency of his
homeland—an ethnopolitical relationship evoked, as we shall see, in the
two men's running quarrel over Home Rule.

As Barbara Belford notes, Stoker was also a perennial "outsider" within the wider "society of London," where Irishness was most often associated with servants, laborers, and the residuum and so bore its own class,
or declassing, inflection.[55] That Stoker was "typed," in Glover's words, "a
big, red-bearded Irishman"[56] automatically put his image at significant
variance with the self-conception of the elite middle-class set in which he
moved and from which he sought recognition. Even Stoker's university
degree, the only one among the Lyceum company, failed to earn him the
respectability he craved, mainly because it was conferred by an Irish institution (which might explain why he decided, at the age of thirty-nine, to
secure an *English* barrister's license that he apparently never intended to
use). But it was Stoker's very quest for respectability, exaggerated as it was
by the ethnic handicap under which he labored, that exposed him to the
public snickering reserved for the arrant parvenu. *Moonshine,* a magazine
of "wit, humour, and satire," which was given to libelous caricatures of
the Celtic race, lampooned Stoker as a man of laughably boundless ambitions.[57] On this score, even Stoker's physical heroism could, to a jaundiced
eye, be accounted against him as mere folly. Stoker's wife, Florence, came
in for similar treatment on the pages of *Punch,* where a cartoon entitled
"A Filial Reproof" represented her as being too socially preoccupied to
give her only child any attention.[58] Lastly, the *Tatler* mocked Stoker's attempt to fit into English club society by pointing to his clumsy Irish inflected
wit, his "horrible dooble ongtong."[59] In the land of the Anglos, Stoker came
to discover, Anglo-Irish usually translated as "mere" Irish. Consequently,
in *occupying* the metropolitan center he paradoxically came to *embody*
the Celtic fringe.

One index of the importance he placed on this insight was his decision
to communicate it to Count Dracula, whose *only* express anxiety in the

entire novel concerns the impediment his pattern and pronunciation of English might pose to his membership in London society: "'Well I know that, did I move and speak in your London, none there are who would not know me for a stranger. That is not enough for me'" (*D* 26). Stoker too carried the evidence of his "foreign" origins in the grain of his voice. But unlike his monster (or his family friend, Oscar Wilde), he took care to preserve his native accent, and his thickish brogue served as both a bait to his more condescending English colleagues and a self-assertive check on his Anglophilia. While busily cultivating the signifiers of English respectability, Stoker persisted in an index of his Irish arrivistism with the power to neutralize or transvalue them. (Remember that while primary codes of racial difference are usually visual, the audible dimension provided the dominant cue for distinguishing the Irish from the English.[60]) Here again, he negotiated the metrocolonial estate by purposefully intensifying and tenaciously attaching himself to its central contradictions.[61]

The most public aspect of Stoker's literary practice, his writing career, proceeded in a similarly cross-grained fashion. Having rejoiced in his deliverance to England as the salvation of his literary prospects, Stoker seems to have shifted or split his allegiance once he was established as a writer there. Not only did he maintain social ties and mutually supportive relations with nationalist literati like Lady Jane Wilde and William O'Brien but he also became a strong supporter of the Irish Literary Society, which carried the cultural nationalist imprimatur of its founder, W. B. Yeats.[62]

In immigrating to England, then, and embracing the "wise kindliness of [its] civilization," Stoker came to discover and to display his Irish voice, in both the literal and the literary sense. Taken in context, his cultural performance both underlined Anglo-Irish distinctions, by setting either register in contrast with the other, and undermined the ontological significance of those differences, by pointing to their mutual constitution and incorporation. Nicholas Daly has usefully written of how all colonial literary production, including Stoker's, addressed an implied metropolitan audience, injecting the resultant text with an "ineluctable hybridity" that requires what Homi Bhabha calls a "'migrant's double vision' . . . to bring into focus."[63] But because Stoker was a migrant and was received as an Irish parvenu, a kind of ethnoclass migrant, he was uniquely positioned to possess and enact, as well as to require, this sort of double vision, which takes account of how the different registers and different audiences for his personal and textual performances informed and even created one another. Apprehended in this fashion, Stoker's public self-presentation not only continued the pattern of political disavowal dating back to his days at Trinity but also built upon his fledgling attempts to convert this pattern into something like policy: a modest, strategically veiled, but not unsophisticated critique of the imperative to ethnic or national self-identity. Stoker realized in London the domestic cosmopolitanism he had formulated at Trinity.

Figured in terms of doubly inscribed, mutually incorporated voices, Stoker's domestic cosmopolitanism seems to have animated his well-known but insufficiently understood support for Home Rule. In an effort to weigh Stoker's nationalist sympathies, scholars have relied almost entirely on his self-description, in *Personal Reminiscences of Henry Irving,* as a "Philosophical Home Ruler."[64] But it is that work's one other anecdote involving Home Rule, unaccountably overlooked to date, that lends conceptual definition to this rather gnomic political epithet. In "The Voice of England," Stoker details his running debate with Henry Irving on the matter of Irish devolution. While Stoker felt that his employer opposed Home Rule out of a "violently" contrary nature, Irving's stated objection to the policy tended more toward quietism. He felt that the "hideous strife of politics," the "bitter thoughts and violent deeds" precipitated by mass mobilization, was alien to "the true inwardness of British opinion," as exemplified by the people of rural England. To prove his point, he hailed a passing policeman, whom he confidently dubbed "the Voice of England," and asked his "'opinion as to this trouble in Ireland.'" The constable replied in dense Irish brogue, "'Ah begob, it's all the fault iv the dirty Gover'mint.'" His "later conversation" further persuaded Stoker "that Home Rule was of little moment to that guardian of law, he was an out and out Fenian."[65] Afterward, Stoker notes triumphantly, allusion to "the voice of England" became an unfailing counter to Irving's complaints about Home Rule.

Whether this incident amounts to embellished fact or Stoker's wish-fulfilling fantasy, "The Voice of England" section of *Personal Reminiscences* seems painstakingly contoured to elucidate and to vindicate Stoker's view on the Anglo-Irish nexus. On the one hand, it stands as an exemplum of the mutual ethnic incorporation that Stoker increasingly took as the bedrock reality of the United Kingdom. The British law has here absorbed the Irishman as both its subject and its agent, and it has been absorbed and subjected in turn to Irish intonations, Irish idioms, and Irish attitudes. There has occurred, in other words, an interpenetration of the "voice of England" and the sociolects of its junior partner. On the other hand, the refusal to own this symbiosis, or to pay due recognition to all of its component parts, engenders the impulse to lawless violence here evinced by the very "guardian of the law." In Irving's easy appropriation of all of the constituencies of Great Britain to the standards, tastes, and interests of the English "folk"—the paradigmatic ploy of internal colonialism—lies the recipe for an explosive dynamic of ethnic imitation and rivalry. Men like this Irish constable, encouraged to identify with the British aggressor and invested with the insignia and authority of that identification, can find a place proper to their social and symbolic mandate only by pushing that identification to the logical extreme of fratricidal aggression and usurpation.

Instead of defending Home Rule on the customary nationalist basis—that Ireland represents a distinct locus and its people a racially distinct entity—Stoker's vignette suggests that Home Rule, by institutionalizing political subdivision consistent with the inherently multicultural nature of the United Kingdom, might serve as an antidote to the *violently exclusionary identity politics undergirding British imperialism and Irish nationalism alike.* From this perspective, Stoker's self-identification as a "Philosophical Home Ruler" does not mean simply that he was an armchair moderate in his commitment to devolution, as is generally supposed, but that his advocacy of Home Rule was theoretically grounded, a matter of principle.[66] It is precisely this theoretical grounding that *Dracula* elaborates, precisely this type of bilateral critique that *Dracula* encodes. Read as an Anglo-Celtic, as opposed to a traditionally Anglo-Irish, fantasy construction, the novel contrives to betray (expose/traduce) the racial imperialism and essentialist ideology that it has seemed to promulgate, deliberately working through the pathos of metrocolonial immixture to an ethos of domestic cosmopolitanism.

2

"The Dualitists":
Prelude to *Dracula*

As noted in the introduction, critics seeking a precedent to authorize an Irish reading of *Dracula* have typically and not unreasonably gravitated to *The Snake's Pass,* Stoker's only novel set on Irish soil and his only narrative rendition of the familiar political allegory of the "metropolitan marriage." But while *The Snake's Pass*'s predictably troubled romance between an English landlord and an untutored Celtic peasant girl speaks more openly *about* the Irish situation than does any of Stoker's other fictions, it does not speak *to* the Irish Question or the metrocolonial condition, as *Dracula* does, in a symbolic register that is itself emblematic of its political referent. The precursor of this sophisticated economy of representation is, as its title indicates, the early short story "The Dualitists; or, The Death Doom of the Double Born," whose reintroduction into the Irish canon of Stoker's work brings into focus the problems of identity, racial and otherwise, that animate it.[1]

"The Dualitists" allegorizes the ambivalence of the metrocolonial subject position as a proto-Lacanian agon of the mirror phase, a psychodrama of imitation and rivalry—not unrelated to that enacted in Stoker's vignette "The Voice of England."[2] Adapted from Dion Boucicault's *The Corsican Brothers,* which the Lyceum first produced, under Stoker's management, in 1880, the plot centers on the young friends Harry Merford and Tommy Santon, whose preternatural intimacy, surpassing the likes of "Castor and Pollux [twins], Damon and Pythias [friends], and Eloise and Abelard [lovers]" (48), raises so much concern in "nurse, and father, and mother" (48) that these authority figures threaten the boys, unsuccessfully, with "whip and imprisonment, and hunger and thirst, and darkness and solitude" should they continue to meet (48). Compelled to secrecy, the boys take to conversing on the rooftops, causing damage to the home of their neighbors, the Bubbs, who demand payment from the boys' "respective sires" to renovate (48). After this attempt to force a parting fails, the boys' parents adopt a different tack, one more along the lines of symbolic communication or subliminal cues. One Christmas, they give each boy a knife, distinguished by his initials, a master signifier of his individual subjectivity. Now since the parents likely feared some manner of homoeroticism in the lads' intimacy (a never distant possibility in Stoker's works), the gift of such an obvious phallic symbol, monogrammed, seems intended to impart to each boy a positive sense of his masculine *gender* identity, predicated upon his assumption of a sovereign and distinct *personal* identity, a sense of absolute self-ownership. The parents, in other words, assume and attempt to transmit the dominant late-Victorian ideal of manliness, which consisted in the autonomizing capacities of self-discipline, self-containment, and self-possession.

Like everything in this story, the boys' response manifests a significant duality. Reasserting their couplehood, on the one hand, the boys compare their prizes with "the fondness of doting parents" (50); they then establish their equality "in size, strength, and beauty," their indistinguishability "but for the initials scratched in the handles" (50); and finally they deliberate upon the vengeance they were to wreak together upon the homes of their respective parents. But heeding, on the other hand, the injunction to separate, the boys "began mutually to brag of the superior excellence of their respective weapons. Tommy insisted that his was the sharper, Harry asserted that his was the stronger of the two. Hotter and hotter grew the war of words" (50). In the end, each boy puts his weapon to the test by "hacking" it against the other. This increasingly forceful effort to draw some competitive and, ultimately, some ontological distinction between the weapons serves to reduce them to a perfectly identical state of dilapidation and impotence. The outcome, however, produces in the lads a manic self-destructive joy—or what Lacan calls *jouissance*[3]— driving them on a continual hunt for paired objects that they might "hack" against one another in an effort to differentiate them by violence. Renewing their insurrectionary partnership, Harry and Tommy all but destroy their parents' extensive home furnishings matched set by matched set to satisfy the "infatuation—a madness—a frenzy," of the game "hack" (52).

Eventually, the boys graduate from inanimate to animate objects and, finally, from figurative to literal children. They entice and trap the belated, beloved offspring of Ephraim Bubb and Sophonisba Bubb, Zachariah and Zerubbabel, a set of loving identical twins, who embody the idealized potential form of Harry and Tommy's own symbiotic "duality." The mischievous boys then begin to mash the infant twins together, and in this "apotheosis of [their] art" (55), they set the stage for the tale's final, manifold, and utterly bizarre tragedy: the wholesale (self-)extermination of the Bubb clan.

The psychoanalytic import of Harry and Tommy's action is both straightforward and compelling. Subject to the familial and social imperative of individuation, the "duality" of the inseparable boys issues in contrary psychic drives: one toward mutual identification, manifest in their ongoing quest to find matching phallic signifiers of selfhood, and a second toward complete disjunction, manifest in the boys' violent efforts to force a recognizable difference between the signifiers. In Lacanian terms, the boys fail to graduate fully from the Imaginary to the Symbolic order pursuant to the injunction to separate. The parental dictum proved so traumatic that it splits the boys' desire in two, producing on one side a deep-seated resistance to the ordinance, manifest in the boys' continued mutual attraction and allegiance, and on the other side a kind of compulsive repetition of the ordinance, enacted in the incessant and violently abrasive polarization of the "hacking" contest. The result is a vicious and addictive cycle in which every fulfillment breeds frustration and vice versa, so that the frenzy and brutality accelerate out of control, exhausting themselves only in a displaced form of self-immolation—the assault on the twins—after which Tommy and Harry slide, as if by magic, into contented, distinguished, and exemplary lives.

Key features of this macabre fantasy, general and specific, indicate that its underlying content involves Anglo-Irish fraternity and antagonism. First, by introducing the boys' surrogate objects of power and desire as their figurative children, which they in some sense become, Stoker introduces the issues of lineal filiation and internecine tribal warfare, which dominated the (Dis)United Kingdom of his day. More pointedly, the inflaming condition of the boys' mayhem is not unlike that which triggered racial tension in late-Victorian Ireland, with similarly ruinous consequences to person and property: a narcissism of small differences, otherwise known as proximateness.[4] In this situation, individuals (like Harry and Tommy) or groups (like the English and the Irish) are constituted symbiotically but defined disjunctively and, as such, can neither maintain clear and stable boundaries nor resolve into happy dyadic union, but struggle, sometimes violently, with an antagonism that is both internal and external, a difference too near to be excluded outright and a nearness too different to be assimilated whole.

Second, by giving the boys' dueling objects such an unmistakably phallic cast, Stoker adduces gender as the ideological medium of this lineal or tribal antagonism. The boys join in a struggle to prove their manhood by desperately trying to feminize one another, a dynamic that captures, on a miniature scale, the discursive contest between the imperialist typology of the feminine Celt and the Irish counterimage of the hypermasculine Gael.[5] This gendering of the dispute is by no means adventitious; it responds, along patriarchal lines, to the inherent sexuality of the metrocolonial condition, its highly charged imbrication of self and not-self, group identity and otherness. Perhaps because of the subtle ethnic differences infusing the Stoker family narratives and structure, Bram himself possessed a peculiar awareness of this sexual ingredient of racial and national tensions, an ingredient that becomes central in his most notorious dualitist, the Irish Dracula.

Finally, and most importantly, by taking the extraordinary step of peppering the account of juvenile outrage with the wildly incongruous language of state administration and policy, Stoker takes care to make legible the story's more sweeping topical analogies to the Irish situation. Phrases like "home authorities" (48), "rumours of war" (47), "schemes of domestic reform," "big with revolution," "ideas of reform" (49), "schemes of improvement" (50), "domestic calamity" (51), "schemes of destruction," "concerted scheme of action" (52), "parental mansion" (51), "deeds of darkness" (48), "national honors" (49), and "plan a new campaign" (53) not only extend the allegory to the world historical level but also allude with some degree of specificity to the political currents in Ireland during the period of the story's conception, composition, and publication, 1880–87. Following the crop failure of 1879, the worst such "domestic calamity" since the Great Famine, the "home authorities" confronted an Ireland "big with revolution" (the New Departure, 1882) and rife with "deeds of darkness" (outrages committed by the mythic Captain Moonlight and the very real agrarian Fenians of the Land League) and "schemes of destruction" to the "parental mansions" of the Ascendancy (the Land War, 1879–82). They responded with "schemes of domestic reform," most notably the Land Acts of 1881–82, and their own "concerted schemes" of action, most notoriously the Coercion policies hatched over the same period. The insufficiency of these Liberal measures and the Tory "ideas of reform" that succeeded them (killing Home Rule with kindness) left "rumours of war" abroad in Britain at the time Stoker was inditing this story, 1886–87, and prompted such nationalist luminaries as William O'Brien and John Dillon, Stoker's cousin, to "plan a new campaign," officially known as "the Plan of Campaign," to which Stoker surely alludes here, as he does in *Dracula* (*ED* 382). The Tory countermeasure was the notorious Crimes Bill framed over two years and finally instituted in the very year Stoker's domestic crime tale was published. At the vortex of these revolutionary, repressive, and reformist maneuverings stood the nationalist demand for Home Rule, which Gladstone tried to pass into law in 1886, with the Government of Ireland Act. In the broadest sense, of course, Stoker's contemporaneous story, "The Dualitists," unfolds as a giant narrative pun on the idea of Home Rule and an allegorical parody of the related domestic struggle over domestic space.

The key to the rhetorical construction of "The Dualitists" is that it denies the reader any basis for taking sides. The boys appear and act exactly the same. By this means, the text positions the reader instead to apprehend the calamitous events of this story as effects of the boys' futile obsession with self-identity. The problem is not that Tommy and Harry are of themselves interchangeable, incapable of sustaining the individuality enjoined by their respective parents; it is rather that in becoming the central occupation of their shared lives, the boys' quest for individuation and differentiation renders them interchangeable, perpetually defeating its own designs. The very attempt to distinguish the dueling phallic marks of identity only refashions their indistinguishability. Like "The Voice of England," this parable bears implications that run directly counter to the ethnic and gender essentialism that increasingly dominated both sides of the Irish Question, counter as well to the ideologies of atavism and degeneration frequently imputed to Stoker himself. "The Dualitists" specifically aims at deconstructing these racial logics, for it narrativizes how the will to lineal distinction and superiority only reproduces and aggravates the circumstance it would resolve: the ambivalent immixture of self and other at the heart of metro-colonial society and subjectivity.

Put another way, just as the title doubles the sign of duality (Dualitists, double born), the narrative doubles the concept of duality, to significant political ends. The *symbiotic* duality of Tommy and Harry is not dissolved, but distorted and debased by the introduction of the paternal law of individual/lineal distinction, which splits the psychic economy of these subjects, leaving a restless *schismatic* duality in its wake. The allegorical relevance to the Irish situation is not far to seek. As Luke Gibbons has noted, "the racial concept of the Irish character" first arose as an instrument of colonial hierarchy, a means of naturalizing and thus essentializing invidious distinctions between conqueror and conquered, and it was then reappropriated in Irish nationalist discourse as an instrument of colonial resistance, a means of mobilizing and justifying demands for independent statehood.[6] At this point, the imperialist assertion of a discrete Irish racial essence turned against itself, undermining the very hegemony it was meant to support. For its part, the corresponding nationalist reification of such an essence took shape, in Gibbons's words, as "an extension of colonialism" in the guise of an "antidote," a "mimicry of Engⷪ.ish life," working to foreclose the more authentically Irish possibility of a multiracial symbiosis.[7]

With his mixed ethnic heritage and his immersion in contemporary racial theory, Stoker was peculiarly situated to appreciate both the necessity and the tremendous difficulty of articulating such an implicitly cosmopolitan vision, and we have already outlined his nonfictional approaches to this task. His strategy in "The Dualitists" is to emphasize the delicate, impossibly vulnerable character of symbiotic duality itself. His key move in this regard is to identify this "native" metrocolonial promise of Ireland with the eroticized innocence of early childhood: Harry and Tommy *before* the repressive parental law. With this extremely clever narrative gambit, Stoker implicitly invokes *both* the Celtic-nationalist trope of precolonial Ireland as an Edenic space of social unity *and* the Anglo-imperialist caricature of indigenous Irish culture and society as a vestigial remainder of humankind's primitive childhood. Stoker then progressively displaces both myths into a new allegorical synthesis, the burden of which is that these partial (in both senses) and essentializing representations of Irishness are the vehicles of a law of "pure" identity that betrays the real prospective paradise of a racially amalgamated Irish nation. Ireland's long-standing fratricidal ordeal, this figural dynamic suggests, is but the essentializing reduction and perversion of its "native" symbiotic promise.

Stoker proceeds to fold the fall from idealized to schismatic duality into the Gothic structure of the narrative. The tale begins by personifying the beatitudes of symbiotic duality in the play of Harry and Tommy, before their parents' fateful intervention, but ends by personifying this blessed estate in the primary participant victims of Harry and Tommy's developing schismatic obsession, Zachariah and Zerubbabel. The exact resemblance of these identical twins to one another, which makes them perfect specimens for the "hack," is but the outward sign for their perfect amity, their unbroken contentment in their duality. Stoker appends verse to this effect, which links the fellowship of the twins to the politically valenced ideal of domestic harmony: "They grew in beauty side by side / They filled one home, etc." (47). But their comfort in their symbiotic status seems to depend upon their remaining sequestered in a presocial bower. No sooner are the twins tempted by Harry and Tommy to advance "boldly into the great world—the *terra incognita,* the *ultima thule* of the paternal domain" (55)—than they find themselves enlisted as implements in the youths' brutal competition, the present aim of which is to coerce the little twins into inflicting fatal marks of difference upon one another. Like Tommy and Harry, the twins cannot cross into the social register without being immediately subject to its primary symbolic law, the imperative to individual and lineal distinction, which cannot but mangle psychic economies predicated upon mutuality and immixing.

Indeed, the subtitle of the story, "The Death Doom of the Double Born," refers specifically to the Bubb twins in their congenital accursedness, and yet it is crucial to note that the Bubbs suffer *not at all* from their native symbiotic duality. They suffer rather from the schismatic effects of an alien standard or mandate of self-identity arbitrarily enacted upon them. Of course, the same is true of Tommy and Harry, who perform the arbitrary enactment or, rather, force the twins to perform the arbitrary enactment upon one another. With this vertiginous doubling and redoubling, Stoker reveals the story's central paradox: that the standard or mandate of self-identity, being socially inherited and unconsciously internalized, is as endemic as it is alien, as desired as it is inflicted, as systematic as it is arbitrary, generating consequences that not only engulf but also *implicate* everyone in its path.

There is, I would submit, something distinctively metrocolonial about this paradox, for it speaks most clearly to a form of subjectivity that has been doubly inscribed in the dominant and subdominant positions of prevailing racial hierarchies, a form of subjectivity whose interests lie in a certain consolidation as well as a certain abrogation of lineal and ethnic distinctions, a form of subjectivity imperfectly enfranchised by existing articulations of the law of social identity. Indeed, one articulation of the historical conditions under which Stoker's work came so plainly to solicit, and even prefigure, psychoanalytic theories of the unconscious might run as follows: to be a metrocolonial subject is always to find oneself inculpated in some unconscious way or at some unforeseeable point in one's own victimization.

Stoker underscores the last point in the climax of "The Dualists," in which his meticulous choice of phrase and his spectacular use of symbolism collaborate in creating a sense of chain-reaction moral responsibility. First, the proud father, Ephraim Bubb, does not just see his sons and heirs being bludgeoned together, but perceives them "being made unconsciously and helplessly guilty of the crime of fratricide" (57). "Baffled in every effort" to bring the practice to a halt, Ephraim chases Tommy and Harry, who are still holding the twins, onto a rooftop and shoots at them with (of course) "a double barreled gun" (57). His purpose, to sever the twins forcibly from their twinned torturers, rings yet another variation on the story's separation/differentiation theme. Ephraim only succeeds, however, in blowing "the heads off his own offspring" and so becomes, unwittingly but culpably, an "infanticide," a term Stoker repeats for emphasis (57). Lastly, the bodies of the twins, tossed from the roof in triumph, crush Ephraim and Sophonisba on their way down, and the twins are said to be "posthumously guilty of parricide" (57). With this outcome, the parental mandate prompting Harry and Tommy's acts of (self-)destruction return upon the parental head of Ephraim as the real self-destruction triggered by his actions. The lifeless "masses" of the Bubb twins land on their parents with the entire weight of a social history defined, like the Irish predicament it allegorizes, by the profound heteronomy of its nonetheless accountable actors, their transmission of a baneful agency exceeding all conscious control.

In a chilling coda, the Bubbs are "found guilty," and by "an *intelligent* coroner's jury" yet, of both "infanticide and suicide on the [false] evidence of Harry and Tommy" (57; emphasis added). That is to say, they are attached as the bearers of the finally unattachable force of divisiveness circulating throughout the neighborhood, and their attachment is literalized for posterity in the "maimed rights" of their burial (58): "They had stakes driven through their middles to pin them down in their unhollowed graves until the crack of doom" (58). The extreme measure answers, of course, to the contemporary belief that (displaced) suicides like the Bubbs might turn into *nosferatu,* vampires, like Dracula, who accosts Lucy Westenra on the suicide seat of Whitby Cemetery after having apparently slain Mr. Swales on the same spot.[8] Given the uncanny circumstances and the strange nature of the Bubbs' criminal "guilt," their method of interment can be seen to introduce an association between the undead and the unconscious, which *Dracula* will bring to fruition. The vampire motif here stands as nothing less than the final testament, as it were, of the "death doom of the double born," the devastation of an "innocent" people by a daimonic social force that is of and yet beyond them. It foreshadows in this regard Dracula's crucial psychosymbolic role as the doppelgänger of the apparently virtuous and heroic protagonists of the novel, a secret sharer at once dangerous and desirable, repudiated and irresistible—in short, an emanation of their own double-born status. And since the disruptive force of duality in this story consists precisely in the attempt to force a law of identity that would proscribe it, we should not be too surprised to find the same peculiar twist of moral logic informing *Dracula*. The real evil of the vampire, uncannily enough, lies in his being the arch-exponent of this identitarian social logic rather than the agent of its degenerative doom.

3

The Metrocolonial Vampire

Ireland and the Irish Question may be said to constitute the "other scene" of *Dracula*, a never fully present correlative to the official narrative concerning the Balkans and the Eastern Question, at once a supplementary shadow term and the novel's ultimate object of reference. Like any proper dream or fantasy scenario, Ireland intersects with the manifest content, here Transylvania, in an overdetermined manner: verbally, topographically, historically, politically. For that very reason, however, the two spaces cannot be aligned in a straightforward vehicle-tenor relationship. As Freud's analysis of dreams illustrates, often to its clinical detriment, overdetermination inevitably passes at some point into its seeming opposite, undecidability. Following this strange logic, Stoker's Ireland and Transylvania engage in a *trompe l'oeil* oscillation, flipping in and out of identification with one another, and through this phantasmal geography, Stoker sets about representing Ireland's otherness to itself, its own undecidability as a national community.

The evidence for this figural connection begins at the level of the signifier. As several critics have noted, the literal meaning of the name *Transylvania*, "beyond the forest," irresistibly suggests "beyond the Pale," which historically refers to the broad expanse of Ireland that remained outside and resistant to British military and political control for most of the colonial epoch. What has gone unremarked, however, is Stoker's deliberate and insistent elaboration of this implicit word play over the course of the narrative. In the first instance, the name of Dracula's self-identified tribal group, the Szekelys, which means "at the frontier or beyond" (*ED* 39 n.

6), reinforces and radicalizes the transnational pun while simultaneously glancing sidelong at Ireland's own position at or beyond the frontier between metropole and empire. When Dracula finally comes into direct confrontation with Jonathan Harker, Van Helsing, and the rest (whom I shall henceforth denominate "Little England"), he derides them as "pale faces" (D 267), an odd ethnic slur considering the Count's own "extraordinary pallor" (24), unless it also functions to signal Dracula's displaced and uncontrolled Irishness, his indomitable Gaelic or Celtic opposition to the Anglo invader (Stephen Dedalus deploys a similar pun in *Ulysses,* indicating its currency).[1]

As if to isolate the political resonance of the Count's epithet, this dramatic encounter with Little England occurs in a London townhouse whose purchase was arranged in Sackville Street, eponymous with the main thoroughfare of Dublin, the very heart of the Pale, here momentarily reinscribed at the center of the metropolitan capital. Moreover, Dracula's phrase picks up on the prior usage of his agent/victim, R. N. Renfield, who complains, "I don't care for the pale people" (245) while perishing in the forced custody of the Little England crew. Thus, this single pun tends retrospectively to mark Jonathan Harker's business trip as an Occidentalist as well as an Orientalist incursion. That is to say, the first "occidental tourist," pace Arata, is not Dracula, but Harker.[2] Colonization in *Dracula* is always already reversed, a point to which we will return.

A founding insight of the Irish *Dracula* school of criticism has been that Harker's observations in Transylvania refer in whole or in part to the features of life in Ireland in the nineteenth century.[3] I think it would be more accurate to say that Harker's observations in Transylvania seem intended to echo or recall prominent treatises, received wisdom, and well-worn remarks, not to mention canards about Ireland. His comment on the immodesty of a peasant woman's native dress, for example, rehearses Edmund Spenser's strictures on Irish women's attire in *A View of the Present State of Ireland.*[4] Harker's complaint about dilatory trains and his comments on the "idolatrous" peasants kneeling by a roadside shrine in a "self-surrender of devotion" (11), like figures "in old missals" (15), would have been familiar enough from Anglocentric travel narratives about Ireland. So too would have been his sense of the general depopulation of the countryside.

Harker's still more horrific observation, the penchant of Dracula and his harem for stealing and eating children, does not derive, to my knowledge, from vampire lore at all; it rather combines salient elements of Irish letters and legend. The child thievery likely comes from tales of Irish fairies, which had been most recently compiled by Stoker's friend and social mentor in Ireland Lady Jane Wilde ("Speranza"), in her *Ancient Legends in Ireland*, published just two years before Stoker began work on his novel.[5] W. B. Yeats's well-known Celtic Twilight poem "The Stolen Child" likewise helped to popularize the lore. Child cannibalism, for its part, finds one primary Irish antecedent in Jonathan Swift's mordant satire "A Modest Proposal," which recommends breeding Irish babies for human consumption as a measure for curing the country's stubborn economic woes. Finally, Harker's description of Castle Dracula, grand but grim, dominant but desolate, recalls the Big House of latter day Anglo-Irish literature, a monument to misrule, now slowly lapsing into genteel squalor and social obsolescence.[6]

From the above catalog, let me repeat, we must not draw the customary inference that the social landscape of Stoker's Transylvania deliberately and directly evokes the conditions of contemporary Ireland, but rather that Harker's report on Transylvania evokes a multigeneric, multiethnic, and multiperspectival construction of Ireland that had developed, unevenly, over an extended period. Only by acknowledging a certain theoretical distance between Harker's express account and the condition on the ground can we begin to appreciate and reckon with Stoker's ironic qualifications of the representational authority that he seems to grant his hero-protagonist. Further, only by articulating the fundamentally *textual* nature of *Dracula*'s geopolitical parallelism can we appreciate that the phantasmatic Transylvanian allegory does not fail, as Glover contends, to capture the identity of its Irish referent,[7] but rather succeeds in indexing the opacity, the hybridity, and the self-alterity of that referent, its intractability to univocal or even coherent representation.

The history shaping Ireland's fate likewise finds its checkered reflection in the Transylvania of Harker's highly mediated chronicle. Like Ireland, Transylvania is a "whirlpool" of ethnic difference (40), and the four distinct nationalities Harker designates as populating the region (Wallachs, Saxons, Magyars, and their subdivision, the Szekelys) provide a suspiciously neat symmetry with the four main ethnicities of modern Ireland (Anglos, Celts, Norse, and their subdivision, the Normans). Indeed, Stoker apparently decided to trim the number of relevant Transylvanian "nationalities" in order to cook this quite precise correspondence.[8] Like the ethnic groups of Ireland, those of Transylvania have, on Dracula's account, undertaken an interminable series of religious, dynastic, imperialistic, and ethnic wars, not just among themselves, but with, for, and against foreign

invaders. As Nina Auerbach and David Skal puts it, "the history of Transylvania is the history of whom it belongs to" (*D* 9), and the same has of
course been true of Ireland, which James Joyce likens to a "pawn shop."[9]
In both cases, the legacy of such long, multilateral contestation is a highly
variable and volatile ethno-national intermixture.

Behind these parallel historical problems looms a more timely geopolitical connection. In placing Transylvania and Ireland in an oscillating
relationship with one another, the metaphorical logic of *Dracula* mirrors
the political calculus of contemporaneous British foreign policy deliberations, in which the Irish Question and the Eastern Question bore upon
and stood in for one another in a number of ways. First, in the words of
the Irish nationalist member of Parliament T. P. O'Connor, "Interest in
the Eastern question" was "obliterated" around 1881 "by the obsession
with Ireland [which] spread like a ghost over every other preoccupation."[10] Even O'Connor's phraseology is consonant with Stoker's Gothic yarn. This obsession, in turn, allowed the Irish Parliamentary party
leadership to hold the Eastern diplomacy of the Liberal party hostage to
the irredentist agenda.

In the end, the Eastern reaches imaged in *Dracula* actually came to serve
as a model within Irish Parliamentary nationalism for a solution to the Irish
Question not incompatible with Stoker's political beliefs—which is also to
say that Stoker's strategy of making Transylvania a wholly other place that
was nonetheless a privileged metaphor of his Irish home had a specific basis in the foreign policy discourse of the time. Annexed to the Austro-Hungarian Empire in 1711, Transylvania was in 1867 placed under the rule of
Hungary, which at that time had achieved the sort of local autonomy shortly
to be sought by moral force Irish nationalists: a semidetached status linking it to the empire solely through the Crown. When Isaac Butt, Stoker's
Trinity College acquaintance, founded the Home Rule movement a few
years later, he floated the Hungarian arrangement as a blueprint for his own
devolutionary scheme.[11] More importantly, Charles Stewart Parnell recir-
culated the Hungarian paradigm in October 1885 as a prospective settle-
ment of the Irish Question, which had by now grown positively explosive,
and his speech earned the approval of both the Tory leader Lord Salisbury,
who judged the plan "reasonable," and Stoker's Liberal favorite Gladstone,
who thought the plan provided a workable basis for future bargaining.[12]
Five years before Stoker began researching *Dracula,* then, and a decade
before he began writing, the circumstance of Hungary galvanized a brief
moment of rapprochement among the main adversaries in the parliamen-

tary struggle over Home Rule. Sometime thereafter, Parnell played with the more hostile strategy of outright parliamentary withdrawal, which represented the very means whereby Hungary ultimately secured autonomy.[13]

Against this backdrop, Stoker's decision to cast the socioeconomic conditions of Transylvanian life in such a desperate light can be understood as a characteristically hedged political gesture reflecting a characteristically ambivalent political temper. Do the "troubles" of Stoker's Transylvania point to the hopeless failure of the colonial status quo in Ireland or do they express acute anxiety over how the still accumulating Anglo-Irish distrust might affect any future devolution? Does his gesture point to the urgency of the Home Rule platform or its increasingly fatal belatedness? Stoker's allegory does not merely decline to make available the answer to such questions; his allegory produces such questions strategically, as a means for conveying the positive unanswerability of the Irish Question generally *within the reigning framework of binary opposition.*

Just as the Irish Question hybridizes and destabilizes the import of Transylvania in the novel, so does the question of Irishness hybridize and destabilize the standing of the Count. Central to the vogue of an Irish *Dracula* has been, well, an Irish Dracula. But to read the Count in an Irish register is to multiply his pedigree, muddle his status, and disseminate his historical and political significance.

Like nineteenth-century Ireland, Stoker's Transylvania has suffered a famine and a plague, and Dracula is symbolically associated with both: the vampire, according to Stoker's working notes, brings on drought,[14] and Dracula represents, of course, a virulent force of contagion (as Stoker underscores by linking the spectacle of Renfield's demise with the report of a death watch during the kind of cholera epidemic Charlotte Stoker had survived to tell about; D 234). These allegorical indices of historical responsibility consist with the novel's Irish-enough scenario, in which a terrorized but restive peasantry serves a hated grandee, who boasts of his "old family" (29), dwells in a Big House, and does a pretty good imitation of an absentee landlord.[15] If this were not enough evidence to clinch an allegorical identification of Dracula with the increasingly vilified Anglo-Irish Ascendancy, Seamus Deane, Terry Eagleton, and others have decoded the Count's fatal attachment to his dirt as a Gothic figuration of the similarly fatal dependency of the Ascendancy ruling caste upon the land that they owned, which was steadily declining in relative value as industrial capital became the coin of the realm and the passport to class regeneration.[16]

From the Nationalist point of view, that dependency had long since

turned the Anglo-Irish patricians into a species of social parasite for which
the dominant metaphor was none other than the vampire. Given the other contextual allusions, accordingly, the figure of Dracula recalls Percy
Bysshe Shelley's comment, long before the famine, that "the Aristocracy
of Ireland sucks the veins of inhabitants" or Fanny Parnell's reprobation
of the same class as "coroneted ghouls." And surely Dracula is intended
to bring to mind Michael Davitt's castigation of the Irish landowners as
"cormorant vampires"—after all, Dracula's initial assault on Lucy Westenra leaves her with "an appetite like a cormorant" (101). Lastly, Van
Helsing's many impassioned admonitions to his fellows chime with William O'Brien's exhortations of the Irish tenantry to "fight like men" against
the landowning "bloodsuckers."[17] In a socioeconomic as well as a political sense, then, Joep Loerrsen seems entirely justified in processing Dracula as a displaced Irish aristocrat, "the undead remnant of the feudal past
battening on the vitality of the living."[18]

Well, perhaps not entirely. The Count's portrait does yield opposing implications. For example, Dracula cherishes his bit of earth specifically for
the blood bravely spilled thereon: "'There is hardly a foot of soil in all the
region,'" Dracula declares proudly, "'that has not been enriched by the
blood of men, patriots and invaders . . . sheltered in the friendly soil'" (27).
Even Van Helsing concedes that the blood so cherished by Dracula has
sanctified the land: "Great men and good women . . . their graves make
sacred the earth where alone this foulness can dwell" (213). The Count's
martial politics thus bear the aspect of a secular religion, with strong resonance of the iconography of Christ's Passion. And such a redemptive, liturgical attitude toward patriotic bloodshed aligns him not with the Ascendancy landowners but with their sworn enemies, the increasingly Catholic
Fenian revolutionaries, who were, at the time of *Dracula*'s composition,
mainly mobilized under the unofficial auspices of the explicitly pro-tenant
resistance organization, the Land League.

The Fenian cult of blood sacrifice and resurrection held Ireland's martyrs to be immortalized by the blood they enthusiastically shed, which
would bring forth successive generations of nationalist heroes to eulogize
and emulate them. Taking the pre-Christian Celtic myth of sovereignty as
its distinctively Irish provenance, this cult took hold after the futile yet
inspirational risings of 1798 and 1803 and the subsequent canonization
of Robert Emmet, whose famous speech before his execution virtually set
the terms of modern Irish martyrology.[19] It received renewed emphasis with
the discovery in 1842 of Wolfe Tone's burial site in Bodenstown, memori-

alized in the poem "Tone's Grave" by the likewise short-lived Young Ire-
lander Thomas Davis.[20] The cult achieved critical mass at midcentury with
the monster funeral the Fenians staged for Terrence Bellow MacManus,
declaring him, in effect, a secular saint, and with the execution of the
Manchester Martyrs, one of whom delivered a paean to blood sacrifice that
was to become the semiofficial anthem of the Irish Republican Brotherhood (Whether on the scaffold high / Or the battlefield we die, / Oh, what
matter, when for Erin dear we fall?).[21]

But the ethos of regenerative blood sacrifice did not come to full expression until the period Stoker set about researching and writing *Dracula*
(1890–97). The breakdown in reformist nationalism after the fall of Parnell, coupled with the near quiescence of advanced physical force nationalism after the unauthorized Phoenix Park murders, created an opening
not just for cultural and literary brands of nationalism, as Yeats observed,
but for a more generalized investment in the politics of gesture and symbol, myth and ritual.[22] As the decade wore on, this performative politics
avant le lettre increasingly centered on commemorating the Rising of 1798,
along with the Emmet sequel, and the stage was set for a powerful resus-
citation of the religion of martyrdom as the centenary date approached.
In brief, rising qua insurrection, the traditional *political* sense of the term
in Ireland, translated into rising qua resurrection, the traditional *religious*
sense of the term. Revolutionary energies flowed backward, as it were, in
order to flow forward. Bodenstown became a shrine for the Fenians—
indeed, for nationalists of all varieties—who shaved off slivers of Tone's
newly erected gravestone as sacred relics. The literary tradition of blood
sacrifice, as expounded by mid-Victorian poets like James Clarence Mangan and Stoker's friend Lady Jane Wilde (writing as "Speranza"), enjoyed
a renaissance as well, supplemented by powerful new treatments of the
sovereignty myth. The latter were exemplified by Yeats's wildly popular
nationalist incitement *Cathleen Ni Houlihan,* which dramatizes Mother
Ireland's call to immortality through self-immolation: "They that had red
cheeks will have pale cheeks for my sake; and for all that they will think
they are well paid: they shall be remembered forever, they shall be speaking forever; the people shall hear them forever."[23] And growing out of this
legendary-historical matrix, cultural institutions devoted to cultivating a
traditionalist mode of Irish manhood, like the Irish Republican Brotherhood–dominated Gaelic Athletic Association, wound up lending at least
tacit support to the ethos of blood sacrifice. It was this social atmosphere,
in fact, that groomed the next and greatest generation of Irish martyrs, the

leaders of Easter 1916. Envisioning and enacting blood sacrifice less as an instrumental measure for winning Irish independence than as an end in itself—the resurrection of Ireland's patriotic spirit in repeated risings—radicals like Joseph Plunkett, Thomas MacDonagh, James Connolly, and, above all, Patrick Pearse gave blood sacrifice its final liturgical and evangelical form and came to be, for future generations, its embodiment.

So too, in a fragmentary allegorical sense, is Dracula. The blood sacrificed in the past, *literally* preserved in the ancestral graves, and then renewed in the blood feast of the present and future, offers Dracula something on the order of a perpetual resurrection, which the vampire himself credits, in a tribal and quasi-nationalistic act of commemoration, to the valor of slain patriots (*D* 27). From the standpoint of Little England, of course, Dracula's reproductive processes look like the permanent rising of a racial-cum-species other. A structural homology is thus sketched between the self-perpetuating dynamics of vampire life and irredentist martyrology. In either case, the seductive thrill of answering the call to "blood sacrifice" dovetails with becoming a part or vehicle of that call and achieving immortality on that basis.

Stoker goes so far as to link this fatal cycle of regeneration explicitly with the heritage of physical force Irish nationalism by casting Dracula in the role of updated sovereignty deity. Just as modern variants of the Poor Old Woman or Mother Ireland transform themselves into beautiful young women by drawing upon the spilled blood of their willing legions, so the similarly aged Count waxes perpetually younger and more vigorous by drawing the blood of his not-unwilling victims ("I did not want to stop him," declares Mina Harker; 251). As a matter of fact, this mythic correspondence underlies what is by critical consensus the most terrifying scene in the book. Jonathan Harker all but collapses when he espies the Count in Piccadilly and, "half in terror and half in amazement," tells his concerned wife: "'I believe it is the Count, he has grown young. My God, if this can be so! Oh my God! my God! If I only knew! if I only knew!'" (155). The uncanny recognizability of Dracula to Harker parallels the uncanny recognizability of the sovereignty figure in the Count to the Irish audience of the time. The Irish might have been expected to read the vampirism of Dracula as a complexly apposite metaphor for the patriotic summons delivered by Cathleen Ni Houlihan: each figure reproduces itself by dealing death and immortality in the same motion, engendering a tribe of the undead—biological/ontological in the one case, cultural/historical in the other. At this point we can understand why the sole indisputably Irish classification of Dracula in Stoker's own working notes consists of a single word, *Fenian*.[24]

There is a further, still more obvious line of correspondence between Dracula and the newly dominant peasant mode of Fenian revolutionary. The agrarian Fenians were "creatures of the night" in much the same fashion as Dracula. They were principally known for, and restricted to, acts of nocturnal mayhem. They even enlisted in this enterprise under a mythical leader, Captain Moonlight, to whom Dracula may well allude, particularly considering how prominently moonlight figures in the vamping of Mina Harker and Lucy Westenra (88, 226).

The contradiction that obtains, however, between Dracula's symbolic connection with the Anglo-Irish Ascendancy and with its political nemesis, the racially mixed but Gaelic-identified Fenian movement, by no means exhausts the conflictual overdetermination of Dracula's Irishness, which evolves over the course of the novel into a full-blown logic of self-alterity. Just as the Draculas seem to have allied themselves with all manner of opposing parties in the Balkan wars,[25] so Dracula's own subject position aligns him with various constituencies in the debate and struggle over Ireland. Through this logic of self-alterity, in turn, the Irishness of Dracula helps to configure other concerns of the novel while registering and working through the ambivalence implicit in the author's cross-grained social and ethnic identity. Nowhere is this more important than with respect to the most prominently discussed and most persistently misunderstood of these concerns, the question of the moral and physical degeneration of the racial stock in Great Britain.

❦ ❦ ❦

A number of critics, including Laura Croley and Kathleen Blake, have proposed that the peril of Dracula and vampirism stands in for the perceived fin de siècle threat of the residuum or lumpen proletariat in England's large industrial centers, a threat typically attached to particular immigrant groups and so conceived along racial as well as class lines. Although Dracula's aristocratic bearing, standing, and pedigree would seem to exempt him from any direct allegorical association with the urban underclass, it has been remarked that the Victorian bourgeoisie often divined a similar laxity, dissoluteness, impropriety, and unrespectability in the aristocratic and working classes, a likeness that the Transylvanian Count, with his rank odor, his nocturnal dissipations, his performance of menial household chores, and his fondness for dirt naps, might well be seen to embody. But what is important to remember for our purposes is that only in Ireland did this convergence of high and low social grades constitute a regular and obtrusive feature of both cultural stereotype and self-representation. On one side, the political cartoons of the day depicted the Anglo-Irish Ascendancy as an altogether tattered and shabby lot; the land they lived on was rapidly becoming, like that of the "Ascendancy" Dracula, the dirt they lived in.[26] On the other side, the Celtic-Catholic cottiers and day laborers often traced an ancient aristocratic, even royal, lineage for themselves ("All Irish. All kings sons," as Stephen Dedalus sardonically notes in *Ulysses*).[27]

Considered in a Hibernian register, the shabby genteel Dracula effectively encodes this distinctively Irish class ambiguity. A recent piece of scholarly confusion attests as much. Having identified Dracula as an absentee Anglo-Irish landlord, Seamus Deane proceeds to observe, ignoring the implicit contradiction, that the Count's conveyance to England is literally a "coffin ship,"[28] the name given to dangerous and disease-ridden vessels carrying the poorest Irish émigrés to foreign shores and, needless to say, enjoying *no* Ascendancy patronage whatever. Not unlike Stoker himself, Dracula appears an Anglo-Irish grandee at home, but looks to be "mere" Irish riff-raff abroad in England. As the phrasing here suggests, however, the question of class in Ireland is finally inseparable from the question of race; the highest and lowest Irish ranks split along ethnic as well as socioeconomic lines. Understood in this light, Stoker's decision to play upon class ambiguity in the figure of Dracula has significant and mostly unexamined implications for his *racial* philosophy. He exploits the conventional wisdom of the ambiguity of Irish class formations to undercut the conventional belief in the discrete racial essences of Anglo-Saxon and Celt.

In the decades following the famine, waves of wretched and bitterly reviled sons and daughters of Irish "kings" took up residence in English inner cities, especially Liverpool and London, where they formed a primary stimulus and target of metropolitan anxiety over degeneration and the residuum. Speaking precisely to this development, the Tory Unionist Lord Salisbury proclaimed, "Ireland is no doubt the worst symptom of the malady [of degeneration]. But . . . it is beginning to affect us in this country, though the stage is less advanced and the form is less acute."[29] Here again, Stoker sustains a careful and detailed parallelism with his infectious Transylvanian immigrant. Just as the character of Dracula's homeland comprises a pastiche of received perceptions of Ireland, learned and popular, the character of Dracula-in-England seems to have been built trait by stereotypical trait as a parody of stock perceptions of the Catholic Irish in England:

1. They live in squalor and spread disease (Dracula's intimate relations with both dirt and contagion are obvious).

2. They are reckless overbreeders (remember Jonathan Harker's agonized vision of the "new and ever-widening circle of semi-demons" to be engendered by Dracula).

3. They are congenitally and pathologically lawless, according to popular assumptions molded by the pseudoscientific findings of contemporary degeneration theory and anthropological terminology ("The Count," Mina Harker confidently declares, "is a criminal and of criminal type. Nordau and Lombroso would so classify him, and *qua* criminal he is of imperfectly formed mind"; 296).

4. Being evolutionary primitives, the improvident Irish of Herbert Spencer's description closely resemble children in their underdeveloped rationality and want of discipline (Van Helsing assures the crusaders of Little England, "'He [Dracula] be of child-brain in much . . . and it is of the child to do what he have done'"; 296). Within a Darwinian context, the primitivism imputed to the Irish by all manner of social commentators—from anthropologists (Robert Knox, Daniel Macintosh) to historians (James Anthony Froude, Sir Charles Dilke) to writers (Thomas Carlyle, Charles Kingsley) to physiognomists (John Beddoes) to popular caricaturists (John Tenniel, Matthew Morgan)—virtually place them in another (lower) species category, as the insistent simianization of the Irish throughout the Victorian period attests. Beyond the Pale of humanity, and in peculiar communication with the animal world, Dracula incarnates the slippage from racial to species other—the missing link phenomenon—to which the Irish were often subjected.[30] Indeed, the verdict rendered in the best-seller *A Tour of Ireland,* that the Irish "form a distinct race from the rest of mankind," chimes closely with the well-known idea of the vampire kind as a race apart.[31]

5. They are alien subversives whose arrival amounted to an "invasion" (Dracula on any conceivable geopolitical reading). And finally,

6. They just drink too much.[32]

As several critics have noted, the name *Dracula* puns on the Gaelic phrase *droch fhola,* meaning "bad blood," a tag that seems to trace the social anomie plaguing the imperial metropole to its Irish occupants.[33] But on the question of the ultimate source and significance of the "bad blood," this controlling Hibernian analogy divides against itself, leaving a *radically* hybridized Count, at once Anglo and Celtic, landlord and lumpen, tyrant and terrorist, the monstrous signifier of Stoker's own political dislocation and ambivalence, his simultaneous identification and disidentification with the antagonistic forms of metrocolonial identity.

Read in terms of Stoker's extensive and systematic Irish-Transylvanian analogy, the "bad blood" that *is* Dracula in London lends credence to Arata's germinal argument that the Count's London expedition—carefully prepared by the study of English history, politics, law, and society—allegorizes the guilt and anxiety-ridden metropolitan fantasy of reverse colonization, in which subalterns of the empire would return, perhaps vengefully, to England's shores, with disruptive effects on English life, degrading effects on English culture, and degenerative effects on the Anglo-Saxon race.[34] The same Irish-Transylvanian analogy, moreover, lends historical specificity to the nightmare of reverse colonialism. For if the return of the oppressed en masse was but the apocalyptic fantasy of a slowly declining imperial powerhouse, it was influenced by the very real mass influx of the Irish-Catholic other. This was not simply the largest and most conspicuous immigrant group during the nineteenth century, but it was also, thanks to the Act of Union, always already there, lurking within the precincts of the United Kingdom, an immigrant group whose menace culminated in the fact that its members were not technically immigrants. In addition, and for the same reason, it was the Celtic-Catholic Irish whom esteemed anthropologists and ethnographers like James Hunt and John Beddoes had labeled the collective embodiment of unregenerate primitivism.[35] In this fantasy, then, the act of vampiric transfusion and transformation stands as a metaphor of the spread of an atavistic or degenerative social malaise and the resulting reproduction of a physically depleted, intellectually arrested, and spiritually infirm race, unfit for the rigors of bourgeois democracy.[36] Jonathan Harker's sense of the Transylvanian peasants as backward, woefully superstitious, and entirely cowed offers colorable evidence for this sort of reverse colonialism fantasy.

But on the terms of the same transnational analogy, the "bad blood" of Dracula at home on his demesne, terrorizing the natives, attaches to a figure of Anglo-Irish rule or Ascendancy, who serves as both a stay and an extension, a garrison, in short, of the British colonial project itself. On these grounds, Dracula would not—or would not *only*—embody a fantasied threat posed by subdominant peoples to the ethno-national health and vigor of the English, he would register—or he would *also* register—the ethno-colonial threat posed *to* subdominant peoples by the English. Here the act of vampiric transfusion and transformation stands as a no less compelling metaphor of social contagion with a contrary political valence: it is a corporeal trope for the racial enervation and cultural dispossession and deracination of one (colonized) group and its reproduction as both mimic and puppet of another (hegemonic) group. Construed along these lines, Dracula's vampirism parodies the "soul-making" mission of British imperialism, the insistence on not only vanquishing but also reacculturating subject peoples and thereby seizing control over the internal structure of their desire. Just as the undead suck the blood of their victims by way of inducing them to internalize the vampiric form of being, so the Anglo-imperialistic agenda proposed detaching the colonized from indigenous belief and value systems by way of inducing them to internalize the self-legitimating tastes, standards, and lifestyles of their conquerors.

According to the theories of the time, from Nietzsche's to Nordau's, the colonizing process could reasonably be construed to entail not just a corruption, *strictu sensu,* of native ways of being but a distinct form of degenerative threat to the subject peoples or races. For if the problems of physical and moral deterioration were imputed on one side to an influx of atavistic racial and cultural forces into the metropole,[37] they were attributed on the other to modernization itself, the pace, complexity, and ease of which was seen to have rendered the most advanced people increasingly neurotic and effete.[38] Carrying the pathologies of industrialized urbanization, European colonizers could be expected to vitiate the simplicity, vigor, and vitality of the "savage" races, even as their exposure to these races threatened to stunt, disintegrate, or overwhelm their own civilized attainments. By making the imperialist vampire, Dracula-in-Transylvania, something of a decadent roué—Max Nordau's widely recognized type of modern elite degeneration—Stoker allows for a specifically Anglo-Saxon role in the transmission of social decline. At this point, Stoker's critique of metrocolonialism passes, unwittingly but irresistibly, into a tacit critique of the more far-flung colonial enterprise that he typically extolled.[39]

On this reading of vampirism as imperialist contagion, all the generally accepted indices of Dracula's reverse colonialism are themselves reversed once more into a kind of cultural unionism, the desperate self-identification with the metropole of a colonial settler class, the garrison of empire, dislocated by its occupation of and exposure to other(ed), less "advanced" peoples. Dracula's cited wish to perfect his English grammar and intonation, his inventory of English social and professional lists, his careful, almost obsessive study of English lore, all these mark him as a subject displaced by the empire he advances and yearning to be fully assimilated to its center. "'Well, I know that, did I move or speak in your London, none there are who would not know me for a stranger. That is not enough for me. Here I am noble; I am *boyar;* the common people know me, and I am master. But a stranger in a strange land; he is no one; men know him not— and to know him not is not to care for. I am content if I am like the rest, so that no man stops if he sees me, or pause in his speaking if he hear my words, to say "Ha, ha! A stranger!"'" (*D* 26). When Dracula voices sentiments on this order or dons Jonathan Harker's clothes and impersonates him or tells Mina, not without an aggrieved air, that he has long "fought" and "intrigued" for the likes of Little England, who would now destroy him, his sentiments resonate less of colonial subversion than of what Homi Bhabha calls "colonial mimicry," the efforts of the superintending colonial elite to imitate and internalize metropolitan norms.[40] If Dracula's self-conscious plan and attempt to perform proper Englishness confesses his continuing distance from fully metropolitan status, it also reveals the impress left upon the shape of his identity and the itinerary of his desire by the imperialist project, which he nevertheless continues to unsettle.

Initially coded as an Anglo-identified aristocrat in a hibernicized Transylvania, where he expresses a telling contempt for the native peasantry (27, 35), and subsequently coded as a déclassé Irish-identified alien in the rookeries of London, Dracula undergoes a wholesale metamorphosis in subject position that outstrips the relatively linear narrative and symbolic logic at work in the conventional reverse colonialism narrative. The Count's fugitive and conflicting allegorical valences, including the type and source of degenerative agency he might embody, are much better recuperated according to Freudian dream logic, which, in disregarding the classical limits of identity, can answer to the split and mixed nature of Irishness. Much like Stoker's own movement from Dublin, where he was marked as a solid "Anglo," to London, where he was marked as a suspect Irishman, Dracula's move from a Transylvanian estate bearing his name to the outcast East End of London condenses in a single action the multiple layers of contradiction implicit in the metrocolonial estate.

While the metrocolonial predicament had not been conceived or analyzed as such in Stoker's time, the schismatic force of social contagion that might be presumed to flow from this estate was represented in the popular press, and precisely in the terms discussed above: as dueling interpretations of the vampire metaphor, images upon which Stoker likely drew for his double vision of Dracula. On October 24, 1885, *Punch* magazine's

premiere political cartoonist, John Tenniel, published a now famous drawing entitled "The Irish Vampire."[41] It depicts a large vampire bat labeled
"The National League" (a Home Rule umbrella organization) poised over
the recumbent female form of Erin peacefully sleeping, harp at her side,
amidst her "four green fields." Insofar as the vampire vaguely resembles
Charles Stewart Parnell, the head of the Land League and the "Uncrowned
King of Ireland," it works a violent inversion on the iconography of the
aisling tradition of Irish poetry, wherein a passive female figure, allegorical of the Irish people-nation, awaits a royal deliverer from across the sea.
Two weeks later in the *Pilot* an anonymous response appeared entitled
"The British Vampire," depicting the same vampire bat, now labeled British rule, hovering above the same figure of Erin, now defiantly armed with
a sword engraved with the insignia of the National League.[42] Both cartoons, with details suitably altered, could serve as models or blueprints
of the fatal scene in which the newly landed Dracula first vamps a slum-
bering Lucy Westenra in the cemetery above Whitby: "There, on our favorite seat, the silver light of the moon struck a half-reclining figure, snowy
white. . . . Something dark stood behind the seat where the white figure
shown, and bent over it. What it was, whether man or beast, I could not
tell" (88). The *Punch* cartoon has been adduced as a decisive background
allusion in *Dracula*.[43] Viewed in isolation it has been taken, unsurprisingly,
to denote Stoker's conventional garrison class anxiety over the social and
political effects of a mass nationalist movement in Ireland. The cartoon
in the *Pilot,* which contributes to the long Irish nationalist tradition of
vampire invective, has been entirely overlooked, despite its relevance to
Stoker's Home Rule sympathies. But it is the dialogical relationship of the
two, rather than their respective partisan messages, that provides the appropriate contextual paradigm for Stoker's doubly articulated construction of Dracula.

To corroborate the point, the symbolic associations infusing the ethno-
national identity of Dracula's main victims split and double along homol-
ogous lines. The name *Lucy Westenra* loosely translates as "Light of the
West," an emblematic phrase frequently seen to enshrine her as an icon of
English racial superiority and cultural refinement and thus of the resulting
legitimacy of British world-historical domination—in short, as a beacon to
less-perfected eastern worlds like Transylvania. And to be sure, the novel
does portray the homeland of Dracula as "East of England" in an invidious sense. As numerous critics have observed, the entire Balkan peninsula
is "orientalized" from the very first paragraph of the text, where Jonathan

Harker records "the impression . . . that we were leaving the West and entering the East" (9) as an explanation for the tardiness of the trains. By the same token, the name *Lucy Westenra* might even admit the punning translation "Light of the West End," which would dub her a personification of enlightened, upper-caste London civilization, a beacon to those poor and barbarous East End immigrants, like the Irish, with whom the intruding vampire is linked. When read, however, against Stoker's likely sources, the dueling vampire cartoons and the aisling verse tradition they invoke, the name of Dracula's victim just as plausibly designates her a typically feminine icon or mythic personification of Erin, the "Western Light" of the British Empire. In a kind of hermeneutic version of the metrocolonial condition, it proves impossible, as a matter of interpretative logic, to choose definitively between these alternatives, which nonetheless exclude one another. That the recherché name Westenra belonged, in point of historical fact, to an Ascendancy family, the Barons of Rossmore in County Monaghan,[44] does not resolve the issue in the least, but rather reinforces its undecidability. Precisely owing to the equivocality of the metrocolonial situation, and the ethno-national subject position that it subtends, Lucy Westenra can appropriately represent her Rossmore namesakes as either/both Irish victims of colonialism or/and Anglo victims of reverse colonialism.

The same contradictory position holds for Dracula's other featured prey, Mina (Murray) Harker. In a coincidence too pointed to discount, her similarly Irish birth name filiates her with native Celts of the name O'Muireadhaigh, which was anglicized to Murray sometime during the colonial occupation, and with Protestant Scotch-Irish planters, the Murrays, who were part of that anglicizing occupation.[45] Furthermore, her full Christian name, Wilhelmina, is the Dutch feminine form of William and, as such, alludes to the most famous Dutch William of them all, William of Orange, who sealed Celtic-Catholic Ireland's doom by defeating James at the Battle of the Boyne, the traumatic event around which all subsequent Anglo-Irish relations have organized themselves. The appendage of the name Wilhelmina to the name Murray thus encrypts the Irish history of ethnosectarian conflict and dispossession in two diametrically opposed forms: it either signals the imposition of an alien symbolic order or law upon the native patrilineal culture, positioning Mina as another personification of the defeated Erin, or it commemorates the foremost champion of the settler class, William, positioning Mina as a living emblem of his triumph. Her bipolar symbolic status likewise fissures the ethnopolitical implications of her vamping.

So what is the ideological rationale animating the comprehensively contradictory "Irish" identity accorded Dracula? A proponent of the idealized enterprise of British imperialism, if not always its actual execution, Stoker was not undisturbed at the much-discussed prospect of metropolitan decline and degeneration. At the same time, as a thickly accented Anglo-Celtic émigré in London, bidding for acceptance among the theatrical elite, yet never to be entirely disaffiliated in their English eyes from his fellow expatriates in the East End, he could not easily concur in the imputation of this social malady to any of the racially inflected classes of Ireland. His literary solution is to imbue Dracula with his own immixed ethno-national status as a means of working a subtle reversal in the prevailing ideological currents that shaped his masterpiece. By fashioning Dracula as the personification of Ireland's racial and national self-alterity, its metrocolonial confusion of high and low stations, dominant and subdominant groups, superior and inferior blood, Stoker entertains the popular association of Irishness with racial inferiority for the express purpose of disrupting the logic of essentialism whereby such an association might be sustained.

The narrative motif of dirt epitomizes Stoker's strategy in this regard. As we have seen, the attachment of Dracula to his dirt figures a degenerative threat that can be imputed, by different inferential pathways, to the Anglo Ascendancy in Ireland and to the Irish immigrants of London's East End. At the same time, the Count's biological need to renew himself by repeated immersions in the native earth of his ancestors installs him as a parodic illustration of Thomas Davis's Young Ireland maxim, "racy of the soil," which summarized his effort to redefine the Irish ethnos on cultural and environmental grounds that would encompass all racial and religious constituencies under a single national banner. Stoker himself showed such environmentalist leanings, as evidenced not only in his 1872 *Address,* discussed above, but also in a later article, "The Great White Fair," in which he envisions economic expansion and technological advances working a change in the Irish character that would take his people "beyond Fenianism and landlordism."[46] Stoker can thus be seen to have hibernicized his monster in order to diffuse rather than fix his racial origins and properties, and hence to refuse rather than reiterate the attribution of atavism or degeneracy to any particular ethnicity or "blood." The logical implications of this method, moreover, cannot be limited to their intended metrocolonial center of reference, but radiate, like all logical implications, toward the universal, thereby serving to challenge the racial ideology not just of

British rule in Ireland, which Stoker openly questioned, but of British imperialism abroad, which Stoker expressly approved. Precisely in writing the eccentric curve of his own social condition into his ghoulish creation, Stoker paradoxically contrived to lurch beyond the reigning ethnological assumptions of his time. In the same motion, he gives the lie to the methodological tendency of latter-day ethnic-based cultural studies to read him (or any other fully situated subject) as the representative voice or symptom of the sociohistorical context that shaped him.

Stoker goes one dramatic step further in complicating the allegorically rendered bloodlines of his vampire and thereby baffling the identity politics of his age and our own. He grafts onto the lineaments of his vampire's Irishness the historical marks and stereotypical traits of another hybrid ethnos that concentrated British anxiety over racial adulteration, the Jews. The Irish and the Jews split the distinction of being white-skinned specimens of the other in fin de siècle Britain, and Dracula's "extraordinary pallor" underlines this shared estate (27), which factored heavily in the sort of domestic cosmopolitanism current among Stoker's devolutionist compatriots (e.g., Stoker's cousin John Dillon proclaimed that the Irish deserved Home Rule "because we are white men"[47]). Each group was derogated specifically as primitive, premodern, and deeply superstitious, and Jonathan Harker judges the peculiar power of Dracula to reside precisely in those qualities; the Irish and the Jews were also distinctive in being European inhabitants subject to ongoing deracination and diaspora, a fate emblematized in Dracula's flights to and from his native earth. Both groups were known for populating the impoverished, miasmic, and putatively degenerative ghettos of East London, specifically Whitechapel, the notorious haunt of Jack the Ripper, a model for Stoker's vampire, who also traverses that fabled neighborhood. The Irish and the Jews shared the stigma of being classified an "essentially feminine" and (like Stoker's *nosferatu*) an ultimately "feminizing" race—hence their joint reputation for *physically* degenerative influence. At the same time, more monied Jews, like the land-owning Anglo-Irish, were thought rapacious, déclassé, and socially irresponsible—hence their joint reputation for *morally* corruptive influence. Moreover, as Gladstone wrote in defense of his Home Rule policy, both groups were often unjustly accused of being inherently unassimilable, a race apart, not unlike the vampire kind.[48] Finally, both the Irish and the Jews crossed and disturbed existing categories of ethno-national definition, as Dracula himself does, partly through his identification with them.

Having usefully unearthed references to contemporary stereotypes of Jewishness in the representation of Dracula, critics such as Jules Zwanger and H. L. Malchow look to the "tradition of anti-Semitism," "Irish" and otherwise, to analyze and explain them.[49] Yet Malchow himself concedes that Stoker did not think of himself as anti-Jewish, publicly exhibited no anti-Jewish sentiment whatever, and, with his biblical first name and odd surname, was probably taken for Jewish on more than one occasion.[50] (This was all the more likely, I would add, since Stoker found himself playing a role, the middle-class parvenu, often assigned to Jews in the popular imagination of Britain.) In 1905, finally, Stoker joined an artists' protest against mistreatment of the Jews (*ED* 413 n. 17). With all of this in mind, the close parallelism between Stoker's deployment of prejudicial Jewish and prejudicial Irish motifs (both Anglo and Catholic) in the construction of Dracula indicates that his monster is no more a piece of anti-Semitism than a racial attack on his own Anglo-Celtic bloodlines, but is rather a vehicle for destabilizing such racial typologies through a proliferation of overlapping categories. This strategy is akin to that he employed in his 1872 *Address,* in "The Voice of England," and, less adroitly, in *The Primrose Path.*

By conjoining without fully intermingling discrepant and sometimes oppositional ethnic and class associations in the figure of Dracula, Stoker renders him a *progressively* indeterminant or catch-all source of racial disease and, correlatively, works to attenuate, and attenuate visibly, the link between the Count's force of social contagion and any particular bloodline or racialized essence he might be construed to possess. That is to say, Stoker suspends Dracula amid a congeries of conflicting ethnic, class, and sectarian genealogies, all of which are underpinned by one explanatory principle, "blood," but which in their untotalizable interaction prevent blood from effectively operating with explanatory finality. On the one hand, Dracula can be apprehended only as a racialized and classed specter; on the other, he is so overwritten in class and racial terms as to disable that apprehension from performing its customary function of ethnological classification and moralization.

In that failure, the burden of responsibility decisively shifts from blood itself as an assumed source of social dysfunction to blood consciousness as the source of this assumption and, with it, the anomie that engenders such dysfunction. And as we shall see, Dracula, the ultimate embodiment of Irish "bad blood," also turns out to be the ultimate practitioner of blood consciousness. With this double inscription of Dracula, the novel pursues a relatively seamless and, I would argue, decidedly modernist passage from a state of undecidability, wherein the responsibility for vampiric corruption exists *in* the eye of the beholder, who cannot make the charge stick, to a discovery that the real vampiric menace originates *with* the eye of the beholder, as a projection of the belief in racialized taint or infirmity. To make this case, we must now direct our attention to the psychodynamics of the beholder-beheld relationship in *Dracula*. This is also to say we will be moving from questions of metrocolonial identity, for which Stoker's Anglo-Celtic status provided an important interpretive key, to questions of metrocolonial subjectivity, for which the explicitly social articulation and experience of his Irishness come more decidedly into interpretive play.

The dialectical construction of the ethno-national allegory in *Dracula,* its vertiginous amalgam of dueling vampiric forces, doubly inscribed victims, mixed gender associations, disjointed yet overlapping spaces of operation, mines the peculiar ambivalence of Stoker's own involuted subject position for two closely related literary-political purposes: to sift the finally irresolvable contradictions animating and encumbering every strain of metrocolonial subjectivity in some measure and to trace in this variegated "state" of contradiction both the impediments to and the intimations of a racial understanding decidedly ahead of its time. Put another way, Stoker seizes in the "proximateness" of the metrocolonial estate—its imbrication of socially opposed, even Manichean elements—the possibility of advancing a progressive, pluralistic thematics of "blood."

   Here again, the means of extracting the text's comparatively enlightened attitude concerning Anglo-Irish relations from its detailed portraiture of contemporary blood consciousness lies not in a return to a pre–cultural studies perspective that would lift novel and novelist from their historical context, but in the development of a post–cultural studies perspective that refuses to reduce novel or novelist to a microcosmic emblem of that historical context. We must analyze how the highly particular conditions of Stoker's imagination helped to mold a work like *Dracula* to be counterrepresentative of the dominant racial ideology of the time. This dimension of counterrepresentivity allows us to distinguish between serious literature, or what we take as serious literature, from popular fiction, or what we are content to treat as such. The former is not *less* socially determined than the latter, as high modernist formalism convinced itself, but determined and constrained otherwise, against the grain. The formal or rhetorical insignia of this eccentric social pattern can be found in some unforeseen wrinkle on those settled generic conventions that shoulder the affirmative or representative burden of popular culture. The double is precisely that stock motif of the Gothic whose possibilities Stoker exploits to innovative literary ends, with correspondingly iconoclastic political implications.

As an immixed, interethnic half-caste, Stoker's effective assumption of a normative male Anglo-Irish identity remains chiaroscuroed by a feminized native Celtic heritage, which, in a self-colonizing gesture, he often elected to conceal by omission. In the process, however, he acquired a sharp awareness of the pressures of colonial identity politics and an unusually comprehensive sensitivity to the problems of psychic and social self-otherness plaguing all ranks of metrocolonial subjects in different ways and degrees—in short, a cosmopolitan capacity for "cross-dwelling."[51] Whereas Franz Fanon's colonial subject "occupies two places at once,"[52] the metrocolonial subject whom Stoker allegorizes occupies a single space subdivided along vertical lines of power and prestige and horizontal lines of tribal affiliation and antagonism—what we earlier anatomized in terms of schismatic duality. Such metrocolonial subjectivity was constituted in and through a conflict between modes of identification, the ethnic and the national, that were generally presumed, in the wake of the great nineteenth-century romantic nationalisms, to be organically continuous with one another. Stoker figures forth the resulting sense of internal dislocation by assembling Count Dracula as both a recognizable specimen and an inimical other of every major Irish caste or estate. At this level, the Irish vampire signifies the vampiric otherness of Irishness itself, as seen through an identitarian optic, its shadowy, fugitive, and adulterate character: to be a metrocolonial subject, Dracula's composite construction suggests, is always to be alienated in what you call home and always implicated in what you call alien.

This internalized form of schismatic duality obtained not only in the ethnic and cultural dimensions but in the geopolitical arena as well. One was either an agent of colonialism—a la Dracula the Ascendancy landlord—who being displaced and disoriented in some foreign locale could only return, vampire-like, to a metropolitan body that was never or no longer one's own. (Witness the consensus, time out of mind, that Anglo settlers in Ireland often grew "more Irish than the Irish.") Or one was the object of colonialism—a la Dracula the Irish urban lumpen—who being incorporated, vampire-like, into the metropolitan nation-state, could never entirely dissociate from the conduct or consequences of empire. (Witness the continued belief among all manner of Home Rule nationalists in the continued Irish stake in administering the imperialist project so bitterly resented at "home.") On these terms, *Dracula* does not dramatize a reverse colonialism, pace Arata's well-known argument, but rather an *impacted colonialism,* which registers the impact of a colonialism enacted within an officially metropolitan state and of the inscription of racial and cultural difference within the space of national self-identity. This problematic is likewise encrypted in the name *Transylvania,* which might just as easily be translated "*across* the forest," athwart rather than beyond the Pale.

Along similar lines, Stoker's experience as a self-exiled Irish parvenu in London put him in a position to suspect that the "proximate" contradiction informing metrocolonial subjectivity ultimately extended beyond the English Pale and *to* the English capital. Poised between grudging acceptance within a given community and persistent suspicion by it, the figure of the parvenu serves as a receptacle for the incertitude, anxiety, and ambivalence that community harbors about its own unifying principles and values, its rules of engagement, qualifications for membership, protocols of self-representation, and so forth. It was largely, if not exclusively, on account of his ethnicity that Stoker found himself cast in this role by London's theatrical elite, the Irish having become just such a liminal point of angst and insecurity for the collective self-conception of greater Britain.

The political dispensation of the Act of Union (1800), followed by the Catholic emancipation (1829), the disestablishment of the Church of Ireland (1869), the Land Acts (1881, 1885), and, finally, the first, failed Home Rule Act (1886), had come to blur significantly the lines between England's entrenched colonial (dis)possession of Ireland and its emergent partnership with Ireland, between immemorial conquest and immanent kinship, a pass exemplified by the structural position of the Liberal party and its leader, Gladstone, "in the vanguard of Celtic nationalism."[53] This peculiar political arrangement spelled a new and potentially disturbing encroachment upon the ego boundaries of the *English* national subject, as evidenced by the free-floating public unease—mistakenly attributed to Stoker—at the specter of reverse colonization. The alarmed hypothesis, what if *they* colonize *us,* with which John Allen Stephenson summarizes the reverse colonialism scare,[54] voiced neither realistic fears nor even plausible fantasies concerning the movements of Britain's more distant colonial wards; it was instead *all about Ireland,* about that "half-barbarous people" (NPH 30) already at and within the gates. Ironically, in its dual role as colonial outpost and internal constituent of the United Kingdom, Ireland turns the latter, predominantly English domain into a simultaneously imperial and colonial space as well, in which a subaltern population was newly enfranchised to do or to impede the work of governing Britain and superintending the empire. This circumstance was dramatically underscored in the 1880s by the Parliamentary obstruction policy of Charles Stewart Parnell. By the same token, this increasingly confident yet still derogated Irish constituency came to represent a kind of subdominant space in the British national psyche, as Stoker's ambiguous position in London society tended to confirm. The citizenship of the Irish in the United Kingdom and their presence within England's shores served to expose the retroactively hybridizing effects of the imperial adventure upon the metropolitan power and its populace.

One of Dracula's main symbolic functions is to conjure forth this nightmare vision of the Irish as an other-at-home.[55] It is therefore appropriate that the most chilling scene in the novel, by all accounts, does not feature blood in any literal or graphic way, but implicitly and metaphorically, as an index of ethnicity. I refer, of course, to the sudden apparition of Dracula on the streets of London, which recalls Stoker's own equally abrupt debut (the Irishman's joyful exclamation at the prospect of going to the metropole—"London in view"—is transposed into Jonathan Harker's fearful exclamation at the arrival of the Irish vampire: "'It is the man himself!'") (155). Writing of this famous scene, Arata locates Dracula's power to terrify the Harkers in his uncanny ability to "pass" as an Englishman.[56] There is certainly something to this contention, particularly when considered in light of the rich Anglo-Irish history of political surveillance and subterfuge. Owing to the absence of fixed, unmistakable visual indices of Anglo/Irish ethnic difference[57]—an absence evoked in Stoker's puns on the word *pale*—the accelerating physical force struggle over Ireland, from the 1798 rising through the Fenian risings to the land wars, unfolded in a thrust and parry of intelligence and counterintelligence, information and misinformation, disguise and exposure, secrecy and betrayal. It thus formed a bridge, one of the more extended bridges, between the enlightenment fantasy of a fully transparent space of unilateral social regulation, modeled after Jeremy Bentham's Panopticon, and the modernist sense of irreducibly oblique and opaque practices of social contestation requiring—and defeating—the most vigilant monition, a multilateral play of feints and guises exemplified in the increasingly pervasive activity of espionage. (Indeed, the British Secret Service was created after the Phoenix Park murders [1882] in an effort to stymie the revolutionary underground in Ireland.[58]) Insofar as Dracula's whole business is infiltration—infiltration of the body, the spirit, the society, the state—his "passing" is in and of itself a means or form of espionage. The London street scene suggests that Dracula is so spooky because he is, in another sense, simply an extraordinary "spook," a Gothic hyperbole of a kind of secret agency at once endemic and peculiar to Anglo-Irish intercourse.

Yet this account of the panic incited by Dracula's startling display of colonial "mimicry" still does not go quite far enough. It comes to rest on the horns of those classic epistemological antinomies: essence and appearance, authenticity and deception, true self and social mask, all of which pointedly depend, in this context, on a prior assumed disjunction between colonial subalternity (what Dracula properly represents) and metropolitan subjectivity (what Dracula pretends to be). But in responding to the metrocolonial circumstance, wherein the latter distinction founders, the documented thoroughgoing duality of Stoker's Irish fantasy functions to jam or disrupt these other, corollary antinomies as well, to confound perceptual errancy with social contradiction even more thoroughly than the protocols of Gothic fiction ordinarily accommodate. Thus, it might be argued that Dracula ultimately proves less terrifying to the Little England crew because he can pass, realistically, as an Englishman than because he in fact *is,* allegorically, a Briton, whose resulting metonymic proximity to the English poses a seeming threat of adulteration to that identity form. His status as what D. G. Boyce calls a "marginal Briton"[59] has the effect of marginalizing Britishness itself. His sudden appearance near Green Park, accordingly, is not just uncanny but doubly so: to be sure, his mimicry is *unheimlich,* estranging, in its effectiveness at making him seem at home, familiar, *heimlich;* but his performance is far more *unheimlich* in registering the reality that, in a sense, he already *is* at home, after all, is the familiar fellow citizen of those he encounters. This point is set in sharp relief by the earlier representation of Dracula's own home, the castle bearing his name. In a clever play on the phrase "more Irish than the Irish," which was coined to express the earliest public anxiety over the colonial Hiberno-hybridization of the English, Stoker appoints the living space of his Irish vampire with all manner of effects and affectations "more English than the English." He thereby evinces the second order "domestic" Hiberno-hybridization that lay at the source of the latest public anxiety over the state of Englishness. More than a secret agent, Dracula is a double agent or, if you prefer, his power of secret agency, his ability to pass, rests upon his double agency, that he is passing in one sense as what he really is in another. Like Stoker himself, Dracula does not represent a foreign arrival so much as an ethnic arriviste, and Jonathan Harker's response to seeing the Count in London compounds a sense of the profoundly alien with a sense of the weirdly accustomed. He registers not the shock of the new but dismay at the (parve)nu.

By the same token, the figure of the Irish Dracula does not so much key a collective fantasy of racial and cultural alterity being transported back to the British homeland as he taps and bodies forth the half-conscious awareness that such alterity is present within those confines and is constitutive, in certain respects, of the "imagined community" it so threatens. This role becomes more obvious given that the Irish, in keeping with their metropolitan adherences, regularly consented to participate in the imperialist venture abroad. As Boyce writes, "If some Englishmen might claim that the Irish were comparable to the Indians, needing a smack of firm government, . . . this was contradicted by the spectacle of Irishmen (Protestant and Catholic) spread throughout the Empire busily ruling (and shooting) black and brown races."[60] This fact surely did not elevate the English-speaking Celt to the status of honorary Saxon, as Sheridan Gilley fondly imagines;[61] it did not even prevent the prime minister of England in 1895, Lord Salisbury, from likening the Irish to the Hottentots in their incapacity for self-rule.[62] But it did place these racial groups in a more complexly companionable form of antagonistic relationship than typically obtained between colonizer and colonized. That Stoker's vampire mounts his occupation of England from the inside out, as it were, by "inhabiting" and mobilizing the subjects of Britain themselves, touches precisely upon the antagonistic intimacy of Anglo-Irish relations.

While Ireland remained, in George Bernard Shaw's convenient phrase, "John Bull's other island," an island housing that presumably inferior racial other over against whom John Bull consolidated his ethno-national identity, the Irish connection had also grown into an increasingly indispensable, if painfully impacted, organ of his body politic.[63] The rhetoric of opposition to any proposed severance of the connection, even the semidetachment of Home Rule, attested as much. Using a clichéd metaphor with special resonance for *Dracula,* Anglo-Unionist politicians periodically suspended their disparagement of the "mere" Irish to expatiate upon how their proposed independence would cut to the "heart," hence the lifeblood, of the British Empire.[64] In their eyes, "since the making of the United Kingdom . . . coincided with the rise of England to the powerful and respected position it now enjoyed, it followed that the rise to power and status must be a product of the making of the United Kingdom as a political entity."[65] But if the United Kingdom itself was the culmination of English supremacy over Ireland, it was also the commencement of Irish penetration into the affairs and the national conception of England. On one side, Irishness named a site of value for the English, a ground of traits (marks/attributes) integral to their sense of *national* completeness; on the other, Irishness named a site of abjection for the English, a ground of subordinate traits potentially corruptive of their *ethnic* integrity. Thus, the defining crux of metrocolonial subjectivity, the "proximate" splitting of race and nationality, turns back upon—rather than returning to—the citizens of the metropole.[66] Indeed, the familiar bipolar stereotype of Paddy, "charming or threatening by turns,"[67] answers to this double articulation of the Irish with the imagined British community. Understood in the light of this charmingly menacing Irishness, Dracula allegorizes more than the British sense of immanent racial crisis at the fin de siècle; he allegorizes the racial crisis constitutive of Britishness itself during the same period, the coexistence of mutually uneasy ethnic communities, and oppositionally demarcated racial strains, within one joint national identity formation.

Stoker himself experienced this sense of identity in/as crisis from both the inside and the outside. As an Anglo-Celt in Ireland, he was in a unique position to appreciate what the symbolic mandate of metrocolonial subjectivity implicitly prescribed: to suture together a self-consistent political and cultural identity by persistently misrecognizing one's own ethnic hybridity (and the hybridity of one's "own," one's designated community) as the property of some external agency or collective that threatened to ensconce and reproduce itself on the "inside." As a self-exiled Irish parvenu in London, Stoker was in a unique position to appreciate the more rankling and invidious consequences of this socially encouraged strategy of projection. For in focusing and amplifying the anxieties of a given community about the coordinates and the permeability of its borders, as I suggested earlier, a parvenu inevitably attracts the residual aggression of that community. Indeed, as my colleague Stephanie Foote brilliantly argues, the parvenu reveals the unity or solidarity of the social group to subsist largely in its concerted resources of other-directed aggression.[68] Because the specific anxieties Stoker aroused in Irving and his intimates centered on ethnic difference, the undercurrent of aggression he withstood took the projective form outlined above. While by no means a marginal figure in the Lyceum Theatre, Stoker did serve as a figure of the margin, a catalyst and receptacle for the company's unease at the seeming erosion of settled grades of ethnoclass distinctions in Great Britain.

The section of *Personal Reminiscences of Henry Irving* sifted above, "The Voice of England," provides some indication that Stoker construed his place in Irving's world along roughly these lines. During an argument over Irish Home Rule, you will recall, Irving appealed to a passing English constable for support, typing him as the bearer of the authentic "voice" (idiom/sentiments/mindset) of the English folk, only to discover a thick-brogued irreconcilable "Fenian" in peace officer's clothing. Stoker's response was to parry all of Irving's subsequent Anglocentric indictments of Home Rule with gibes about this embarrassing misapprehension. The point of these teasing references, beyond the immediate policy dispute, was to puncture his employer's naively insistent faith in the virtues of a quintessential Englishman no longer in existence and, by implication, to hold forth his own brand of ethno-national hybridity, here instanced in a wandering policeman, as the very pattern of British identity. As Stoker well knew, having served as court clerk for Her Majesty's government, the English law had long been consecrated the plenary public expression of distinctively, perhaps exclusively, Anglo-Saxon racial mettle. By isolating a figure who represented and enforced that law in Irish accents echoing his own, Stoker adumbrates for his readers a certain synchrony between his present standing as an ethnic arriviste in the England of Irving's imagination and the arrival of a new racial order in the England of historical fact.

(That Gladstone periodically recommended a similarly hybrid model of Britishness, to be formalized in a multinational state, better explains the support Stoker gave him than does the more straightforward unionism sometimes attributed erroneously to the novelist.[69] Like Gladstone, however, Stoker did prefer to view this new racial order in the United Kingdom as strengthening rather than threatening the empire beyond its shores. He most clearly embodies this belief in the hero of his late novel *The Lady of the Shroud*, the imperialist adventurer Rupert Sent Leger, who not only possesses Stoker's Anglo-Celtic Irish background but also is raised, upon his mother's death, by a Scottish aunt, thus completing the British ethnic trifecta.[70] The respective emphases laid upon the component parts of his background and his impossibly brave and daring service to the empire suggest that an internally differentiated confluence *of* the races of Britain at home conduces to shared conquest *by* the races of Britain abroad.)

In reading "The Dualitists" as a political allegory, we witnessed how Stoker's multilateral purchase on Anglo-Irish/Celtic-Irish relations enabled him to grasp their current state of schismatic duality—the reproduction of lineal identities in and through their antagonistic interdependence— but also to discern their historically grounded potential for symbiotic du- ality, the reproduction of lineal differences in and through their interpen- etration. Read as personal allegory, "The Voice of England" registers a similarly parallactic vision of the broader English-Irish nexus, rooted in a similarly multilateral participation therein. Having first internalized the pressure to consolidate a self-consistent metrocolonial identity and hav- ing then encountered the social aggression of others responding to an analogously problematic mandate, Stoker here gives narrative voice to the notion that such a symbolic mandate is not only impossible to fulfill— even the "Voice of England" is other-wise inflected—but for that very reason *unnecessary to assume* as well. Since Englishness, the local gold standard of elite thoroughbred ethnicity, was itself alloyed or compro- mised in its most cherished institutional enactments, as Stoker's "Fenian" lawman epitomizes, the bio-anthropological basis and *raison d'être* for a politics of identity among the so-called races of Britain evaporates. Un- der these metrocolonial conditions, ethnic admixture and cultural hybrid- ity would constitute first terms, coextensive with the symbolic order, and there would be simply no redoubt of pure or proper blood heritage left to defend. To the contrary, plenary and universal ethno-national identi- ty formations could be said to emerge only as ideological afterimages, metaleptic illusions, of the otherwise futile defensive practices themselves. That is to say, the collective psychic projection onto some menacing external(ized) other, like the Irish, would not protect or preserve a fully unified ethno-national profile, such as Englishness, so much as create the continued imagination of such a profile *precisely by establishing the col- lectively recognized need to preserve and protect it.* In this way, the de- sire for a self-identical ethnicity or nationality not only conceals its op- eration but also conjures forth, on however untenable a ground, the phantasmal object of its own satisfaction.[71]

On this scenario, however, and this is its most far-reaching consequence, the ultimate source of racial pathology, contagion and menace inheres not in some minoritized or stigmatized otherness but in the neurotic structure of racial self-identity, which must manufacture the perils of contamination and mongrelization to purify *itself* into existence. What is more, such per- ceived perils are immediately transformed into unconscious warrants for the continued viability and value of that self-identity, for the anxiety they generate in the racially minded and entitled subject serves as living testimony, powerfully felt evidence, that she or he does indeed have something essential (in every sense) to lose and, more importantly, *has not yet lost it.* Hence, such anxiety comes freighted with an implicit counterbalancing sense of relief, which can make it both intoxicating and addictive. Like the mythical status of manhood discussed above, imaginary "blood" identities are most acutely experienced as substantial and irrefutable when they come under a convincing if no less imaginary threat. Like the dread of feminization undergone by Stoker's vampire fighters, racial anxiety necessarily comprises a certain *jouissance,* a fulfillment of desire that both encompasses and exceeds simple pleasure or satisfaction. This is not to endorse the conventional psychoanalytic view that racial anxiety supplies the psychic justification for the enactment of aggression, which affords an enjoyable release of libidinal energy. Just the reverse. In providing visceral relief as to the continued being and value of an otherwise notional ego-identity, racial anxiety partakes directly of a *jouissance* that may, in turn, fuel aggression as the mark of its own validity.

The Henry Irving of Stoker's vignette is a perfect specimen of this enjoyment-in-anxiety. In the aftermath of the "Voice of England" episode, he is reported to have repeatedly deprecated schemes of Irish autonomy only to drop his objection as soon as he received the expected riposte from Stoker, a taunting reference to the incident itself. Why then did Irving raise the Irish Question if not to elicit that riposte, if not to raise the specter of the voice, law, and blood of England suffering inflection by the Irishness it aimed to "incorporate and neuter?"[72] And why would he raise that specter if not to take some perverse homeopathic satisfaction at its return? The Fenian policeman can be understood as a vehicle of a special kind of *frisson* for Irving, a sense of something about to go completely awry that, being repeated or re-cited, makes sure that everything is still all right. Because this species of enjoyment can be taken only unconsciously, in the guise of misgiving or dismay, it must be displaced in its very emergence, preferably onto the vehicle of the secretly ludic threat. Nothing can more securely conceal the pleasure lurking within anxiety than the misapprehension that it belongs to the source of the anxiety. This helps to explain why racial subalterns are so frequently stereotyped as possessing superior powers of enjoyment, from imaginative wonder to sexual passion or potency, from culinary gusto to verbal facility and inventiveness. For Irving, this figure of projected delight may well have been our man Stoker, who so evidently relished the repeated opportunity to invoke his "Fenian" surrogate as a trump card.

At the very least, this episode casts a telling sidelight on the import of Stoker's uncomfortable situation as ethnic parvenu. Leaving aside his marvelous managerial efficiency—a perhaps too perfect imitation of English economic rationality—the racial distrust and unease aroused by Stoker did not substantially damage his professional status because they were part and parcel of a still deeper psychosocial office that he unwittingly performed for his colleagues: to confirm the value of their Englishness in and through his vexing encroachments upon its preserves and prerogatives. He sustained his entrée, paradoxically, in being outré, held his place in Irving's inner circle precisely by being perpetually suspect as an outsider. On his side, this gnawingly double-voiced acceptance at the Lyceum Theatre reinforced what the biographers tell us was the most characteristic feature of his mature temperament: a proclivity for resenting those, like Irving, with whom he nonetheless continued to ingratiate himself.

Discerning the impact of this dual motive in the construction of Stoker's masterpiece makes available an as yet untapped vein of its political fantasy, while helping to illuminate why this region of *Dracula*'s "crypt" has proven so difficult to crack. As all of the Irish (and the English) readings of *Dracula* concur, the vampire is the very avatar of racial dis-ease. But as these surrounding pieces witness, Stoker diagnosed this strain of dis-ease as culturally psychosomatic, regarding Anglo-Irish differences as benign in reality and problematic strictly as a matter of perception. In this assessment, of course, he found himself significantly at odds with the particular set and the larger society into which he wished to be accepted more fully, in all of his Irishness; and it is in the light of this dilemma that *Dracula* yields up its discursive agenda: to critique the racial assumptions and attitudes of these respective communities without forfeiting the author's self-styled membership in them.[73] It is to this end that the novel delivers its political import wrapped in dense layers of hieroglyphic irony and ambiguity. It is to this end that the vampire in particular is fashioned as a doppelgänger who can be readily construed, at one level, as the atavistic, degenerative bogey of (Little) England's nightmares, but can also, with another turn of the deductive screw, be interpreted as a fantasy effect, a materialization, even an exponent of (Little) England's blood consciousness.

Such ambiguity operates all the better as a strategic blind, indemnifying Stoker against the likely reactions to his critique, because it also happens to constitute a serious expression of his own ethnic ambivalence. Previously, I detailed how the signifiers of Dracula's Irishness systematically devaricate along class, ethnic, and sectarian axes so as to render the vampire emblematic of the double/divisive inscription of metrocolonial subjectivity. But the same constellation of antithetically coded properties also serves to render the vampire emblematic of the similarly fractured psychodynamics that such a "proximate" state tends to foster or aggravate.

On one side, Dracula figures the return of the repressed self-otherness of the metrocolonial subject as an alien and hybridizing incursion, specifically a sexual penetration that is *automatically procreative* of a certain difference in kind or blood; the alterity-within getting out, and into public view, is transposed into an alterity-without getting in, both sexually and racially. To throw this ideological ruse into relief, Stoker specifically provides for his Dracula, unlike the original Vlad the Impaler, to succeed by erotic seduction rather than brute force, that is, by a means that finds its corrupting agency secretly lodged in the desire of its object or recipient. Stoker's Irish vampire is always just under the skin of his prey, at once an intimate, eroticized part of them—a corporeal manifestation of their own wishes and attitudes—and yet radically dissociated from them—that which they must react against in order to be themselves. In this respect, he is designed to give narrative shape to the constitutive yet haunting interpolation of socially designated and ethnically defined otherness within the official precincts of metrocolonial subjectivity.

On the other side, Dracula embodies the threat of a hybridizing incursion as the ongoing sexualized fulfillment of the metrocolonial's desire to sustain a fully consolidated ethno-national identity; the specter of that alterity-without getting in helps to secure the assumption that there yet exists a racial immanence to be protected. By the reverse logic of racial anxiety, which affrights in order to reassure, Dracula stands surety of lingering and even enduring blood purity precisely insofar as he represents an always *prospective* corruption, a taint ever more about to be. Stoker specifically provides for this paradox in his allegorical fashioning of vampirism. Whereas Dracula's signature practice comprises a simultaneous exchange of blood and species identity, invoking the widespread fear of racial pollution and attendant degeneration, the ends or effects of his practice do not consist in any adulteration of the blood or in any mongrelization of racial or species makeup. To the contrary, the vampire's sexualized possession of his victims issues in their metamorphosis into members of his own more powerful kind, their purified "reproduction" as the undead, and leaves no vestige of hybridity in its wake. Such a seamless marriage of erotics and eugenics looks less like the British fears of admixture than the British hope, formally articulated in Matthew Arnold's "decomposition thesis," that sexual commingling with the Irish might tend to their racial "conversion." ("Intermarriage, for instance, was not counted miscegenation," R. F. Foster writes, "but rather a valuable conversion process."[74]) Beyond translating the inner otherness of metrocolonial subjectivity as an external threat to that subjectivity, the vampiric transaction in *Dracula* implies a fundamental reversal of that otherness into a capacity for homogenization, for incorporating blood differences to a single racial type or kind.

Considered along these lines, Dracula's campaign enacts something like the dispensation of blood purity and racial hegemony that his sworn adversaries have rightly been seen as endeavoring to defend. Conversely, their enmity toward Dracula amounts, in an overdetermined sense, to fraternity-in-denial. The collective disposition of Little England to "deny" or contain the racial other that Dracula is taken to be places the group in a denied or misrecognized fellowship with the racial imperialism that Dracula in fact epitomizes.[75] Vampire and vampire fighter alike hold the blood to be, if not "the life" (*D* 130), then the primary site of moral properties, positive and negative, which are subject to transfer and incorporation. "'We Szekelys,'" Dracula boasts, "'have a right to be proud, for in our veins flows the blood of many brave races'" (33), while the doctors of Little England pride themselves on harvesting only the purest blood for transfusion into Lucy Westenra. In sum, vampirism may be said to represent the acute blood consciousness of Little England as a form of blood lust, which is why the corrective blood transfusions likewise bear an expressly erotic cast, being likened to marriage and designated an occasion for sexual jealousy (158). In this metaleptic twist of symbolic logic lies the organizing principle of the novel's politics of blood. The racial peril advanced or "caused" by Dracula folds back at another level into a phantasmatic effect of race consciousness itself, which breeds in its turn substantive moral and social ills *likewise allegorized in the person and the practices of Dracula.*

This ingenious gambit weds the traditional psychic dualism of the doppelgänger with the full-scale ontological dualism of *nosferatu;* it gives us the undead (the living dead) as the unreal (the fantasy real), that is, a figment of a certain race-based Imaginary, who is also the emblem and vehicle of the very real consequences produced by that sort of Imaginary.

Stoker thereby fashions his vampire to incite and to undermine contemporary blood consciousness in a single motion, offering a kind of internalized critique of the ethnic obsessions in which his variously identified compatriots were so steeped. If Dracula is indeed a degenerative nightmare, he is a nightmare that reflects back upon the mentality conceiving him.

4

Double Agents

While Stoker was not responsible for inventing the doppelgänger gloss on the undead, he did elaborate it more comprehensively, more innovatively, and in greater detail than had been done before. For he premises each vampiric transaction upon a simultaneous partnership and polarization between violator and violated, a deathless antagonism that is also a secret sharing. Jonathan Harker, you will remember, deliberately courts the danger of an undead visitation by flouting the Count's warning to abide within his own quarters for the night. What is more, he subsequently welcomes with sexualized languor the "grains of dust" heralding the vampire's approach: "I watched them with a sense of soothing, and a sort of calm stole over me. I leaned back in a more comfortable position, so that I could enjoy more fully the aerial gambolling" (D 48). Lucy Westenra likewise participates in her ghoulish fate: first by sleepwalking to a known suicide seat, a fixture associated with the breeding of vampires; then by repeatedly breaking the protective confines of her virginal boudoir, an action that signifies her libidinal investment in being vamped; finally, by removing, in the throes of sleep, the garlic flower that would defend her, an action that, like her sleepwalking, signals the unconscious pursuit of that investment. Wooed by a narcotic mist, Mina Harker also entertains the voluptuous advances of Dracula, at least initially, while Renfield intermittently imagines himself the Count's disciple and deputy, then casts about to do his bidding. Van Helsing, finally, confesses himself "moved by the mere presence of [the vampiress] even lying as she lay in a tomb fretted with age and heavy with the dust of centuries, though there be that horrid odour" (319). Stoker goes so far as to institutionalize this collusive motif via a number of invented supplements to the conveniently obscure inventory of vampire lore, such as the rule that a vampire cannot enter a building, a metaphor for the body, without some type of invitation from an inhabitant, or the notion that "no painter can make a likeness of him. [The vampire] always winds up looking like someone else."[1] With additions like these, which betoken the fundamentally transferential role of the vampire, Stoker clearly aims to make the doppelgänger interpretation effectively his own.

It is therefore ironic that this dimension of the novel has quietly deposited something of a wedge between its two main critical schools. The doppelgänger has proven central to psychoanalytic exegesis, the general but embryonic development of which at the time of the novel's composition sedimented the text with references to "unconscious cerebration," the "dual life," and "double consciousness," a phrase likely taken from Sigmund Freud and Josef Breuer's *Studies in Hysteria* and J. M. Charcot's experiments in hypnotism (*ED* 97, 235). In the wake of Lacan's "return to Freud," the vampire stands forth as a Gothic figuration of "the Thing," the innermost vortex of *jouissance* around which the subject both forms and splits or, rather, forms by splitting. The Thing accordingly bears what Lacan calls an "extimate" relation to the subject, best exemplified in the vampire's relation to his victims: each is profoundly alien in and through its *interiority*, its bodying forth of an intimate yet unrecognizable desire.[2]

The Irish studies take on Dracula, by contrast, has greatly emphasized one of the conflicting aspects of the vampire's doppelgänger function, polarization. Following in the wake of mainstream postcolonial theory, the Irish school of criticism has typically found in the novel the Manichean oppositions dear to imperialist ideology—self and other, ruler and ruled, enlightened and backward, superior and subaltern—and have ascribed them to Stoker's anxiously normalizing impulses made articulate in the bourgeois pieties of Little England. This approach's momentum has been to credit the protagonists' official narrative of diametric opposition between the living and the undead, as epitomized in their repeated pledges to free the world of the vampiric enemy.

I believe a more nuanced historical and psychobiographical taxonomy has the power to obviate this particular breach in Stoker scholarship. For the strange curvature of intimate polarization characteristic of the psychoanalytic subject encapsulates the metrocolonial subject *position*, as I have anatomized it, and provides for an alternative reading. Indeed, from our perspective, Stoker's openness to the nascent psychoanalytic conception of *split* subjectivity may well have followed from his lived sense of metro-colonial *double* agency, an economy of mutually inimical yet secretly in-termingled interests and attachments. At the same time, it was Stoker's conversance with cutting-edge notions of the divided mind, his readiness to bring early psychoanalytic models of the unconscious to bear on his Irish allegory, that enabled him to narrativize the sense of double agency in the first place, to inject into the outer world of social determination the fun-gibility of roles, states, and identities ordinarily reserved for the inner world of private fantasy. In the Lacanian lexicon, Stoker conceives the problem of the other (positive social differences) in terms of the Other (the uncon-scious condition as differential structure), an approach rooted in a pecu-liar confluence of intellectual and geopolitical history.[3]

The primal scene for any psychoanalytic interpretation of Stoker's vam-pire is the celebrated mirror episode at Castle Dracula. Still confident of his host's goodwill, Jonathan Harker begins to shave one morning after but a few hours of sleep. Hearing the Count greet him good morning, Harker peers after Dracula in his shaving glass, but finds no image of him there: "There could be no error, for the man was close to me, and I could see him over my shoulder. But there was no reflection of him in the mir-ror! The whole room behind me was displayed; but there was no sign of a man in it, except myself" (*D* 30–31). Now Harker's last formula harbors a muted or half-buried pun, which represents one of Stoker's most char-acteristic and most frequently overlooked devices for extending and com-plicating the allegorical framework. The phrase *in it* bears a denotative English reference—"in the glass"—that invokes the legend that a vampire manifests no reflection, having no soul. But the phrase also carries a col-loquial Hibernian sense—"presence," "there," "in existence"—that sug-gests Dracula possesses no being at all "except" as an emanation of the "self" who beholds him, a state perfectly consistent with his elusive resis-tance to any form of objectified reproduction (photography, painting, mirror reflection, shadow). While the first meaning surely seems the most obvious, the time of day authorizes the second. According to common folklore of *nosferatu,* if the Dracula apprehended in this episode were a "real" vampire, he could not be abroad *and* empowered in daylight. Van Helsing testifies to this effect later (211), passively undercutting Harker's testimony, which he is elsewhere much concerned to affirm and advance. Even the Harkers remain doggedly unconvinced of the objective facticity of Jonathan's ordeal: Mina continues to query if it was truth or imagination, while Jonathan confesses to a persistent "hue of unreality" about the incident (168).

In what is surely a calculated narrative arrangement, the entire experience of Jonathan Harker, Mina Harker, and the other members of Little England unfolds from this undecidably (self)-reflexive inter-view with the vampire. Startled by his confusion as to Dracula's actual presence, Jonathan Harker cuts himself slightly, and unable to dispel his "vague uneasiness," he "saw that the cut had bled a little, and the blood was trickling over [his] chin" (31). This is the first letting of blood in the novel and it is, significantly, *self-induced*, a result of the protagonist's anxieties. No less significant, however, is the way Harker immediately interprets his accident as inciting his host to "demoniac fury" and an abortive (and hence merely speculative) assault (31). It is *only* at this point, with this self-inflicted wound, that Harker's sense of collegial security quite abruptly evaporates, and he pronounces his lodging a "veritable prison" (32).

This primal mirror scene may be construed as an instance of *anamorphosis*, a disturbance of the visual or experiential field that externalizes and positivizes some unconscious desire or complex animating the viewer's perspective, that is, a perceptual manifestation of the logic of self-reflexivity. Anamorphosis is, in the words of Parveen Adams, a "distorted" projection that "unhinges the whole point of view."[4] As such, an anamorphosis remains effectively unintelligible, a mere blur or lacuna, unless the viewing subject undergoes a fundamental change of perspective, an "anamorphotic shift."[5] Harker himself never resolves this moment of scopic disruption, never fully clarifies Dracula's nonappearance in the mirror, precisely because his anamorphosis symptomatizes his deeply transferential, even self-replicative, relation to the vampire.[6] Indeed, Harker's speculative encounter with Dracula establishes the novel's general paradigm of vampiric intercourse as a densely mediated and mystified mode of *self*-relation. As we shall see, it is but a prelude in this regard to the more collective anamorphosis of Little England, which drives the main action, and a foil to the "anamorphotic shift" undergone by Mina Harker, which provides the action with its central turning point.

Like the spectacular game of "hack" devised by Harry and Tommy in "The Dualitists," the mirror-play of Jonathan Harker and Dracula reveals how the most personal of psychic frameworks constitutes a protosocial and micropolitical theater of operation. As with Harry and Tommy, the illicit homoerotic component of Harker and Dracula's doppelgänger relationship is entirely bound up in a lineal contest of imitation and rivalry, and as in "The Dualitists," Stoker embellishes the interpersonal drama with allegorical indices of ethnopolitical concerns pertinent to Britain and its empire.

When Dracula fails to materialize upon the screen of Harker's conscious reflection, thereby showing himself *in absentia* to be the projection of Harker's unconscious desire, Harker simultaneously finds himself projected, in *propre persona,* into the visual frame notionally reserved for Dracula ("no sign of a man in it, except myself"), thereby showing himself to be the unwitting counterpart of his fearful adversary. The line between demon and daemon proves excruciatingly fine. The psychic mirroring of Harker and Dracula models the sociopolitical logic of the larger Transylvanian narrative, in which Harker apprehends in Dracula not only the weirdest specimen of a thoroughly exoticized locale but also a figure weirdly sympatico in several areas crucial to Harker's public, professional, and political identity. The very type of the stranger, Dracula turns out to be:

1. Someone whose occupational temper and expertise are unexpectedly cognate with Harker's own, but of superior merit, perhaps even forming something of an ego-ideal for the younger man. "He would have made a wonderful solicitor, for there was nothing that he did not think of or foresee," exclaims Harker, who still thinks of himself, despite a recent promotion, as a solicitor's clerk (21, 37). In this context, the word *solicitor* carries a subterranean sexual valence that hints at an erotic tinge to Harker's professional identification with Dracula and to his resulting complicity in the vampiric assault upon him. To extend the double entendre, Harker is indeed a solicitor's assistant on the verge of becoming a solicitor's "partner" (140).

2. An exponent of the glories of British law, forms of life, and social hierarchy, whose Anglophilic adherences answer directly to Harker's social fantasies and aspirations.

> In the library I found, to my great delight, a vast number of English books, whole shelves full of them, and bound volumes of magazines and newspapers. A table in the centre was littered with English magazines and newspapers, though none of them were of very recent date. The books were of the most varied kind—history, geography, politics, political economy, botany, geology, law—all relating to England and English life and customs and manners. There were even such books of reference as the London Directory, the "Red" and "Blue" books, Whitakers Almanack, the Army and Navy Lists and—it somehow gladdened my heart to see it—the Law List. (25)

Harker's shamefacedly excessive emotional investment in the Count's powerful Anglo-identification—an identification with old or traditional England specifically—adumbrates a parallelism between Dracula's status as an ethnic arrival in England and Harker's status as a class arriviste among the aristocratic–haute bourgeois circle of Little England.

Stoker carefully draws out this parallelism in his plot construction. Just as Dracula's arrival on England's shores spells an immediate success for his special brand of ethnic adventurism, giving him access to the blood of London's "teeming millions" (161), so Harker's delivery *back* to England yields immediate dividends for his class and professional prospects: his employer, Mr. Hawkins, unexpectedly installs the novice solicitor as partner and heir of his entire legal enterprise. The now beloved Hawkins obligingly expires directly thereafter, and it is *upon returning from his funeral,* strikingly enough, that Harker beholds the chilling spectacle of a younger, sprucer Dracula mixing easily in the street life of the metropolis. Mina Harker proposes a connection between the events, wondering if the distress of losing fatherly Mr. Hawkins has not reactivated a "train" of delirious memories associated with Jonathan's recent "brain fever." Since Dracula himself represents both a "partner" (doppelgänger) and a father figure (professional ego-ideal) of some sort, Mina's inference seems eminently plausible, though not for the reason she imagines. The timing of Dracula's triumphant appearance as a fully naturalized Briton at the very moment Jonathan formally becomes a naturalized bourgeois casts the vampire as a sinister figure of unconscious wish fulfillment.[7] At this juncture, that is to say, he acts as a hieroglyph of Jonathan Harker's necessarily repressed enjoyment in his sudden social assent. Self-conscious recognition of this grimly reaped enjoyment could not but bedevil Harker's sense of social propriety and moral rectitude. That is why his momentary vision of its veiled signifier, Dracula, not only fills Harker with terror but profoundly disorients him as well, unsettles his sense of self and reality, causing him to collapse into hysterical amnesia. His professed, racially inflected fears for his society are in part an unconscious defense (projection) against the seemingly magical fatality of his own upstart ambitions, which have, ironically, left him a more fully authorized shareholder in that society's racially inflected imperialism. It is hard to miss in this intersection of social ambitions fulfilled and ethnic phobias aroused an uneasy and yet cathartic exercise in authorial self-portraiture.

3. An agent, as Dracula himself later observes, of imperialist geopolitical hegemony, hence a martial, diplomatic, and administrative comple-

ment to Harker's commercial and juridical mission: "'They played wits against me,'" Dracula subsequently proclaims, "'against me who commanded nations, and intrigued for them and fought for them, hundreds of years before they were born'" (251–52). In this light, we can see Dracula's virulent contempt for the peasants who populate his demesne (27, 35) to be the ideological correlative of Harker's smug condescension toward "the East" (9)—the same imperialist attitude filtered through disparate social grids.

By the same token, inasmuch as Harker's national pride, his professionalized mode of authority, and, above all, his business of property law are all symbiotic with the conduct and ends of empire, the Count's practices, even those depredations that so harrow the young solicitor, amount to parodic reflections of Harker's ambitious being-in-the world, a jaundiced image of his own *bildung*. Thus the scene wherein Harker stands accused of an infanticide committed by Dracula while wearing Harker's clothing is but the flip side, the tain, of the mirror scene in which Harker first discovers himself "framed" in the space of the Count. Dracula can so successfully impersonate Harker because in terms of social fantasy and political function he is *of* Harker, "no man . . . except myself" (31).

Stoker underlines this point with deliberate force. When the bereft mother shows up to demand the return of her baby, she accuses Harker instead of Dracula in apparent accordance with the Count's plan of disguise. But, and this is the most important but, she fingers Harker *not* on the basis of his dress, the sole instrument of Dracula's imposture, but strictly on the evidence of Harker's physiognomy. "She was leaning against a corner of the gateway. When she *saw my face* at the window she threw herself forward, and shouted in a voice laden with menace:—'Monster, give me my child'" (48; emphasis added). The reigning consensus that she has simply been deceived by Dracula's ruse only demonstrates how the reader might be misguided by Harker's benign self-conception and self-presentation, how easily we might participate in the constitutive *meconnaissance* of his subjectivity, accepting his ego as a reliable index to the unconscious depths of his being.[8] This is not to dispute that Stoker's portrait of the solicitor is sometimes morally sympathetic, but to suggest that Harker's sympathetic nature, imbricated as it is with vampiric monstrosity, is meant to throw into relief the ethical and political contradictions at the heart of metrocolonial respectability.

Indeed, Stoker crafts Harker's most celebrated instance of heroism, his scaling of the castle wall, to extend and reinforce his doppelgänger bond with Dracula. Harker first regards Dracula's egress from the castle in borrowed dress as not simply terrifying but well-nigh impossible: "I saw the whole man . . . begin to crawl down the castle wall over that dreadful abyss, *face down.* . . . At first I could not believe my eyes. I thought it was some trick of the moonlight, some weird effect of shadow" (39). Yet he still proceeds to emulate Dracula's preternatural feat and in fact expresses from the very start a seemingly unwarranted confidence in his ability to pull it off: "Where his body has gone why may not another body go? I have seen him myself crawl from his window; why should not I imitate him and go in by the window?" (49). Here Harker *thrusts himself* into the fantasy space occupied by Dracula, mimicking the vampire's unreal power of bodily control, and as he reports his resolve to attempt the geste, the idiom of his journal takes the impress of the Count's slightly fractured English syntax. Harker writes, "why should not I" instead of the more common "why should I not" and "why may not another body go" instead of the more obvious construction "why may another body not go" (49). The overall effect is to confirm the psychosymbolic kinship of the two figures in the pursuit of exploits resonant of imperialist mercantile and political appropriation. Dracula is an "effect of shadow" for young Harker, the darkened emanation of his own private desires and professional designs. Harker's admission, immediately prior to these incidents, that "I start at my own shadow" (38), is more telling than he realizes.

But if Dracula embodies, at least in the first instance, a disturbing projection of Harker's unconscious fantasy life, then this projection would logically extend beyond the event of being vamped, the generally acknowledged focus of Harker's censored sexual longing, to the ethos and enterprise of vampirism itself, the generally unrecognized focus of Harker's underlying sociopolitical identification with the Count. The structure of vampirism presupposes and externalizes precisely this confluence of an erotic experience of self-abandon, the ecstatic surrender of one's own socially cultivated individuality, and the new eugenic attachment to an "ever-widening circle" of similarly motivated and constituted subjects. Since the essence and telos of any vampiric interchange lies in vampiric reproduction and recruitment, the unconscious wish to be vamped, to undergo the radical hybridization of the undead, can pass immediately into the unconscious wish to vamp, to enlarge the domains of the undead, understood as a race or species apart. The anticipation of the former as a sexual prospect may well testify to a certain identification with the latter as a social project.

The ideological *jouissance* of vampirism, allegorically construed, might even be said to emerge specifically in the overlap between these two modes of psychic investment, that is, at the point where an eroticized anxiety over the prospect of racial immixing is converted, like affective fuel, into an aggressive delight at the possibility of racial incorporation. Such a conversion from anxiety-ridden exposure to triumphant interiorization virtually defines ethnically based politics on both sides of the colonial divide. This is evidenced in a wide array of activities from terrorism to tourism, cultural nationalism to imperialist ethnology, all of which aim to transform what Mary Louise Pratt has called "contact zones" into zones of possession.[9] Even before he meets his avid new client, Harker exemplifies an imperialist version of this politics in his approach to the East, suggesting that vampirism is, in a symbolic sense, a part of his social makeup from the beginning. Confronted with the exotic, seemingly backward, and sometimes terrifying customs of Irish-Transylvania, he indites a series of memoranda reminding himself to retrieve and collect some of the more interesting tidbits about the place. Like a good ethnologist, for instance, he purposes to interview a native, the Count, on the array of local superstitions he has observed. Like a typical tourist, he repeatedly thinks to get his wife recipes for the national dishes he has sampled and enjoyed. As the latter case directly involves the act of physical ingestion, it begs comparison with the practice of vampirism, especially since blood represents the national dish, as it were, of the undead.[10] Dracula can thus be seen as introducing Harker to yet another new culinary recipe, one that crystallizes Harker's own tried and true cultural recipe of exposure and incorporation.

When it comes to the Anglo-Irish nexus, the motifs of racial and cultural incorporation are not bound by literary conceit alone, but by a geopolitical framework whose founding metaphor, the metropolitan marriage of masculine Britain and feminine Ireland, specifically delineates the resulting colonial affiliation in terms of *lineal consubstantiality.* The parodic bearing of vampirism upon this assimilative paradigm is dramatically underscored during the narrative climax of *Dracula,* the vamping of Mina.

Given her undecidably Anglo/Celtic-Irish birth surname and her pointedly allusive first name, Wilhelmina Murray Harker is, you will recall, paired with Lucy Westenra in representing the assault of the vampire as, in one allegorical dimension, an assault *on* rather than *by* Irishness, specifically an assault on the feminine persona of Ireland, Erin. It is therefore of crucial importance that Stoker takes pains to have Dracula ritualize his aggression as a travesty of the Christian marriage ceremony, with special emphasis on that part of the liturgy which solemnizes the incorporation of the wife to the spiritual and legal identity of her husband. "'And you,'" the Count intones, "'are now to me flesh of my flesh; blood of my blood; kin of my kin . . . my companion and my helper'" (252), a decree he enforces by constraining her to drink of his blood before making her his "wine-press" (252). His sacramental rendition of the blood feast, in turn, consists perfectly with his initial role as a doppelgänger of Jonathan Harker, bringing the meticulously elaborated correspondence between the pair's imperialist attitudes back home to the domestic sphere.

With her arguably Irish ethnicity already folded into a dominant British, not to say English, nationality, Mina Murray stands to see the last trace of her Irish heritage, her surname, effaced upon her marriage to Jonathan Harker, which, accordingly, amounts to a lowercase specimen of the "metropolitan" variant invoked and enacted by Dracula. Jonathan himself, of course, lies in the bed with "the white-clad figure" of his wife as she is vamped by Dracula, leaving his role in the proceedings a very live question (246–47). From the context we have established so far, the Count's sexual incorporation of her literal blood may well stand as a symbolic complement of Jonathan's marital assimilation of her metaphorical blood, her ethnic lineage.

The marital quietus to Mina's already muted and uncertain Irish identity is paralleled in the text by her maritally inspired, gender-mandated sacrifice of personal and professional independence. Mina begins the novel as an assistant school mistress and, as such, part of a female labor aristocracy especially noted for its growing social emancipation and economic self-sufficiency.[11] She is occupationally situated, in short, as a likely New Woman. What is more, she discloses a certain professional identification with a still more radical element of that sorority, the "lady journalists" (56). In the context of courtship and marriage, however, Mina conspicuously breaks with this attitude of solidarity, tartly chaffing New Women for their reputed gender presumption: "Some of the 'New Women' writers will some day start an idea that men and women should be allowed to see each other asleep before proposing or accepting. But I suppose the New Woman won't condescend in future to accept; she will do the proposing herself. And a nice job she will make of it, too!" (87). Now Mina's words here have generally been taken to reflect Stoker's opinion on this emergent feminine "type."[12] But their highly specific frame of reference, once fit into the larger narrative puzzle, suggests instead that while Mina wears lightly the normative demands on femininity in most areas—

so much so that the old patriarch Van Helsing pronounces her a miracle of constructive androgyny (295)—she has with an anxious and almost defensive enthusiasm internalized the rules and embraced the institutions of amatory and connubial respectability. Thus, with her own nuptials on the horizon, Mina sets about pondering and consulting with her fiancé on how she might train her otherwise marketable skills—for shorthand, typing, administrative organization, managerial assistance—onto the task of becoming his amanuensis. Her lineal appropriation under the name and ethnicity of her husband is, accordingly, to be supplemented by the appropriation of her gendered labor and energy to the enterprises of her husband, completing the symbolic correspondence between the metropolitan marriage and their own.

The lineaments of the Harkers' "Act of Union" tend to confirm Jonathan, his personal character notwithstanding, in the structural role of vampire, a figure who incorporates Mina—blood, flesh, and agency—entirely into himself. Once again, Dracula paradoxically serves to protect the protagonists from having to confront the monstrosity they assume, in all of its systemic, quotidian, and intractable force, by presenting it to them in an alien and inconceivably aberrant form. Stoker ingeniously contrives to insinuate as much through his narrative deployment of the principle vampiric stigmata. After Dracula feeds upon Mina, on her forehead appears a token of her pollution and continued enthrallment, a "red scar," the removal of which is explicitly equated with the larger task of eliminating Dracula and his vampires: "If it may be that with all the others we can be so successful, then the sunset of this evening may shine on Madam Mina's forehead all white as ivory, and with no stain!" (260). But the "terrible scar" itself is merely a duplicate, a contagious transmission, of the scar inflicted upon Dracula's forehead by Jonathan with a shovel, the symbol of his desire to rebury the walking dead. In other words, Mina ultimately receives the mark of the beast, quintessential sign of her contamination, not from the beast per se, but from an ordinary English gentleman, a fine husband and future paterfamilias, whose very being depends for its consistency upon his blindness to the ethical and political implications of his social position. Perhaps Dracula's famous pronouncement "'Your girls that you all love are mine already'" (267) seeks to force precisely this recognition: not that he has "already" taken their women from them, but that he "already" possesses their women in *their* possession of them. That Jonathan is in some phantasmatic sense a vampire figure not only finds considerable support in the painstaking reversibility of his relation to Dracula, but it helps to unriddle a series of narrative lacunae that have frequently been overlooked or imputed to Stoker's carelessness.

1. As he awaits his conveyance to Castle Dracula, Jonathan Harker observes a crowd of people suddenly gathered about his lodgings, "all [of whom] made the sign of the cross and pointed two fingers towards me" (14). A "fellow passenger" then refuses to decode these signs for Jonathan until informed of his foreign status, at which point "he explained that it was a charm or guard against the evil eye" (14). Jonathan infers from the apparent sympathy of his interlocutors that the manual sign is intended to protect him from some still unknown curse. But the pragmatics of the gesture and the manner of its verbal translation argue to the contrary. Whether the sign described is a specimen of *mano fica, mano cornuta,* or *mano pantea* (*ED* 11 n. 40), it functions to protect the person making it from the malevolent power of the figure on the receiving end, while at the same time expressing aggression of one kind or another toward that figure. Hence, unlike the crucifix that Harker's innkeeper gives him, the power of the pointed fingers, like the force of "the finger" today, is not really transferable. It is directed against the person at whom it is flashed. That is why Harker's fellow passengers must be convinced of his terminal cluelessness and vulnerability as a foreigner before venturing an explanation that might otherwise give offense and incur supernatural vengeance. That is to say, the collective indigenous reading of Harker pauses over whether he really is a prospective victim to be feared for or a closet vampire to be feared. The natives, it should be noted, direct the very same sign at Mina when she arrives in Transylvania as a scarred bride of Dracula.

2. After Jonathan Harker's encounter with the trio of vampiresses, he records his apprehension that "those awful women . . . were . . *are* . . . waiting to suck my blood" (*D* 44). But the question arises, how does he know this since, as Leonard Wolf observes, "bloodsucking has not been mentioned or witnessed so far in the book" (*ED* 55 n. 1). Harker knows, we are to deduce, precisely because he already desires; his occulted appetite affines him from the start with the vampire kind, and his affinity in turn affords him an occult(ed) knowledge.

3. Stoker signals as much in another unsolved mystery of the text, Harker's uncanny and erotically fraught intuition that he "seemed somehow to know [the] face" of one of the vampiresses (*D* 42). Here again, Harker's inexplicable acquaintance with vampire life at once derives from and betokens his preexisting symbolic and subliminal kinship with the undead. In this sense, it is intriguing to know, Harker avows no familiarity with

the two "dark" vampiresses with "aquiline noses," but solely with the one who was not just "fair" but "fair, as fair can be," not just blonde but "with great wavy masses of golden hair," not just blue-eyed but "with eyes like pale sapphires" (42). In sum, he recognizes *only* the female figure whose vampiric exoticism is relieved, even replaced, by her hyperbolic conformity to the dominant Anglo-Saxon standard of beauty. Since Harker's recognition of her coincides with his overwhelming attraction to her, and hence with his susceptibility to seduction by her, and evidently by her alone, this decisive scene would seem to peg vampiric corruption less to racial immixing as a mode of reverse colonialism than to the transmission and reproduction of tribalist attachments and antipathies through the powerful circuitry of sexual desire; less to the erotic fetish of racial difference than to the erotic taste for racial purity, exclusivity, and superiority. *What makes Harker vulnerable to the undead, what is already vampiric about him, is ironically the ethnocentrism that energizes his defense.* This moment of Harker's confused familiarity, with the accent on familial, thus typifies the inside-out logic that coordinates the sexual and racial currents of the novel. Just as the vampire seems a straightforward sexual predator, but turns out a fantasy effect of forbidden desire, so it seems a racial other, but turns out the fantasy affect of embattled identity.

4. A subsequent instance of Harker's unaccountable gnosis (and there are too many to be accidental) pushes this logic still further into the realm of vampiric reproduction. On his second foray into Dracula's chapel, while watching Dracula enjoy his postprandial nap, Harker suddenly seizes upon the dire consequences of his commercial venture in Transylvania and contemplates them in terms consonant with both reverse colonialism and racial degeneration: "Then I stopped and looked at the Count. There was a mocking smile on the bloated face which seemed to drive me mad. This was the being I was helping to transfer to London, where, perhaps, for centuries to come he might, amongst its teeming millions, satiate his lust for blood, and create a new and ever-widening circle of semi-demons to batten on the helpless. The very thought drove me mad" (53–54). The obvious question to be posed is, how does Harker know how vampires multiply? (*ED* 67 n. 27). How does he even know *that* they multiply? Nothing in his adventures to this point substantiates the conclusion he draws. In the original and still authoritative edition of *Dracula* (1897), the answer is exactly the same as in item three: Harker's precognition of vampire protocol and laws of being, like his recognition of unencountered vampire faces, testifies to the likelihood that vampirism is partly the ef-

fect of his unconscious cognition, the "return" of his social, sexual, and professional fantasy life. Harker's public role in admitting the proliferant undead to his homeland merely serves to externalize his psychic implication in the very existence of the vampire life that he apprehends. Harker's reiterated feelings of incipient derangement support this line of analysis. Instead of suffering blank, bone-crushing terror at the indomitably malignant force descending upon his person and his nation, Harker experiences the vampiric threat as his own descent into madness, an unraveling of his personal identity from the inside, as if the social canker were already lodged there. To the extent that his vision of Dracula is still governed by *anamorphosis*, of course, this is precisely the case.

In the subsequent American edition of *Dracula,* published two years later, Stoker introduces a dramatic revision that consolidates the narrative grounds for Harker's seemingly unaccountable insight, while calling further attention to the self-reflexive logic upon which that insight rests.[13] On the evening prior to his cited confrontation with a dormant Dracula, "gorged with blood" (*D* 53), Harker overhears the Count command his female cohorts to wait twenty-four hours before feeding upon their guests: "'Your time is not yet come. Have patience. Wait. Tomorrow night, to-morrow night, is yours'" (52). But the American edition interpolates a crucial phrase explaining Dracula's reason for insisting on the delay: "'To-night is mine'" (*D* 52 n. 1). Now if the Count is as good as his word, Harker's understanding of vampiric multiplication may be taken to germinate in the wake of his being bitten, which presumably amounts to a form of initiation into the mysteries of the undead. The blood on which the Count is presently "gorged" presumably belongs to the young solicitor and marks the inaugural stage in his conversion, of which his spontaneous and arcane knowledge is an index. But the same disclosure also transforms the episode in question into a kind of inverted replay of the mirror scene, its own mirror image, if you will. In the earlier scene, a confused Harker gazes after the Count in the mirror and finds only himself, thereby betraying his psychic implication in the Count's very existence; in the latter scene, a clear-eyed Harker contemplates a glutted Dracula and fails to see himself, his blood, and so fails to recognize his *material* immersion in the Count's existence. Taken together the scenes encapsulate the political dimension of Harker's doppelgänger relation to Dracula, wherein his secret partnership with the vampire (qua racial imperialist) is predicated on his phobic dissociation from the vampire (qua racial other).

5. As Leonard Wolf observes, the vampiric "lore, verging on law promulgated [by Van Helsing] leaves us wondering . . . how is it that in Transylvania, Dracula's feeding ground for hundreds of years, there were not
thousands, if not millions of vampires (*ED* 261 n. 15). Or to draw a still
finer point, how is it that with the vast hosts supposedly vamped and thus
corrupted by Dracula and family, we see but one, for which Harker himself stands accused? Why is Transylvania, of all places, not pullulating with
vampire life? Once again the point seems to be to mitigate the standing of
Dracula as an objective racial threat and to reinforce his role as a fantasy
effect or projective disturbance. What better device for incriminating the
eye of the beholder in a contagious horror than to restrict the contagion
to the scope of that eye?

Stoker further relies on this stratagem to extend the dream work from
the individual to the collective level, in keeping with the ethno-national
import that Dracula carries. Once the vampire makes land in England,
his victims share some more or less intimate connection with the band
of people who are his sworn adversaries and chief aficionados. Why
would Dracula's *fatal* strikes be so rigorously limited to the bailiwick of
Little England, if not to raise the possibility that the strikes are the effects of their collective fantasy, if not to encourage the inference that there
is something fatal in the bailiwick itself? This metaleptic inversion of
vampiric cause and effect, moreover, manifests itself in a collective anamorphosis or visual projection no less prominent and noteworthy than
Harker's mirror scene. When Van Helsing, Seward, Morris, and Godalming break into the bedroom where Dracula is vamping Mina Harker,
his "face was turned from [them], but the instant [they] saw [they] all
recognized the Count—in every way, even to the scar on his forehead"
(*D* 247). With its strangely intransitive use of the verb *saw,* this report
begs the question, how could the men recognize the forehead scar of the
Count, which they have never seen before, when his face is "turned from"
them, that is unless they, like Jonathan, harbor concealed knowledge
grounded in unconscious kinship?

The following section explores a related and still more compelling warrant for this last inference: a detailed pattern of affinities and correspondences that align the vampire with the various vampires fighters in London, much as he is twinned with Jonathan Harker in Transylvania. In both
cases, Stoker's basic strategy is to develop formal, distinctively Gothic symmetries between the partisans that convey moral and political correlation,
if not equivalence, between them.

❦ ❦ ❦

In "The Irish Vampire," Michael Valdez Moses usefully catalogs the "highly suspicious and shadowy connections" between one of the vampire fighters, Quincy Morris, and his arch-nemesis. I have reduced his list to the most strongly documented items:

> Morris is the first . . . to suggest that Lucy has been bitten by a vampire bat. Lucy's condition unexpectedly deteriorates rapidly *after* she receives a transfusion of blood from Morris. . . . During a scene in which Dracula is first named as their enemy Morris leaves the group and then fires *into* the room where the vampire-killers are assembled. . . . After Dracula makes a hasty escape following his critical assault on Mina Harker, Quincy is inexplicably seen running *from* the house and hiding in the shadow of a great yew tree outside the asylum.[14]

To Moses, "these details suggest that Quincy, although he ultimately sacrifices his life in an effort to kill Dracula, is nevertheless secretly allied with the Count."[15] Moses further speculates, on impossibly slender evidence, that Morris is to be taken as figuring Irish-American antipathy to the British Empire, while Stephen D. Arata, culling the same data, supposes Morris to be a figure of the new American imperialism challenging traditional British domination.[16] Both critics, in other words, explain Morris's linkage to the vampire in terms of his own ethno-national separateness from Little England and his corresponding opposition to the dominant faith of Little England, liberal British imperialism.

Two problems with this interpretive line spring immediately to mind. First, Morris comes to participate in the councils of Little England only on account of his having previously joined the dominant Brits, Arthur Holmwood and Jack Seward, in globetrotting imperialist adventures. Indeed, his first action in the novel is to send Holmwood a dinner invitation that reveals how deeply their friendship and his own categories of perception have been dyed by their cooperative and companionable experiences as agents of Anglo-American influence:

> We've told yarns by the campfire in the prairies, and dressed one another's wounds after trying a landing at the Marquesas; and drunk healths on the shore of Titicaca. There are more yarns to be told, and other wounds to be healed, and another health to be drunk. Won't you let this be at my campfire tomorrow night? I have no hesitation in asking you, as I know a certain lady is engaged to a certain dinner-party, and that you are free.

There will be only one other, our old pal at the Korea, Jack Seward. He's coming, too. . . . Come! (*D* 62)

Whatever competitive tensions existed between the world-historical designs of their respective nations, the relationship between Morris and his "old pal[s]" has not been fashioned to represent them.

Second, as our discussion of Harker in Transylvania indicates, the symbolic alignment of Morris with Dracula proves the rule rather than the exception; it is, I shall demonstrate presently, the mark of his honorary membership in the Little England crew, rather than of his outsider status. Even before we profile the others of this circle, we can illustrate this point in the most relevant area of all, the pragmatics of vampire-fighting.

As the crusaders await their climactic London confrontation with Dracula, Seward reports, Morris "laid out our plan of attack and, without speaking a word, with a gesture, placed us each in position," exhibiting the kind of tactical leadership he had "in all our. . . adventures in different parts of the world" (266). Despite this commanding performance, however, the arrival of Dracula—less than a half page later—finds Seward complaining that "it was a pity that we had not some better organized plan of attack, for even at the moment I wondered what we were to do" (266). On the strength of these sentiments, the relatively trouble-free escape of Dracula from the ambush seems a plausible addition to Moses's bill of attainder against Morris: given his record as an unfailingly dependable tactician, the collapse of his "plan of attack" on this occasion might tend to corroborate his "hidden," perhaps subliminal, allegiance to the Count. But the charge of unwitting conspiracy would have to be expanded to include the remainder of his crew as well. By Seward's report, he and Holmwood (Lord Godalming) "renewed instinctively" their "old habit" of obeying Morris's instructions "implicitly" (266). The qualifiers *instinctively* and *implicitly* signify a virtually organic connection among this cadre and, as such, even their botched and disorderly execution of the vampire trap should be read as answering to some joint, and jointly misrecognized, purpose. That is to say, the men of Little England here act *in synch* to the effect of self-confusion and *in concert* to the ends of self-sabotage. And they do so because they remain unconsciously in league, on one symbolic plane, with a figure whom they desperately wish to destroy one another. As we shall see, such aiding and abetting of their quarry is likewise more the rule then the exception for these gentlemen.

Taking these points together—that Morris does not instance the tension within Western imperialism but gives voice to the homosocial romance of its enactment and that his "shadowy" confederation with Dracula is representative rather than atypical of Little England—argues for a surprising reversal in the received geopolitical interpretation of vampirism in *Dracula*. Instead of representing just a potent enemy or an odious consequence of British imperialism, the vampire emerges over the course of the narrative as its secret avatar, precisely in being the protagonists' secret sharer. This is not to discount Stoker's Liberal brand of support for the global imperialism of Great Britain or his heartfelt enthusiasm for its heroic legends, organizational achievements, technological éclat, and the myth of Euro-Aryan supremacism that they undergird, all of which surface more prominently in his later novels and memoirs.[17] It is rather to say that his skepticism about specifically *domestic* colonialism and the racial attitudes promoted therein, filtered through his deep-seated ambivalence about his own interethnic subject position, impresses the textual unconscious of *Dracula* with a ramshackle but extensive system of correspondences between the vampiric project, the penetration of the body in the cause of blood, and the imperialist project, the penetration of the world in the cause of "blood."

Considering the crux of Stoker's ideological conflict, it is pertinent that the character bearing perhaps the most varied metonymic and metaphorical links with the Count is Van Helsing, whose Dutch residency and ethnicity, compounded with his titular and strategic leadership of Little England, are clearly meant to recall the watershed historical occasion when England looked to Holland for its national salvation. I refer of course to the invitation issued William of Orange to depose and succeed James II. The upshot of that "Glorious Revolution," the defeat of the Jacobite king and his predominantly Celtic-Catholic supporters on Irish soil, finalized their colonial subjugation by the British garrison, under the oppressive color of Penal Law. Stoker's decision to cast Van Helsing as a Roman Catholic does not blunt the allusive force of the latter's crusade so much as it focuses the ironic possibilities of metrocolonial life, wherein disparate yet overlapping social distinctions and hierarchies, each contested in its own right, vie for priority in defining a particular situation or, as in Stoker's case, an individual subject position.

The symbolic correspondence of Van Helsing and Dracula runs the gamut from the physical to the temperamental, the expressive to the pragmatic. Let us begin with an apparently nugatory physical trait, which has the virtue of epitomizing the allegorical method in the novel: a strategy of displacement whereby Stoker seems to identify with and speak for the metropolitan middle-class elite, even as he conducts a guerrilla critique of their social attitudes. Late in the novel, in yet another play on the ideas of atavism and degeneracy, Mina and Van Helsing concur in classifying Dracula as a "criminal type," according to the forensic model of Cesare Lombroso, and the reader is thereby alerted to the close fit, on several points, between Jonathan's physical description of the Count and Lombroso's anatomy of his prototypical malefactor. One of these points is Dracula's eyebrows, which Jonathan gives as "very massive, almost meeting over the nose" (23). The eyebrows of Lombroso's "criminal man" are "bushy and tend to meet over the nose" (*ED* 403 n. 25). Before we take this evidence of Dracula's constitutional miscreancy to the bank, however, a couple of items demand our consideration. First, Jonathan counts himself a "physiognomist," someone who self-consciously appraises the character of his acquaintances by decoding their facial construction according to the current authoritative taxonomies. So he presumably shares Mina's familiarity with Lombroso, whose interpretive grid might well have slanted his perception, and he has presumably shared his physiognomical account of Dracula with her, influencing the verdict she ultimately renders. Second, the one figure in the novel whose eyebrows are said to fit Lombroso's category, "bushy," is Van Helsing. His eyebrows are so conspicuous in this regard that Jonathan no sooner meets the good doctor than he volunteers a characterological gloss on them. He does not of course find Van Helsing's eyebrows indexical of an innate proclivity to lawlessness, but just the opposite, the sign of overwhelming moral courage and self-confidence. Like the perception of vampirism, then, the detection of embodied criminality in Dracula is referred to the eye of the beholder. The differing estimations of Dracula and Van Helsing's looks do not finally hinge on empirical evidence but on some moralized preconception.

Stoker even insinuates that such preconceptions might be racially freighted. But in a classic bit of strategic indirection, he fastens this possibility on Renfield's response to Van Helsing instead of Jonathan or Mina's response to Dracula. One of the prominent traits of the Lombrosian ne'er-do-well, "a thick boned skull" (*ED* 403 n. 25), also happens to fit the British stereotype of the Dutch, to which Renfield gives impassioned vent (*D* 225). The reader is left to deduce how regularly the anatomical categories of Lombroso's criminology meshed with and reinforced the fabric of various ethnic caricatures.

This textual feint brings us to the second crucial parallelism between Van

Helsing and Dracula: their respective ethno-national differences from the remaining Anglo-identified characters, differences manifested most richly in their eccentric and sometimes faulty speech patterns.[18] Dracula of course frets that his nonnormative pronunciation and sentence construction will inevitably mark him down, in every sense, as a "stranger," and critics of the novel have generally paid him the compliment of prophesy by treating his toxic power as a Gothic corollary of his immigrant status. Let us keep in mind, however, that the far more tortured idiolect of Van Helsing does nothing to disqualify him from anchoring and commanding the Little England crew. On the contrary, Stoker seems eager to flaunt the malapropisms that mark, without in any way undermining, the doctor's authoritative pronouncements. With this sort of gesture, he troubles or complicates the ideology of blood entertained at different points in the novel, insisting on the gap, a deep if narrow one, between metropolitan defensiveness and metrocolonial ambivalence. Whereas the vampire taken in isolation may accord with the popular view of *Dracula* as a xenophobic invasion narrative, the vampire taken in tandem with Van Helsing, as with Jonathan Harker, stages a reverse discourse cognate with "The Voice of England," in which the kind of ethno-national difference that the protagonist (like Irving) fears turns out to be constitutive of the very identity formation to be protected.

Any passionate struggle implies some point of joint investment. In the case of Dracula and Van Helsing that point is ironically their mutual commitment to the novel's main object of critique, the forms of blood distinction and gradation, based on race and class alike. Indeed, vampiric reproduction itself is a perverse literalization of the obsessive concern with "breeding" that Van Helsing, like Dracula, displays. This, the third layer of abrasive affinity between the opposing leaders, manifests itself in both celebratory and denigratory terms. Just as Dracula's contempt for "the peasant" (27, 35) is mirrored from the start in Harker's condescension toward "the East" (9), so it is subsequently mirrored in Van Helsing's quietly disdainful estimate of the lower orders or serving classes, which in late Victorian London were frequently populated with Irish immigrants. Peter Stallybrass and Allon White have taught us how, by way of a metaphorics of dirt, the maidservant came to be regarded as an agency of social contamination and demoralization uneasily harbored within the otherwise respectable confines of the Victorian home (not unlike, we might add, the popular construction of the vampire as a similarly undercover agent of social degeneracy housed within the perimeters of polite society and, ultimately, the well-bred body).[19] Van Helsing aggressively concurs in this bourgeois viewpoint, creating a nice analogy with the aristocratic contempt of Dracula toward his socially appointed underlings. Dracula charges the peasant with an inbred want of the physical fortitude that represents the most cherished virtue of his own feudal warrior class; Van Helsing suspects the house servants of an inbred want of the moral steadfastness that represents the approved virtue of the newly preeminent middle and professional classes. Accordingly, he refuses to allow the Westenra maids any part in the vigil over their failing mistress. Still more pointedly, though in desperate straits, he objects to considering the maids as blood donors for Lucy: "I fear to trust those women, even if they would have the courage to submit. What are we to do for some one who will open his veins for her?" (136). Finally, he inclines toward corporal discipline of the same servants when they fall prey to Dracula's wiles: "Flick them in the face with a wet towel, and flick them hard" (134).

On the celebratory side, Dracula's cited self-congratulation on the noble virility of his bloodlines, a boast conflating class and ethnic distinction, finds a close parallel in the exaltation Van Helsing expresses at transfusing into his languid patient the aristocratic vigor of Holmwood's blood and the manly puissance of Morris's:

"He is so young and strong and of blood so pure that we need not defribinate it." (114)

"A brave man's blood is the best thing on this earth when a woman is in trouble." (136)

In either instance, the professional judgment of Van Helsing, like the martial judgment of the overlord Dracula, consists primarily in turning, or troping, blood qua material substance into blood qua caste morality. Stoker underscores this agreement by having the doctor second the historic worthiness of the Count's blood in ethnic terms: "The Draculas . . . were a great and noble *race*" (212; emphasis added).

While Van Helsing's commentary indicates that he shares an ideology of blood with Dracula, the transfusions themselves instance a shared technology of blood to go along with it. His transfusions require a form of injection that plainly replicates in another key the horror of vampiric penetration. Van Helsing even designates the procedure his "spell" (122), archly likening it to the occult practices associated with Dracula. This occult connection strengthens later in the narrative when Van Helsing answers

Dracula's mesmeric seduction of Mina with a similarly mesmeric interrogation of her, going so far as to "order [Mina] about as if [she] were a bad child," much as Dracula does upon vamping her (300). Now the commonsensical interpretation of these measures, that they are homeopathic inversions of the invasive techniques of the vampire, generally holds at the basic narrative level and should not be ignored or dismissed. But Stoker also exploits this condition of reversibility to leave the suggestion of a deep structural affinity between Van Helsing and Dracula, grounded in their compatible forms of blood consciousness. In this play of diegetic surface and symbolic depth, we can detect the author's signature parvenu strategy: to encrypt in advance his criticism of the English community he would join for the social biases that vitiate his belonging.

An additional reason to suspect Van Helsing is in structural complicity with the vampire can be found in the contradictory and often self-defeating strategies he devises for hunting Dracula. The following catalogue of Van Helsing's unwitting service to the enemy is by no means exhaustive. First, he delays acting upon or apprising others of his diagnosis of Lucy's malady, and, as a result, necessary safeguards for her welfare come into place only gradually, increasing the likelihood of successful vampiric incursion. Later, in his effort to prove Lucy the "Bloofer lady," Van Helsing claims to have saved an infant "just in time" from being the latest in a series of her tiny victims (177), and yet he quits the churchyard with his protégé, Seward, without taking any steps whatever to curtail Lucy's nocturnal blood drive. Since each new victim potentially adds to Dracula's "ever-widening circle of semi-demons," Van Helsing appears to assist the vampire by omission. On a subsequent expedition to Lucy's haunts, Van Helsing repeats the omission in a more conspicuous fashion. Having apprehended the specter of Lucy, he concedes to Seward the advisability of dispatching her forthwith.

> "If I did simply follow my inclining I would do now, at this moment, what is to be done; but there are other things to follow, and things that are a thousand times more difficult in that them we do not know. This is simple. She have yet no life taken, though that is of time; and to act now would be to take danger from her for ever. But then we may have to want Arthur, and how should we tell him of this? . . . If you know of this . . . and yet of your own senses you did not believe, how, then, can I expect Arthur, who knows none of these things, to believe?" (180)

The doctor is speaking here to a special provision of vampire lore newly invented by Stoker, according to which persons taken "in a trance," like

Lucy, remain substantially guiltless of their transmutation and so exempt from the attendant perdition, at least until their subsequent deeds merit that punishment (179). As Van Helsing notes, the existence of this provision makes his duty a relatively "simple" affair; in this case, he knows "what is to be done." By the same token, the provision makes his deferral of the necessary deed all the more inexplicable. By allowing Lucy to roam the night, Van Helsing is not putting the lives and souls of innocents at risk to save Lucy from damnation; he is not exposing society at large to an exponential cycle of vampiric reproduction for the narrow personal aim of conserving Lucy's immortal hopes; no, thanks to the ad hoc provision, by declining to eliminate her when "she have yet no life taken," he is risking innocent lives, imperiling British society, *and* jeopardizing his beloved Lucy's salvation *in a single blow.* And he takes this unthinkable set of hazards on a pretext that is strained and speculative at best, as the tortuous formulation "we may have to want Arthur" indicates. No reasons for informing Arthur as to the particulars of Lucy's after-death remotely compare in gravity and urgency with the reasons for bringing it immediately to pass. The reader is, accordingly, compelled to look elsewhere for an explanation, and the collateral evidence points to the psychoanalytic dimension, where Van Helsing and Dracula function as dualists.

It might be objected, of course, that Van Helsing's decision is finally dictated by the imperative of Gothic plot construction to build suspense from circumstances of certain yet somehow avoidable doom. On this brief, which is not irrelevant, Van Helsing thinks he "may have to want Arthur" strictly because the story needs him to want Arthur. But Stoker does not downplay or naturalize Van Helsing's decision or soft-pedal its dangerous irrationality, as might be expected if he were merely intent on suturing the narrative into apparent coherence. To the contrary, Stoker quite insistently denaturalizes the doctor's resolution; the fact and phrasing of his concession, not to mention the invented provision to vampire lore, all call attention to the unaccountability of the course he has adopted and raise suspicion about its underlying motivation. With Van Helsing, as with Harker, Stoker cannily manipulates narrative opacities so that they will draw the reader into an unconscious dimension wherein the darker stirrings and structural attachments of the protagonists can be discerned.

After the men forge their phallic brotherhood over the impaled body of Lucy Westenra, Van Helsing hatches the policy of excluding Mina Harker, heretofore a key operational associate of the vampire crusaders, from further participation in their enterprise. While he professes a chivalric desire to spare Mina the dangers and hardships of engaging with Dracula, Van Helsing's plan produces just the opposite affect. Cut off from the main occupation of the group, abandoned for all intents and purposes, Mina is left *more vulnerable,* in both a physical and a psychic sense, to Dracula's nocturnal intrusions, which culminate in the much discussed vamping episode. No sooner, in fact, does Mina enter into her solitude than she becomes sleepless, "full of devouring anxiety," and, though she had "never cried on [her] own account," she becomes hysterically "weepy" (226).

Stoker underlines this unintended consequence with a conventional Gothic play on the concept of darkness. Shortly before her exile, Mina advocates a collective effort based on full and mutual disclosure: "We need have no secrets amongst us; working together and with absolute trust, we can surely be stronger than if some of us were in the dark" (197). Since her immediate objective is to gain access to Seward's "cylinders," despite and even because they contain the record of his private and suppressed grief over Lucy, the phrase *in the dark* signifies not only "without knowledge or consciousness" but also "alone with one's unconscious feelings," always a weakened state in vampire fiction. The dual meaning of the phrase reasserts itself in the persistence of Mina's response to her sudden exile: "It is strange to me to be kept in the dark as I am today" (225). In short order, Mina finds herself in the dark with a vengeance, in the dark of the night and in the dark of her censored desires, which "did not want to hinder" the forces of darkness embodied in a vampire dressed "all in black" (251). Van Helsing thinks to leave Mina "in the dark" and in the process he relegates her to the darkness, in every sense of that term.[20] Dracula's other main doppelgänger, Jonathan Harker, reinforces the confusion retroactively. Noting the enervation of his wife after she is sequestered, Jonathan mistakenly interprets it as evidence of the propriety of the sequestration itself: "She looks paler than usual. . . . I am truly thankful that she is to be left out of our future work, and even of our deliberations. It is too great a strain for a woman to bear. I did not think so at first, but I know better now" (223). The irony, of course, is that Jonathan consigns Mina to Dracula's violations precisely in committing her to Van Helsing's law.

While Stoker was toiling away on *Dracula,* Freud was busy developing, formalizing, and popularizing the long-standing literary conceit that a pun or double entendre could be the vehicle of unconscious cognition or activity, understood as a paradoxically intentionalized form of inadvertence. In keeping with this diagnostic insight, Stoker is concerned to indicate that the isolation of Mina was not a casual blunder by Van Helsing so much as a motivated lapse in judgment.

To that end, he first makes it clear that the doctor's ordinance flies in the face of his own strategic principles. Van Helsing does not just share the robust collectivist ethos of Mina; he goes so far as to designate the "power of combination" (210). Little England's foremost advantage over the vampire, whose selfish nature (a consequence of his "child-brain") restricts him to solitary industry (294). So Van Helsing, of all people, can be presumed to know that the moral quarantine of any member of his group will handicap that person, who must play the "game" on Dracula's turf and without the group's best weapon. Van Helsing's stated rationale for the quarantine—he seeks to protect Mina from burdens inappropriate and overtaxing to her gender—does resonate with patriarchal common sense. But it also contradicts Van Helsing's description of Mina as an instance of triumphal androgyny and thus an exception to the very "separate spheres" ideology that he decides to enforce. Stoker carefully juxtaposes the description and the decision in order to draw out this inconsistency:

> "Ah, that wonderful Madam Mina! She has man's brain—a brain that a man should have were he much gifted—and woman's heart. The good God fashioned her for a purpose, believe me, when he made that so good combination. Friend John, up to now fortune has made that woman of help to us; after tonight she must not have to do with this so terrible affair. It is not good that she run a risk so great. We men are determined—nay, are we not pledged?—to destroy this monster; but it is no part for a woman. . . . Tomorrow she say goodbye to this work, and we go alone." (207)

Van Helsing's conviction that Mina possesses certain definitive parts of a man, without ceasing to be the very pattern of womanhood, completely disrupts the statutory gender dichotomy upon which his claim "it is no part for a woman" is necessarily predicated. His abrupt reinscription of that dichotomy, accordingly, seems to flow less from his faith in its ontological truth than from his commitment to its ideological effects, the creation of paternalistic/fraternalistic hierarchies of will and agency legitimated through the sacrifice and the suffering that the men reserve for themselves. As we have seen, the gender politics of patronizing exclusion advanced in Van Helsing's edict serves as both the domestic analogue and the structural correlate of Britain's self-styled imperial mission, with special application to the land of Mina's feminized ancestors.

In an irony too pointed to be devoid of deliberate political significance,

Mina does ultimately achieve the sort of providential destiny Van Helsing professes to safeguard, but that destiny turns out to be a leading role in the very struggle from which he would keep her. Moreover, she fulfills her destiny only once the rest of Little England *stops* excluding her from their deliberations and Dracula *starts* excluding her from his, attempting to cut off the psychic telepathy that had grown between them since their mock marriage. A deft narrative ploy on Stoker's part, these reciprocal gestures of exclusion translate the temperamental ideological kinship of Van Helsing and Dracula into a strategic parallelism that reveals the self-reflexivity of the war on vampirism in the means of its enactment. The methods of the doctor and his disciples repeatedly founder or turn against them precisely because the vampire objectifies their social mentality, whose decisive component, the refusal of (self-)difference, prevents them from recognizing as much. As the experience of Jonathan Harker in Transylvania so strongly suggests, the men of Little England are at war with their own "shadow" (39), their dark side.

The final repeal of Mina's internal exile does not even take effect with the spectacular demonstration of its wrong-headedness. To be sure, in the immediate aftermath of her vamping, "the first thing decided" is "full confidence" among all parties. Mina draws the obvious moral of recent events for the group: "'There must be no more concealment. . . . Alas! We have had too much already'" (253). The chief architect of this concealment, however, remains imperfectly persuaded, discovering new ground for the now revoked policy: "'But dear Madam Mina, are you not afraid; not for yourself, but for others from yourself, after what has happened?'" (253–54). And within four days, he and his protégé, Seward, can be found successfully conspiring to deny Mina access to all future plans, reducing her once again from agent to protectorate of the mission. Since, in Van Helsing's words, "'Madam Mina, our poor, dear Madam Mina is changing'" into a vampiric consort, "'she must not more be of our council, but simply be guarded by us'" (280–81).

Now given the disastrous consequences of secrecy for both Lucy Westenra and Mina Harker, "one would have supposed," observes Leonard Wolf (*ED* 382 n. 20), "the two physicians would have learned their lesson." Yes, indeed, but given their failure or refusal to learn so plain and insistent a lesson, one would have also thought the distance between the ideological perspective informing their decisions and the ideological perspective underlying the representation of them would be more widely appreciated.[21] *Dracula* and its author regularly stand accused of embracing and promoting the misogyny displayed by the protagonists, in, for example, the euthanasia-rape of Lucy Westenra. The case of Mina Harker, however, in which the perseverance in condescending patriarchal attitudes gives such evident aid and comfort to the vampire, in which a sexist order (directive/regime) spells the ruin of its own professed ideal (the cultivation and protection of "Woman"), such a case importunes a strongly revisionist account of the novel's sexual politics. What the Mina affair does is illustrate in the clearest terms yet how Dracula, qua universal doppelgänger, serves a hermeneutic function as a kind of negative touchstone, whereby the text appraises and critiques the sensibility and the conduct of the other characters.[22] In particular, this unfortunate episode asks us to notice that Stoker's staging of misogyny, like his staging of anti-Semitism or his allegory of Celticism, is not a simple endorsement but a veiled indictment.

The last testament to Van Helsing's correspondence with Dracula moves us from technology to teleology, from means to ends. After much debate over the appropriate tactical response to the ravishing of Mina, her husband issues a call for immediate action: "'Then in God's name let us come at once, for we are losing time. The Count may come to Piccadilly earlier than we think'" (D 258). "'Not so,'" Van Helsing replies and precedes with an explanation no less chilling in manner than matter: "'Do you forget,' he said, *with actually a smile*, 'that last night he banqueted heavily, and will sleep late?'" (258; emphasis added). Alerted to the pain his words have caused Mina, Van Helsing exclaims against "his thoughtlessness," but the "smile" that accompanies his callous reminder, the smile that so shocks the narrator (Jonathan), registers an aggressive, even malevolent mode of erotically tinged satisfaction that is not so much thoughtless as *unconscious*. Although, being similarly implicated, Jonathan cannot accede to full comprehension of the fact, he has caught the esteemed professor vicariously savoring the sinister pleasures of vampirism (note Van Helsing's opulent phrasing, "banqueted heavily"). Jonathan is prompt to excuse the inveterate tactlessness of the old man—"he had simply lost sight of her" (258)—but his very eagerness (not to mention his anamorphotic trope) bespeaks an effort to elide a more deeply disturbing provocation, the sense that Van Helsing takes enjoyment, however repressed, *in* Dracula's enjoyment. Or to turn things around: for Van Helsing in England, as for Harker in Transylvania, the vampire is a condensed figure, a spectral embodiment, of obscure appetite unspeakably gratified.

With this extensive and multi-tiered symmetry in place, a passing and seemingly far-fetched speculation by Jack Seward, that his mentor might be responsible for the death of Lucy Westenra, acquires increased force and a rather different currency. Skeptical of Van Helsing's occult forensics as "outrages on common sense," Seward wonders, "Is it possible that the Professor can have done it himself? He is so abnormally clever that if he went off his head he would carry out his intent with regard to some fixed idea in a wonderful way. I am loathe to think it, and indeed it would be almost as great a marvel as the other to find out that Van Helsing was mad; but anyhow I shall watch him carefully. I may get some light on the mystery" (181–82). The reader, of course, has been placed in a position analogous to that of Seward. We too seek "light on the mystery" gradually unfolding in the narrative and are now prompted "to watch [Van Helsing] carefully" for a solution. Taking Seward at his word, and within its enunciative framework, Gothic fantasy, we may indeed find Van Helsing strangely inculpated in the crime of Lucy's death, not in the dimension of "reality" that the narrative reports, but in the usually censored logic of fantasy that the narrative enacts. The professor is not deranged in the normal sense of the term, as Seward intermittently hazards; rather he represents, in his systematic correlation with the vampire, the derangement of the normative, the madness at the heart of those hegemonic racial and sexual regimes that he upholds.

In this regard, Van Helsing epitomizes the ideological proclivities of the male vampire fighters at large, as emphatically displayed during the second destruction and final disposition of Lucy's body in the churchyard crypt. The band of men engage Lucy as a compound and bipolar racial and sexual stereotype—as both a cherished (sexual) ideal to be delivered from eternal ravage ("Lucy as we have seen her in life, with her face of unequaled sweetness and purity"; 192), and as a vicious (racialized) other to be annihilated from the face of the earth ("The foul Thing that we had so dreaded and grown to hate"; 192). With this double move, they convert the regrettable necessity of dispatching Lucy into an act of violently erotic penetration with clear analogies to the phallic bite of the vampire. Consider the following "climactic" passage.

> Arthur placed the point over the heart, and as I looked I could see its dint in the white flesh. Then he struck with all his might.
>
> The Thing in the coffin writhed. . . . The body shook and quivered and twisted in wild contortions; the sharp white teeth champed together till the lips were cut, and the mouth was smeared with a crimson foam. But Arthur never faltered. He looked like a figure of Thor as his untrembling arm rose and fell, driving deeper and deeper the mercy-bearing stake,

whilst the blood from the pierced heart welled and spurted up around it.
(192)

The "dint" of the stake in Lucy's "white flesh" plainly recalls, in word and image, the "hard dents" of the vampire's teeth on "the supersensitive skin of [Jonathan's] throat" (43). The quasi-orgasmic "spurt" of blood as the stake cleaves Lucy's breast clearly anticipates the "spurt" of blood with which Dracula coercively breastfeeds Mina: both women are described as having their mouths "smeared" with blood (247).

Most tellingly, Stoker seals the bond between Dracula's vamping of Mina and the male vampire fighters' destruction of Lucy by recourse to his much favored and densely allegorical marriage motif. Just as Dracula assumes the role of bridegroom in his murderous sexual assault upon Mina, so the sexualized slaughter of Lucy is reserved for her prospective bridegroom, Arthur. Moreover, since in trumpeting his bloodlines earlier, Dracula invokes the Norse thunder God as a totem of his own warrior tribe, the comparison of his fellow bridegroom, Arthur, with "the figure of Thor" intimates that he has become a likeness, even an honorary member of the Szekelys, has been married into the clan. This symbolic kinship is significantly enriched by its vehicle. At the time of the novel, the figure of Thor was a popular, incipiently racist icon of Nordic-Aryan purity.[23] Given this context, he simultaneously marks the difference *in* pedigree between Dracula and the men of Little England and their joint preoccupation *with* pedigree, thereby condensing in a single leitmotif the novel's determination to frame the so-called facts of race as the fantasy effects of race consciousness.[24]

The root of such tightly drawn analogies between the vampire and the vampire fighters has rarely been traced to the politically saturated worldview of Little England, and, as a result, their specific critical force has gone largely neglected. In a similar way, the multiple violations committed by the Little England men against the law and even the principles that they proposed to defend have either been exempted as compulsions of war, a view first promulgated by Van Helsing himself, or they have been read as evidence, in Moses's words, that the men of the group have "become what they beheld," that Liberal England's commitment to "peace, justice and freedom" suffers the "infectious" taint of Ireland's political irrationality, figured forth in the vampirism of Dracula.[25] But insofar as vampirism allegorizes the illiberal, statutory, tribal adherences embraced by Little/Liberal England no less than irredentist Ireland, it would be more accurate to say that in Dracula the vampire fighters "behold what they already are," and that in engaging him, they automatically enact their own ambivalence toward the emancipatory ethos they espouse and the democratic institutions they endorse. Far from tainting Little/Liberal England's commitment to "peace, justice and freedom," the political irrationality figured in vampirism reflects, as in Jonathan Harker's mirror, the taint within. Once again, Stoker brings to bear the psychologizing impetus of the Gothic form on his historically specific, metrocolonial problematic in order to treat the fantasies lining the course of political events *on their own terms.*

The voice responsible for the rhetorical construction of Lucy's (un)death scene belongs to Jack Seward, the man who suspects Van Helsing of homicidal dementia. Notwithstanding his doubts, Seward confesses to his own perverse enjoyment in the prospect of slaughtering Lucy—"had she then to be killed, I could have done it with savage delight" (188)—and his words crystallize the erotics of bloodshed viscerally linking the self-styled crusaders to their depraved enemy. Seward also possesses a more particularized affiliation to vampirism, however, which further illustrates the deliberate care Stoker took in planning his meticulous formal symmetries for the purpose of political critique. As the student and unofficial deputy of Little England's patriarch, Seward is paired not with the vampire, the great obscene father, but with *his* acolyte and unofficial deputy, the mental patient R. N. Renfield. In a still more precise calculation, Stoker constructs this medial relationship to turn on the question of social connectivity itself, on the relative continuity or discontinuity among differently ranked orders of being.

From the outset of his case study of Renfield, Seward seems more concerned with maintaining his authority over "his lunatic" than with curing him. His first mention of Renfield concedes that contrary to his lofty mission and sworn duty, "I seemed to wish to keep him to the point of his madness" as a means of "making myself master of the facts of his hallucination" (61). Seward's desire to penetrate and control the innermost truth of Renfield, the substance of his fantasy, soon passes into a struggle for recognition reminiscent of the master-slave dialectic in Hegel and bearing a similarly specular form:

His attitude to me was the same as that to the attendant; in his sublime self-feeling the difference between myself and attendant seemed to him as nothing. It looks like religious mania, and he will soon think that he himself is God. These infinitesimal distinctions between man and man are too paltry for an Omnipotent Being. How these madmen give themselves away! The real God taketh heed lest a sparrow fall; but the God created from human vanity sees no difference between an eagle and a sparrow. Oh, if men only knew! (96)

The discrimination Seward jealously guards between orders of institutional authority—doctor and attendant—clearly serves as a metonymy for the more decisive separation he elaborates between the responsible exponents and the egocentric opponents of social authority and symbolic order per se. He introduces a new category into the gallery of dangerous others, the madman, who has the virtue of tapping a whole range of distinctively Irish stereotypes—Paddy as prodigal, unstable, hysterical, violent—while keeping the allegory focused upon politics in its internal dimension.

The governing irony of the passage is that Seward gives himself away in precisely the same exorbitantly self-important manner that he imputes to his patient. The "sublime self-feeling" he depicts in Renfield's neglect of the distinctions "between man and man" is but the projected image of the "sublime self-feeling" prompting Seward to inflate the legitimacy and the importance of such distinctions. Thus, even as he takes Renfield's carelessness of rank to forecast some delusion of deistic grandeur, Seward identifies himself with a God's-eye view that commands even the narrowest and subtlest social gradations. In the act of absolutizing his own perspective, moreover, he sets about absolutizing the gradations themselves; he converts contingent distinctions in institutional rank into fixed, divinely ordained divisions among species of being, in this case the eagle and the sparrow. His naturalizing conception of social hierarchy, which was so characteristic of contemporary blood consciousness, finds a distinct echo in the likewise scripturally derived credo of Renfield, "The blood is the life!" (130), which encapsulates his demented practice of consuming animals whole in the ascending order of their evolutionary development. The biospiritual Darwinism of Renfield, his attempt to amalgamate ever-higher degrees of "life force," parodies the social Darwinism of Seward, his belief that different social degrees may be likened to different animal orders.

As we have noted, in combating the incursion of racial otherness embodied in Dracula, the men of Little England show themselves to share in the vampire's pathological obsession with "blood." Stoker thereby leaves us to infer that the threat they *perceive* to their collective identity is largely an effect of the restrictive manner in which they *conceive* that identity. Seward's abrasive relationship with Renfield replays the political logic of the novel on a smaller and more self-conscious scale. In the act of dissociating himself from Renfield the egomaniac, Seward reveals himself to share in his patient's pathological brand of self-exceptionalism. The reported slight to Seward's professional dignity is largely symptomatic of his over-weening sense of that dignity rather than of Renfield's mental disturbance. These coordinated narrative vectors meet in the figure of Dracula, whom Little England takes to be the supreme egoist, precisely by virtue of the atavistic nature of his "blood." If the self-isolating egomania of Renfield paradoxically makes him a perfect vessel or medium for the vampiric other—and he is the vehicle giving Dracula access to the headquarters of Little England—then Seward and the others are morally implicated on the same grounds. That is to say, Renfield is indeed a medium, in the sense of a *tertium quid*, between Little England and the vampire kingdom. He reflects into himself, as it were, the logical twist that the problem to be excluded, which Dracula personifies, is but the supplemental effect of the effort of exclusion. Or, in other words, he reflects into himself the para-dox that the vampire fighters' unnerving and unintended connection to Dracula, their acute blood consciousness, arises from their refusal of a certain type of social connectivity.

Stoker took special pains to translate Renfield's peculiar symbolic niche, the *pivotal* figure of *failed* mediation, into a homologously peculiar nar-rative role: in the great struggle against Dracula, he emerges as the *pivot-al* agent of *non*-influence. From the start, of course, his zoophagy sends a strong danger signal of the presence of Dracula, which Seward overlooks to his chagrin: "Strange that it never struck me that the very next house might be the Count's hiding-place. God knows that we had enough clues from the conduct of the patient Renfield" (199). But this is just prelude to a more telling species of blindness in Seward. Recall that the ideological affinity of the vampire fighters' with their vampiric enemy bleeds directly into unwitting complicity with his maleficent designs. The men repeated-ly fail to recognize the unholy alliance that they have already joined, which is to say that they fail to apprehend their own moral and political duality—the burden, in allegorical terms, of the metrocolonial condition. Obverse-ly, Seward's temperamental kinship with his purportedly egomaniacal patient results in his refusal to recognize that Renfield might afford Little England some *assistance* or *cooperation* in its mission, which is to say he fails to apprehend Renfield's prospective duality. The exclusionary mode of racial and class identity formation critiqued in the novel is undergirded by a Manichean logic that prevents the protagonists from understanding that, morally and racially speaking, a man might be both one thing and

another. Or that he might, under the Gothicized dispensation of metrocolonialism, find himself *condemned* to be both one thing and another, and
to be so in especially palpable and persistent ways.

Renfield offers faint glimmers of dual allegiance in his early replies to
Seward, which oscillate between the biting and the worshipful. Shortly after
he offends the doctor's professional *amour propre* by lumping him together
with the "attendant," he singles Seward out from the same company for
an expression of fealty that establishes the doctor as a kind of alternative
master to Dracula (102). But it is upon the entry of Mina Harker that
Renfield begins to express his bilateralism with a clarity difficult, though
evidently not impossible, to ignore. Having ascertained her identity and
current lodgings, Renfield immediately instructs Mina to flee. Since Seward
has on that very day discovered Renfield's involvement with the Count,
one might expect the doctor to be on the alert for the betrayal of any advance information. But he remains heedless of Renfield's warning, focusing instead, with tedious predictability, upon a perceived encroachment
upon his authority. When Renfield abruptly alternates into panegyric mode,
affirming his loyalty and esteem for Seward, the latter can only applaud
the change, but continues to displace the credit, and hence any renewed
credibility, from Renfield himself. "I positively opened my eyes at this new
development. Here was my own pet lunatic—the most pronounced of his
type that I had ever met with—talking elemental philosophy, and with the
manner of a polished gentleman. I wonder if it was Mrs. Harker's presence which had touched some chord in his memory. If this new phase was
spontaneous, or in any way due to her unconscious influence, she must have
some rare gift or power" (206). In keeping with the self-reflexive dynamics of *Dracula,* Seward "positively opened [his] eyes" only to espy yet again
the shadows of his preconceptions. He makes a classist equation between
bourgeois norms and mental health then intimates that Renfield has assumed an elite standing he cannot really sustain, that he has put on the
"manner" of a gentleman without possessing the inbred matter. Seward
transfers credit for the newly respectable demeanor of his patient to Mina
Harker, in keeping with her presumptively authentic gentility that, according to Victorian domestic ideology, she would naturally express in the
exercise of an unobtrusively refining influence upon the rougher sex.

Through this conventional division of gender and class agency, Seward
spares himself the necessity of reckoning with the prospect that Renfield may
be one of "us" as well as one of "them"—a potential Little Englander as
well as the vehicle of a hibernicized vampire—and hence with the still scar-

ier prospect that "us" and "them" might be correlates, even versions of one another. Viewed allegorically, Seward avoids confronting the fundamental metrocolonial problematic. In the same self-consoling stroke, however, he also denies himself the opportunity to profit from any active if ambivalent expressions of solidarity on his patient's part, such as Renfield's dramatic valedictory blessing to Mina Harker: "'Goodbye my dear. I pray God I may never see your sweet face again. May He bless you and keep you!'" (207). With these words, Renfield in effect informs Mina that he is on her side—he wishes only her safety—and that, in a structural sense, he is on the other side: her safety depends upon her being removed from his vampirically envenomed presence. While Seward can react with sympathetic "astonishment" to this touchingly phrased piece of intelligence, he cannot read the sympathetic warning, grounded in fellow feeling, that it contains. As a result, he takes no steps to preserve Mina from the peril shortly to befall her. It is ironically Seward's inability to see double, to register the possible double agency of Renfield, that gives his own relationship to vampirism, his own agency, a double cast, cooperative in its very antagonism. Seward's decisions, like those of Van Helsing earlier, symbolically enact the Sisyphean pragmatics of metrocolonialism, which must continually defend the social hierarchies it has imposed against the exaggerated hybridity that it continually produces.

The next inspection of Renfield, conducted four days later by the whole Little England crew, save the Harkers, ratifies this overall assessment decisively. As if sensible of Seward's earlier skepticism of the gentlemanly "manner" he had affected, Renfield sets out immediately to impress each of the men in turn with his bourgeois credentials: his sense of decorum and discernment, his knowledge of the world at large and the particular social orbits of those assembled, his respect for personal distinction, and his qualifications to receive such respect in turn. It is difficult to avoid seeing in his courtly and accomplished self-presentation a displaced caricature of the parvenu efforts of a certain ambitious Irish author to ingratiate himself with the show business aristocracy of the Lyceum Theatre.

Renfield begins his campaign, significantly, with the only high-born member of Little England, Arthur Holmwood (Lord Godalming), apprising him of their unsuspected familial association: "'I had the honour of seconding your father at the Windham; I grieve to know by your holding the title, that he is no more. He was a man loved and honoured by all who knew him; and in his youth was, I have heard, the inventor of a burnt rum punch, much patronized on Derby night'" (215). With his report on having seconded the lord at an exclusive gentlemen's club, corroborated by his show of familiarity with details of Godalming's legacy to high society custom, Renfield lays claim to prior and, to use his word, "honoured" membership in the uppermost reaches of the social sphere encompassed by the Little England circle. That is, he claims to be, Seward's skepticism notwithstanding, to the "manner" born. He amplifies and recalibrates this basic message of belonging in his successive appreciations of the importance of Morris's native state to future American greatness, of the *specific* nature of Van Helsing's medical achievements and renown (the first the reader learns of it), and of the full range of Seward's professional competencies (likewise).

His immediate purpose, of course, is to establish an unimpeachable warrant for his petition to be released. When Renfield confidently declares, "'You, gentlemen, who by nationality, by heredity, or by the possession of natural gifts, are fitted to hold your respective places . . . I take to witness that I am as sane as at least the majority of men who are in full possession of their liberties'" (215), he is in fact predicating his title to freedom less on the stated comparison with "the majority of men" then on his demonstrated social resemblance to *these* men, his affinity for the places they hold, his participation in their systems of tastes, values, and assumptions, including their shared investments in the various figurative modalities of blood: "nationality," "heredity," "natural gifts." Although his claim on their fellowship proves insufficiently convincing to win his parole, his decorous mien does succeed in making Seward feel that he acts "brutally" in refusing his patient (216). This amounts to a reversal in the categories of civilized and barbarous consonant with the narrative and symbolic twists aligning the Little England men with their hibernicized vampiric other.

Renfield's insinuation of solidarity with his captors, moreover, is not purely strategic and self-serving. As in the previous interview, Renfield desires separation from this assembly in part because he identifies with them and knows that his presence can serve as a conduit for Dracula's intrusion into their space and, ultimately, their bodies. Once his appeal, pressed through a diapason of rhetorical tones and emotional intensities, seems irrevocably lost, he combines one last reminder of his gentlemanly stature with a hint that Seward and his colleagues militate against their own interests in denying his request and must take responsibility for the consequences:

When I was leaving the room, last of our party, he said to me in a quiet well-bred voice:—

"You will, I trust, Dr. Seward, do me the justice to bear in mind, later on, that I did what I could to convince you tonight." (218)

Now Seward allows as he would have "taken my chances of trusting" an "ordinary lunatic," but rejects Renfield's pleas because "he seems so mixed up with the Count in an indexy kind of way. . . . He may want to get out and help him in some diabolical way" (219). As we have repeatedly witnessed, however, no one is more "mixed up with the Count in an indexy kind of way" than the double agents of Little England. Here, the substance of this commingling, their exclusionary social and political sensibility, once again passes into a decision beneficial to the cause of vampirism.

Indeed, at this moment, the dualist relationship between the men of Little England and Dracula is not only reinforced but also redoubled. On the grounds that he might secretly assist his sometime "lord and master," Renfield is thwarted in the sincere attempt to free himself of Dracula's influence by men who are "pledged to set the world free" of Dracula (279), but who unwittingly lend him assistance at almost every turn. This incident not only continues the extended progression of suspiciously self-thwarting moves undertaken by Stoker's heroes to this point in the novel, it crystallizes the political implications thereof: when subjectivity is doubly inscribed—and Renfield merely exemplifies that condition, shared by everyone in the novel—the assumption of identity (in every sense) is not *under* threat, it *is* the threat, a form or vehicle, paradoxically, of *self-betrayal*.

With this overlapping series of doppelgänger relations between Little England and Dracula, Stoker characteristically adapts a signature Gothic device to the task of charting the operations of what we might now call the metrocolonial unconscious. While metrocolonialism circulates and consolidates authority by way of interlinked hierarchies of blood—ethnicity, nationality, and class—it also creates the conditions for the hierarchized differences themselves to be profoundly hybridized one with another. As such, this estate both foments and frustrates, demands and defeats, individual and collective adherence to imaginary constructs of discrete caste identity, driving the attempt to impose social order on this basis into ever more brutal and monstrous forms. Stoker establishes Dracula as the very personification of this process, both in its surface misrecognitions and in its underlying reality. As we elaborated in the previous section, Stoker scissors each of the Irish motifs metonymically attached to Dracula into opposed sets of political valence and association: Anglo and Celt, landlord and peasant, mandarin and residuum, imperialist and nationalist, ancien régime and revolutionary vanguard. Consequently, Dracula constitutes a menacing social other *as* and *for* every party to the Irish Question, that is, *in the guise of each and from the perspective of each such lineally defined group.* (The dual allegiance of his disciple, Renfield, translates this relentless allegorical division into practical narrative terms.) As elaborated in this section, however, the practice defining Dracula and the threat he poses, vampirism, is a metaphor of identity formation in its violently reifying aspect, something that kills the living tissue of social connectivity to create a breed apart, an animate but rigidified leftover: the ethnic subject, the class ego, the national character, undead agencies all. On this account, Dracula's affiliation with each Anglo/Irish caste or type reflects its common engrossment in the politics of blood identity.

The men of Little England react to Dracula under the first (metonymical) rubric: they see him as a racialized other infiltrating, via the emblematic bodies of Lucy Westenra and Mina Harker, their cherished Anglo-bourgeois civilization, which so often posed as civilization per se, particularly in contrast with Irish "savagery." But in so doing, and this is the core enigma of Stoker's ethno-national fantasy, they expound the very ethos that Dracula embodies under the second (metaphorical) rubric, the assertion of enclosed classes or ranks of social beings that grow monstrous in proportion to their ultimate unsustainability. It is this recursive political configuration that Stoker narrativizes in the repeated, unconsciously motivated complicity of the vampire warriors with their diabolic foe. In analogous fashion, the central narrative peripeteia, leading to Dracula's destruction and the conventional "happily ever after" ending, comes about only when the tribalist creed of Little England begins, perforce, to mutate.

The agent of this mutation, and hence of the peripeteia, is Mina Harker.

5
Beyond Blood:
Defeating the Inner Vampire

If Seward errs, and errs fatally, in ascribing Renfield's first startling transformation entirely to the civilizing female influence of Mina Harker, it
is nonetheless true that the inmate and the helpmate possess a special
bond in which the Victorian construction of her gender importantly fac-
tors. Just as Renfield would continue to enjoy unimpeachable membership in the general society of Little England were it not for his perceived
disability—his intermittent mania and zoophagy—so Mina would continue to enjoy unqualified membership in the inner councils of Little
England were it not for her perceived disability—her feminine delicacy
or weakness. The personal rapport the two display stems in fact from
their shared status as wards of Little England, figures of a certain social
marginality, condescension, and confinement. Stoker dramatizes this parallel by way of tendentious narrative counterpoint. First, Seward abruptly
curtails Mina's interview with Renfield—ignoring the hints that his patient telegraphs concerning her imminent peril—in order to "meet Van
Helsing at the station" (*D* 207), where the two immediately conspire to
exclude Mina from all future deliberations. In successive scenes, then,
Renfield is effectively silenced on the subject of Dracula, and Mina is relegated *to* silence on the subject of Dracula.

   All of this might be written off as mere coincidence had Stoker not elected
to reinscribe the contiguity immediately in reverse order. Van Helsing and
Seward convene a war room meeting at the end of which Mina is debarred,
for the duration, from further access to the tactical plans of her intimates

("'you no more must question'"; 214). She is then told, like a child, "'to go to bed'" (214), where she records the entire incident in her diary. Even as she makes the entry, the men embark for their group interrogation of Renfield, on which occasion Seward will finally reject his appeal for relief and, once again, turn a deaf ear to his inklings of impending disaster for all. In simultaneous scenes, then, Renfield is locked away with his dangerous knowledge and Mina is imprisoned in her dangerous ignorance. And, what is more, as we learn from Mina's diary and Dracula's subsequent pronouncements, even as the men pursue their interrogation of Renfield, Dracula makes his *first* in a series of visits to a sleeping Mina to have her "veins appease [his] thirst" (251):

> I remember hearing . . . a lot of queer sounds, like praying on a very tumultuous scale, from Mr. Renfield's room, which is somewhere under this. And then there was silence over everything. . . . Not a thing seemed to be stirring, but all to be grim and fixed as death or fate; so that a thin streak of white mist, that crept with almost imperceptible slowness across the grass towards the house, seemed to have a sentience and a vitality of its own. . . . The mist was spreading, and was now close up to the house, so that I could see it lying thick against the wall, as though it were stealing up to the windows. The poor man was more loud than ever, and though I could not distinguish a word he said, I could in some way recognize in his tones some passionate entreaty on his part. Then there was the sound of a struggle, and I knew that the attendants were dealing with him. I was so frightened that I crept into bed. . . . I was not then a bit sleepy . . . but I must have fallen asleep. . . . The mist grew thicker and thicker. . . . The last conscious effort which imagination made was to show me a livid white face bending over me out of the mist. (226–28)

The upshot, then, of the men's disposition of their respective wards is that both find themselves abandoned to Dracula's abuse, and the climactic effects of this practice are likewise rendered emphatically in adjacent and complementary scenes. Hearing that an "accident" has befallen Renfield, the two physicians rush to his side, only to find him badly mutilated by the vampiric assault. As he languishes toward death, Renfield reveals that he has indeed seen Mina's "sweet face again" (207), with the disastrous consequences he had dimly bruited: "When Mrs. Harker came in to see me this afternoon she wasn't the same; it was like tea after the teapot had been watered. . . . It made me mad to know that he had been taking the life out of her" (245). Although the gravely ill Renfield reports fighting with his master on Mina's behalf—"'I didn't mean for him to take any more of her life'" (246)—the doctors abruptly forsake him, in clear violation of their Hippocratic oath, and barge off to the Harkers' bedroom, where they discover a matching spectacle of vampiric depredation.

This is yet another instance of the narrative syntax secreting implications at variance with and more telling than the narrative point of view controlled by the individual protagonists would seem to admit. Renfield and Mina are paired as inlets for the great spectral stranger because both, notwithstanding the wide differences in their present stations, have been alienated to some degree from their community and consigned to a shadowy corner of their world. It is within the terms of this social correlation, furthermore, that those wide differences acquire a special symbolic and thematic significance.

Renfield occupies a particularly abject and pathological social margin, which was attracting increasingly intense concern as the nineteenth century drew to a close: a species of masculine breakdown involving a cluster of nervous disorders classified and treated medically, but identified with a kind of moral incontinence.[1] In the case of Renfield, vampiric inhabitation serves as a Gothic trope of this emasculating malaise, indexing its subversion of both individual integrity and, given the male's presumptive social leadership, the collective sovereignty of the modern ethnos or nation. As discussed earlier, the prevailing code of "muscular" manliness took austere self-reliance and rigid self-containment as its defining norm, and so made the voluptuous self-surrender figured in vampiric seduction both a powerful temptation, as Harker and Van Helsing illustrate, and a synonym of male ruin. *Thus constituted in an allergic relation to otherness, the gender ideal of Victorian masculinity tends not only to encourage but also to encode the sort of defensive xenophobic racial mentality that Dracula both arouses and espouses.*

Renfield clearly accepts, even as he defaults upon, this masculine standard. He acts out his vampiric inhabitation, his failure of boundary maintenance, by orally incorporating an evolutionary chain of other creatures, in an attempt to enlarge his own vital capacity. In other words, his express allegiance to Dracula centers on an identification with his hypermasculine mastery, which Renfield tries to assert on his own behalf. By the same token, when he ultimately endeavors to break with Dracula, he struggles to couch his appeals and admonitions to Seward in the idiom of bourgeois manliness, of which his chivalric protectiveness toward Mina is perhaps the most assured exhibition. For that very reason, however, his communication with the men of Little England does more to reinforce than to alter the existing social dynamic. He desperately wishes to demonstrate how akin to them he is, down to justifying their tribalistic code of values, which unfortunately mandates his own exclusion. His warnings can only confirm the vampire warriors in a mentality that (through the self-reflexive logic of the Gothic fantasy) is at the root of the villainy they confront.

Mina, by contrast, occupies a minoritized and yet *idealized* social margin, that of *properly* feminine fragility, dependency, non–self-sufficiency, heteronomy in sum, which came to attract increasingly intense cultural investments with the fin de siècle emergence of its antitype, the New Woman. Insofar as the traditional "womanly woman," which Mina consents to play at this juncture, exists primarily *to be protected* and thus to confer legitimacy and purpose upon an anxious British patriarchy, the infiltration of Mina's body and spirit by Dracula signifies utter catastrophe, the evisceration not just of her essential role within the hegemonic cultural script but of her essential role in underwriting the script itself. But insofar as that essential role is predicated upon women's socially mandated heteronomy, vampiric inhabitation is uncannily continuous with her interpellation to the enshrined "feminine" virtues of unselfishness, submissiveness, other-directedness. Indeed, the long-established, intuitively obvious identification of vampiric bloodsucking with maternal breast-suckling speaks precisely to this continuity.[2] For beyond the physical acts themselves, this identification, however parodic, points to a close psychosocial analogy between the doppelgänger transaction of vampirism and the dyadic pre-Oedipal engrossment of mother and child, each of which involves a mode of connectivity that tends to confound or dissolve the borders of selfhood so prized by patriarchal liberalism.

Since the maternal care and nurture crystallized in the act of nursing was deemed to be at once the highest and the most natural office of a woman, the gold standard of her womanliness, any supposed compromise of her ego boundaries would register less as a default on the phallic law of assured self-ownership than as compliance with a conflicting imperative promoted by that very same law as its necessary supplement: a sentimental adhesiveness or connectivity that ensures species survival in both its animal and social dimensions. More than an alternative ethics, this conventionally "feminine" supplement represents an ethics of alterity—an openness toward, responsiveness to, solicitude for, and self-sacrificing identification with *others*—that crucially informed the Victorian sense of the family home, women's domestic preserve, as a "haven in a heartless world."

Constituted in a kind of rudimentary and limited xenophilia, normative femininity could serve Stoker as a model of the ethnic ideal of domestic colonialism that he wished to advance. We should not be surprised, therefore, to find him relying strongly upon this gender typology—not, as has often been assumed, to confine his women within traditional stereotypes (Mina's masculine intellect, after all, is repeatedly noted)—but rather to vindicate the ethical disposition traditionally associated with womanliness in general and maternity specifically.[3] Working from this conceptual base, Stoker develops and contextualizes Mina's vampiric inhabitation so that it can signify *beyond parodic catastrophe to redemptive possibility*, with Mina in the role of transformative agent.

To showcase the alembic potential of Mina's seemingly conventional ethos, Stoker revisits the dream logic of metalepsis with a (gendered) difference. As the phantasmatic racial/racist other, Dracula personifies and elicits the violent abrogation of social connectivity already implicit in the blood consciousness of Little England; and, as a result, the men's tactics against the Count tend to facilitate his campaign of incorporation and recruitment. However, as a phantasmatic transfusion of blood identity, at once compulsory and desirable, the vampiric exchange itself, divorced from its telos of conversion, both objectifies and intensifies the sense of radical social communion already implicit in Mina Harker's extraordinarily maternal-being-in-the-world; and, as a result, her repeated vampings ultimately redound to the detriment and even the destruction of Dracula and his campaign.

Stoker underlines the significance of this process/project divide in the respective fates assigned his differently minded female protagonists. Lucy Westenra, who exhibited no particular maternal bent in life, is fully converted to *nosferatu*. In this condition, she reappears as an archetype of the evil mother: she waylays little children, feeds upon instead of feeding them, and then casts them callously aside. Mina Harker, by contrast, remains suspended *within* the dynamics of vampiric transfusion, neither incorporated in nor disentangled from Dracula. And in this condition, she extends to new breadths and depths an already capacious maternal sympathy, which moves her to comfort most of the other characters in their hour of need.

It is worthy of notice, moreover, that Mina's long record of motherly service bears a close and unbroken affiliation with vampirism from the start. Her first maternal display has her wandering into the night to retrieve the sleepwalking Lucy Westenra, her erstwhile student and charge, from the

suicide seat to which Dracula has lured her for his nightly repast. In an
arresting proleptic reversal of Lucy's performance as the "Bloofer Lady,"
Mina leads her friend home, like a lost child, taking special care to protect
both "her health" and her "reputation" (88–89). Her second such display
occurs in a Budapest hospital, where she *begins* her marriage by "attend[ing]
to her husband" (101) as he suffers the effects of his doppelgänger encounter
with Dracula. Almost a month later, she reports, "Jonathan wants looking after still. . . . Even now he sometimes starts out of his sleep in a sudden way and awakes all trembling until I can coax him back to his usual
placidity" (141). For Mina, it would seem, the vampire is a wish-fulfilling
nightmare, compelling her to satisfy her penchant for profound fellow feeling, which tends to seize upon each occasion of emotional attachment as a
site of maternal care and concern.

The third conspicuous exercise of Mina's prompt motherly instinct involves comforting Arthur Holmwood in his "hysterical" grief over the
ruination of his fiancée by Dracula. A full citation of this well-known episode is in order:

> He grew quite hysterical, and raising his open hands, beat his palms to-
> gether in a perfect agony of grief. . . . I felt an infinite pity for him, and
> opened my arms unthinkingly. With a sob he layed his head on my shoul-
> der, and cried like a wearied child, whilst he shook with emotion.
>
> We women have something of the mother in us that makes us rise above
> smaller matters when the mother-spirit is invoked; I felt this big, sorrow-
> ing man's head resting on me, as though it were that of the baby that some
> day may lie on my bosom, and I stroked his hair as though he were my
> own child. I never thought at the time how strange it all was. (203)

This passage has been rightly deemed crucial for making explicit the cen-
trality of the maternal ideal to Mina's self-image, to the evolving social
economy of Little England, and, by extension, to Stoker's sexual politics.
But it is equally crucial for our purposes because in the same stroke it
unfolds a visual and conceptual rhyme between the mother-child dyad and
the vampiric couple. Mina's reflexive accommodation of Arthur's impor-
tunate hunger for comfort ("opened my arms unthinkingly") recalls the
unconscious gesture of permission or consent that is necessary for the
vampire to press his suit. The bodily attitude of the pair, Arthur poised on
her "shoulder," his face presumably turned toward her neck, evokes a classic vampire tableau, while Mina's simile displacing the action from her
shoulder to her "bosom" nudges the reader to draw the bloodsucking/

breast-suckling parallel. Finally, Mina's sense of being called outside of herself by the invocation of the "mother-spirit" extends the analogy to vampirism from one of physical posture and activity to one of spectral visitation and inhabitation. With all of this in mind, her reflection, "I never thought at the time how strange it all was," unwittingly references the scene's uncanny resemblance to and reversal of the parody of motherhood in vampirism.

A still stranger and more decisive reversal is in the offing. During the above interlude, a subtle turnabout of roles transpires. As the pressure of the man-child/vampire's demand for consolation subsides, the mother/host comes to be possessed *of* as well as *by* the active and spectral power, here troped as "mother-spirit." It is as if in not being held to the masculine law of disciplined self-enclosure, Mina is not only able to enjoy, in an intimate eroticized manner, responding to the solicitation of fellow feeling, but also able to *draw* abnormal emotional strength from being *drawn upon* in this way. As opposed to building herself up through acts of incorporation, the masculinized, colonial form of aggrandizement favored by Renfield and his master, she secures enhancement through an outpouring and divestment of the self, a strategy that requires her to remain within the moment, as it were, of interdependency and exchange. With Arthur finally becalmed, she evinces an immediate willingness to renew her maternal efforts on behalf of his comrade-in-mourning, Quincy Morris, whose inferred urgency of grief elicits from her an offer, a proposition, that is not simply bold and unexpected, but, for her time and class, forward to the point of impropriety:

> He bore his own troubles so bravely that my heart bled for him . . . so I said to him:—
> "I wish I could comfort all who suffer from the heart. Will you let me be your friend, will you come to me for comfort if you need it?" (204)

So hard upon her tête-à-tête with Arthur, so comprehensive in the avowed scope of its desire, Mina's gesture unmistakably evokes and inverts the motif of vampiric recruitment. She seeks out recipients for her "heart" blood instead of donors, dressing, in each case, the collateral wounds left by Dracula. In the very next scene she makes her critical visit to Renfield, taking *her* campaign of maternal consolation directly to the vampire's minions.

One more strand of this narrative warp needs to be traced, for it simultaneously marks and points beyond the last remaining limit to Mina's motherly largesse of spirit. Immediately prior to her encounter with Arthur,

Mina ponders the fate of Dracula himself, now that her menfolk are so doggedly in pursuit: "I suppose one ought to pity anything so hunted as is the Count. That is just it: this Thing is not human—not even beast. To read Seward's account of poor Lucy's death, and what followed, is enough to dry up the springs of pity in one's heart" (202). Mina's rationale for denying Dracula her compassion (literally, "feeling-with") is in true Little England fashion inextricably racial and moral: his ontological foreignness—neither man nor beast—naturalizes a moral debasement that absolves her of an otherwise painful but necessary exercise of the sympathetic imagination. Still, Mina's evident discomfort in not reaching the highest standard of magnanimity that she can envisage might well account for her subsequent zeal to afford solace to virtually everyone else. More importantly, this moment of doubt leaves in her mind—and the reader's—the intuition of a regulative ethico-political ideal of *caritas,* comprising a finally unconstrained willingness to acknowledge one's imbrication with others through a generous emotional investment in them. It thereby lays the ground for a truly decisive turning point in the novel, when Mina fully assumes this seemingly impossible empathetic mandate.

After being vamped, Mina calls God's pity on herself, adducing a life of virtue as grounds for his consideration—"'What have I done to deserve such a fate, I who have tried to walk in meekness and righteousness all my days'" (252). But as with Job, to whom her biblically phrased sentiments allude, Mina's bitter fate enables her to reach new heights of meekness and righteousness, to extend her call for mercy to the great Reprobate who brought her to this pass.

> "I want you to bear something in mind through all this dreadful time. I know that you must fight—that you must destroy even as you destroyed the false Lucy so that the true Lucy might live hereafter; but it is not a work of hate. The poor soul who has wrought this misery is the saddest case of all. Just think what will be his joy when he too is destroyed in his worser part that his better part may have spiritual immortality. You must be pitiful to him too, though it may not hold your hands from his destruction." (268–69)

While her compassion cannot be allowed to preempt the spectacle of "destruction" compulsory to the genre, it does augur a change in its symbolic significance. Thus, when her husband reverts to form, ventilating his undiminished "hate" of Dracula in contemplation of his "spiritual immortality" in "burning hell" (269), Mina repeats her demand that he reconsider his asperity, reminding him of their own blood tie to the vampire tribe: "'Oh hush! oh hush! in the name of the good God. Don't say such things . . . or you will crush me with fear and horror. Just think, my dear—I have been thinking all this long, long day of it—that . . . perhaps . . . some day . . . I too may need such pity; and that some other like you—and with equal cause for anger—may deny it to me!'" (269). The "pity" Mina summons (in both senses) might be more accurately termed compassion, the same feeling-with that she expressly withheld earlier. While her grievance against Dracula has surely grown more serious in the interim, it has also germinated a certain identification with him. She overtly predicates her charitable sentiments toward her tormentor, those she would inculcate in her loved ones, on her coerced family resemblance to the vampire. *We* cannot utterly cast Dracula off, she declares in effect, because *I* am now of his party as well, so much so that I can envision my loving husband as "some other" who justifiably abhors me.

In presuming that her change of blood automatically spells a spiritual deterioration, Mina's *method of reasoning* remains faithful to the established Little England creed that moral properties reside in blood makeup, be it race (Harker's slovenly Orientals), class (Van Helsing's feckless servants), or the most common anthropological transcription of race, "species" (Dracula as hibernicized "brute"). But Mina's transitional *state of being,* between the living and the undead—plainly a temporal metaphor of "mixed" blood—defies any easy or absolute correlation between ethnic status and ethical stature. What is more, this transitional state affords Mina access to a privileged moral and political vantage in its own right: her multiple identifications allow her a more prismatic understanding and thus a finer strain of empathy than has been attained heretofore in the novel. Mina alone has a glimmer of the irrevocable linkage between the knight-errants of Little England and the nightstalkers of Transylvania, and this awareness, while a suspicious, identificatory effect of her enthrallment to Dracula,[4] paradoxically proves the means of individual, group, and even national deliverance from him.

The representational strategy underlying Mina's carefully circumscribed transcendence of the Little England mindset is vintage Stoker, a testament to his parvenu facility for sly, self-insulating criticism of the community whose approval he continued to demand on his own, Irish-inflected terms. Instead of directly challenging the racial essentialism that tended to cramp his own social prospects, Stoker makes it the epicenter of an internecine conflict, and he adapts, in the person of Mina, a broadly Christian rheto-

ric to celebrate the Utopian possibilities of ethnic hybridization. On both
counts, he closely follows the script he first wrote for "The Dualitists." Just
as the various counterpart relationships between Little England and the
vampire kingdom rehearse the schismatic form of duality displayed by
Harry Merford and Tommy Santon, so Mina's acceptance of the vampiric other in herself and her intimates transposes, in a distant but still recognizable key, the symbiotic duality of the Bubb twins. Moreover, just as
the symbiotic blessedness of the Bubb twins is embellished with Irish resonances, which index the aptitude for social connectivity buried deep within the often divisive metrocolonial condition, so the enhancement and
refinement of Mina's compassion unfolds under Irish colors. As noted
earlier, Mina's birth surname encrypts a deeply hybrid Irish heritage—at
once native and settler, Anglo and Celt, Catholic and Protestant—which
her infiltration by a similarly hybrid, hibernicized vampire can be seen to
have activated, augmenting her inherited potential for entertaining alterity. As Stoker knew, the Irish prided themselves on a communitarian *Weltan-
schauung* that distinguished them from the more atomized individualism
dear to John Bull, and the English did not dispute them on this point,
doubtless feeling that such other-directedness consorted well with the "essentially feminine" character of the Celtic race.[5]

The metaphor clinching this ethno-national association is precisely that
of maternity. With her allegorically weighted name and her metropolitan
marriage, Mina invokes a long, storied line of female personae of Ireland
and personae of a feminized Ireland—the Shan Von Vacht, Cathleen Ni
Houlihan, Hibernia, the Speirbhean or Sky Woman, and Erin, among others. As the Blessed Virgin Mary became the dominant personification of
the national ideal, reflecting the increased political power of Catholic Irish–
Ireland during the Victorian era, the entire array of female icons came to
be consolidated under the figure of Mother Ireland, who provides a perfect allegorical "fit" for Mina's role in the novel. Insofar as Mina's ethics
of profound connectivity, imaged in and intensified by her vampiric inhabitation, represents a distinctively feminine and maternal supplement to
phallic self-containment, it articulates a cultural ideal with special pertinence to Ireland, one that coheres with that country's national symbolism
and positively transvalues the half-embraced stereotype of its people as
emotional, impulsive, sentimental, "essentially feminine." It is surely no
accident that Mina has already been cast in the role of the Blessed Mother by the Catholic Van Helsing, nor that he does so in the process of announcing her fateful exclusion from the conferences of Little England:

"'You must be our star and our hope, and we shall act all the more free that you are not in the danger, such as we are'" (214). These words endow Mina with the iconic attributes of "Mary, Star of the Sea," the merciful patron of voyagers, and they usher her off to bed where she will shortly be forced to "mother" that seaborn "Irish" voyager so in need of her "pity," Count Dracula.[6]

Ironically, however, the very elements coding Mina's ethics of alterity "Irish"—the intimate yet iconic experience of motherhood coupled with the sectarian yet universalizing discourse of Christianity—speak to interpersonal relations so fundamental and so sweeping that they automatically extend the pertinence of her sentiments beyond the metrocolonial problematic to all manner of social intercourse.

Mina's "sweeter counsels" of sympathy for the vampire do prevail over Jonathan's hatred, reducing the men to tears and effectively turning her personal insight into a collective decision.[7] She not only reconciles herself to the racialized taint of the vampiric contagion; she also convinces the men to accept her on these terms, which is to say, to accommodate a virulent strain of otherness at the heart of their community. At this moment, a conversion narrative suddenly irrupts within the conquest narrative of *Dracula,* and the implications of this modal shift for the novel's political fantasy are decisive, touching upon its central self-reflexive conceit. As we have seen, in violently dissociating themselves from Dracula qua racial other, the men of Little England only testify to their unconscious projection of Dracula qua specter of racism, and this fantasy dynamic takes narrative form in the symptomatic persistence with which their schemes to subdue the vampire seem rather to abet him. It thus stands to reason, as a matter of symbolic logic, that in suspending this unconscious complicity, Mina's acceptance of racialized otherness in herself and her persuasion of her menfolk to do likewise would mitigate or even reverse the self-defeating trajectory of Little England's campaign against vampirism. That is *exactly* what happens, as Stoker accentuates through a painstaking juxtaposition of events.

In the scene just *before* the "sweeter counsels" of Mina prevail, the men have their climactic London confrontation with Dracula, which provides perhaps the most egregious instance of their collective, unconsciously motivated ineptitude. Despite cornering Dracula in a classic ambush, with numbers on their side, with ample time for their strategic ace, Morris, to devise the perfect "plan of action," and despite possessing the concerted will to advance "with a single impulse," they nevertheless wind up empty-handed (266). As Dracula eludes their grasp, the experienced reader of thrillers is left, or rather asked, to wonder exactly what advantages, if not these, would finally permit this platoon of heroes to corral their diabolic counterpart.

In the scene immediately *after* the "sweeter counsels" of Mina prevail, the answer surfaces; Mina herself hits upon what proves to be the *single dispositive means* for hunting the vampire, as it were, to ground. Divining that her blood-suckling of Dracula has laid down an intimate, subliminal line of psychic contact with him, she tells Van Helsing, "'I want you to hypnotize me!'" (271), on the supposition that, being a channel for the vampire's mental impressions, she can serve as a homing device for his movements. With its play on the doppelgänger motif, this pre-Vulcan mindmeld is an ingenious plot contrivance typical of the Gothic adventure genre, which the last third of the novel, a protracted chase scene, otherwise plays out rather perfunctorily. But the stratagem also—and this is the chief part of its ingenuity—perfectly encapsulates Mina's transformative significance in the novel, her incubation of a badly needed ethics/politics of connectivity.

Taken by itself, the men's violent confrontational tactics play into the vampire's hands insofar as he is but the phantasmal emanation of their own antisocial tendencies, their commitment to a metrocolonial ideology of domination and absorption. Their agonistic approach to Dracula only ratifies the depth of their identification. Mina's tactic of subterranean communication reverses this self-reflexive curve. Her secret sharing with the vampire, which registers a certain degree of identification, paradoxically breaks with, stands against, and finally defeats the egoistic agenda and racist ideology he advances.

As the active expression of radical self-absorption and aggrandizement, both individual (egoism) and collective (tribalism), the vampiric act seeks to impose unilateral mastery at a most intimate point of social intercourse, the exchange of bodily fluids, turning the participants into possessor and possessed, respectively. The mindmeld is, from Dracula's perspective, an extension of this violent erotic economy. He is the one who originally enjoins the psychic commerce as a device for monitoring and manipulating his newest "helpmeet" (252). Mina herself is under no illusions on this score: "'he may have used my knowledge for his ends'" (297). But in self-consciously embracing the interior alterity that the mindmeld entails, she effectively restores the reciprocal character of interpersonal exchange and thereby escapes being controlled by the vampire, which is to say by the ideology of expansive self-enclosure.

As Little England enters upon the "great hour" of its offensive into Transylvania, it is given to Van Helsing to translate this ethico-political allegory into the lexicon of Gothic narrative. Confirming that Dracula "'has so used [Mina's] mind'" for his own purposes, Van Helsing describes how and why he will be hoisted on his own petard—in a kind of mirror image of the vampire fighters' earlier contretemps. Dracula's selfish "child-brain" never foresaw that the mindmeld could bind him into a bilateral social relationship, one in which his authority and his desires were not final. He believes he can dispose of Mina as he will, but precisely because she has put herself at his disposal, suspending the collective fixation with mastery, he cannot do so after all.

> "He think, too, that as he cut himself off from knowing your mind, there can be no knowledge of him to you; there is where he fail! That terrible baptism of blood which he give you makes you free to go to him in spirit, as you have yet done in your times of freedom. . . . And this power to good of you and others, you have won from your suffering at his hands. This is all the more precious that he know it not, and to guard himself have even cut himself off from his knowledge of our where. We, however, are not all selfish." (297)

Like his doppelgänger, however, Van Helsing "only saw so far" (297). Assuming that he and his crew "are not all selfish," he overlooks how far their much celebrated norm of manhood, with its emphasis on assured self-possession, self-containment, and self-mastery, is constituted in an allergic relation to otherness, and so carries the seeds of a certain kind of "selfish"-ness within it. The power that Mina has "won" from her maternal "suffering" is the power to persuade her colleagues to relieve their anxious manliness with the unqualified compassion and other-directedness necessary to defeat the egoistic force of Dracula, that is, to effect a conversion that counters *in spirit* the "blood" conversion of vampirism. As a corollary to this conversion, the men once again allow Mina to be an active participant in the campaign rather than its mascot, abandoning the effort to aggrandize their collective male ego by reducing her to a passive and helpless type of the feminine.

With this narrative turn, it should be noted, Stoker bids to effect his own conversion in the racial and gender currencies of Irishness. He tropes the gender ambivalence of his Anglo-Celtic heritage into an alternative value structure. The hysterical heroism/heroic hysteria that has marked much of the vampire hunt begins to give way at this point to another "feminine" style of heroism, which entails confronting and conquering one's innermost xenophobia.

Van Helsing concludes his account of Mina's psychic telepathy by exhorting the others to "'follow'" Dracula "'even if we peril ourselves that we become like him'" (297). With its play on the meaning of the word *follow,* the last proviso has typically been taken to express Stoker's concern about the corrupting effects on otherwise high-minded British liberals of a violent struggle against a lawless colonial resistance.[8] Our analysis, to this point, however, frames Van Helsing's remarks as a belated and still subliminal recognition of the family resemblance that has always subsisted between the members of Little England and their vampiric double. The occasion of his words is significant in this regard, since his recognition is not just induced by but is virtually emergent in his understanding of how the mindmeld operates. Moreover, in acknowledging, first, the possibility of their collective kinship to what has seemed an unspeakably alien figure and, second, the consequent need for the group to guard against its own vampiric aggressions, Van Helsing's address participates in the subtle but seismic shift facilitated by Mina in the symbolic stakes of the vampire hunt. Even as the action reported in the journal entries flattens into a conventional conquest adventure in an exotic locale, the introduction of the conversion narrative has leavened the symbolic register in which the action transpires. Instead of an intrusive spectral signifier of some outward racial caste (the Irish) or condition (degeneracy), a focus appropriate to more conventional imperialist romance, the vampire becomes a literalized or embodied signifier of an inward racial attitude.

☙ ☙ ☙

One problem facing Stoker was how to map this inward turn, with its localized psychic terrain, onto the broader geopolitical landscape allegorized in the novel. His ingenious stratagem was to coordinate the successes enjoyed by the Little Englanders in their crusade with their increasing willingness to "turn Irish" in their means and manner of pursuing it. That is to say, in one of the more sweeping Gothic symmetries in the novel, Stoker counterbalances the colonial mimicry of Dracula, his strategic simulation of English metropolitan ways of being, with the *reverse* mimicry of the Little England crew, its adoption of presumptively Irish methods of combating him. And just as, owing to the impacted political conditions of "the union," the Irish Dracula poses or passes as what he in some sense already is (a Briton), so the members of Little England come to embrace—

on duress at first and gradually by design—an otherness proper to or at least indissociable from their "true" ethno-national selves.

From the outset of the novel, some of the most potent defensive measures undertaken against the vampire derive from the liturgical rites of the Roman Catholic church, which in the Britain of Stoker's day were far less prominently associated with the historic sectarian enemies, France and Spain, than with the restive Irish people-nation.[9] The first such instance sees Jonathan Harker outwardly expressing his discomfort at the receipt of a crucifix that, "as an English churchman, I have been taught to regard ... as in some measure idolatrous" (13). During the mirror scene, however, he comes to regard the crucifix as his salvation from the advances of Dracula (31). In the second instance, Van Helsing seals the grave of the undead Lucy with the Eucharist, for which he claims a papal dispensation. Van Helsing does speak elsewhere of the need to rely upon superstitious traditions in the war on vampirism, but being a Catholic, he certainly does not regard the Sacrament in this light. Nor are the occult uses of the Eucharist greeted with more than momentary shock by his Protestant cohorts, who shortly find themselves escorting the Host and holding their own crucifixes aloft in an effort to drive Dracula from the body of Mina (247). In this validation of beliefs and observances typically associated with the backward, "idolatrous" peasantry of Ireland, there is an understated inversion of the single most pivotal event in Anglo/Irish history. Instead of a Protestant Dutchman, William III, being called across the water to save England from the perils of Catholicism and, by the time of the Boyne, from its Irish exponents, Stoker gives us a Catholic Dutchman called across the water to save England, and William's namesake, *with* the sacred objects of Catholicism and, by extension, the sectarian markers of Irishness.

One of the more prominent aspects of Irish Catholicism eschewed in Anglican culture was marialotry, a zealous, some would say excessive devotion to the Blessed Virgin, which left a deep imprint, in turn, upon nationalist symbology of Irish-Ireland. As noted above, with the growingly Catholic leadership of both the Home Rule and Republican movements, Mary was often conflated with the ancient goddesses Hibernia, Erin, and Cathleen as figures of "the sovereignty," hortatory symbols of an independent Ireland whose honor and dignity her sons were enlisted to avenge. So when Van Helsing proclaims the hypermaternal Mina "'our star and our hope'" in "'danger,'" exalting her as an avatar of Our Lady, Star of the Sea, he implicitly organizes her champions in a symbolic economy that unmistakably recalls contemporary Irish Catholic Fenianism. After Mina's surprising plea on behalf of Dracula and her ensuing entry into telepathy with him, events that catalyze the group's more conscious accommodation of otherness, Van Helsing progresses from mirroring the iconography of advanced Irish nationalism to echoing its philosophy. His quoted comment that Mina has "won" power over Dracula "'from [her] suffering at his hands'" articulates the cardinal principle underlying the Fenian-identified ethos of blood sacrifice and anticipates Terence MacSwiney's celebrated formula: victory comes to those who endure suffering rather than those who inflict it.[10] Blood sacrifice is, of course, a policy of the dispossessed. It aims to make a virtue out of necessitousness, if you will, out of an absence of resources beyond the fully committed bodies of those involved. The avowal of this ethos by Little England, Van Helsing's express belief that Mina's suffering of a "blood sacrifice" may itself prove the key to victory, amounts to a marked structural identification with the disempowered yet dangerous element of Irish patriotism that Dracula has often been taken to allegorize.

A certain topical allusion, highly provocative for Stoker's contemporary audience, not only underlines this cross-ethnic/cross-class identification but also calls attention to the self-consciousness with which Little England assumes it. In his journal, Seward calls the vampire fighters' entire strategy of pursuing Dracula into Transylvania their "Plan of Campaign" (*ED* 383), and since he uses the uppercase letters that turn this colloquial expression into a proper name, he can only be read as affiliating their effort with *the* Plan of Campaign, a scheme undertaken between 1886 and 1890 for the Irish tenantry to secure the right of collective bargaining through systematic rent strikes and boycotting.[11] At the primary level, Seward's use of the term as a corporate self-description identifies the struggle of the Little Englanders against Dracula with a moral force resistance movement undertaken by their ethnic and class antipodes. There is, as usual in *Dracula,* a vertiginous exactitude to this arrangement. The change in Little England's moral and political objective, allegorically considered, from defeating the vampire without (the racial other) to defeating the vampire within (the racialist predisposition) forms a precise corrective reversal of the form of projection demanded of the metrocolonial subject, the displacement of the otherness within onto some external threat. Hence, the change in moral and political objective is not merely accentuated or even supplemented, but literally realized and to a degree explained by the transmutation of metropolitan Anglo mandarins into barbarous Irish aliens.

But the gesture enacted in Seward's journal entry carries still greater evidentiary force and political resonance. In the Plan of Campaign, Seward hits on more than an event in Irish history with which *Little* England might identify, he hits on a conspicuous site in the history of *liberal* England's identification with the Irish tenantry during the so-called Union of Hearts, which covered roughly the same period. What made the Plan of Campaign such a salient political movement was less its direct effects on landlord-lessee relations, which were negligible, than its indirect effects on the way certain more advanced, progressive constituencies of English liberalism came, in despite of the party leadership, to view the plight of the Irish, that is, its capacity to mobilize in historical fact the sort of sympathetic imagination that Mina Harker mobilizes in Gothic fiction. Initiated by Stoker's cousin John Dillon, among others, the Plan of Campaign was designed to bait the largely Ascendancy landlords into staging ruthless evictions that would hopefully be witnessed by English visitors invited to Ireland for that purpose.[12]

One such prominent visitor was a Liberal party member of Parliament from Cornwall, Charles Conybeare, who wound up assisting, even joining the resistance efforts of evicted tenants in Donegal and was for his trouble arrested, convicted, and jailed on the charge of criminal conspiracy. Since the "clinching evidence" turned on Conybeare giving "three cheers for the Plan of Campaign," one might reasonably infer that he was punished for the crime of identifying with the disaffected Irish by being treated as one.[13] Another Liberal party politico, George Lansbury, was motivated to organize a Radical club delegation to the Plan of Campaign by a preexisting Irish identification, which has a special pertinence for *Dracula*. Having moved as a boy to the Whitechapel neighborhood of the East End—the haunt of Dracula in London and the ground of certain of his racial affiliations—Lansbury lived, in his words, "among what may be described as a mixed population—Irish and Jews and foreigners, of all nationalities."[14] Here Ireland became the center of a radiating countercultural web of subaltern loyalties and adherences spun right in the heart of the metropole:

> The Irish boys at our school were all 'Fenians'; consequently, when the wall of Clerkenwell Prison was blown down and three Irish martyrs executed in Manchester because a police officer was accidentally killed, very great excitement prevailed in our classes and playground. The teachers tried to make us understand how wicked the Irishmen had been on both occasions, but my Irish friends would have none of it, and when a few months later T.D. Sullivan's song *God Save Ireland* came out, we boys were shouting it at the tops of our voices every playtime.[15]

The last sentence adumbrates a developing solidarity between elements of the English and Irish communities in England, a bond that proved crucial to the Home Rule policies of Stoker's political favorites and found still more strenuous expression in the Plan of Campaign that they opposed.

By having the English Seward place the final, ultimately successful push against Dracula under the sign of the Plan of Campaign, Stoker looks to rivet text and context, history and fantasy, literary and geopolitics from both ends. On one side, through the association of the Plan, and more specifically English participation in the Plan, with the happy resolution of a hibernicized nightmare of blood, Stoker offers his support, characteristically encrypted, for those advanced Liberals who seized the occasion to fashion links with the moral force Irish independence movement, fulfilling the political posture implicit in "The Voice of England." On the other side, insofar as these elements sought a resolution to the Irish crisis in a self-conscious revision of England's ethnic attitudes, Seward's replication of this gesture further attests to the self-reflexive turn the vampire hunt has taken.

The construction of the novel's denouement, the pursuit and execution of Dracula, illustrates the last point compellingly. When the vampire fighters arrive at Galatz, looking for the box containing the Count, they are directed to the office of Immanuel Hildesheim, whose presence elicits an outburst of anti-Semitic vitriol from Jonathan Harker (D 302). In keeping with the dream logic of the novel, this racist fulmination magically conjures forth an objective correlative with direct bearing upon Little England's quest: the man to whom Hildesheim directs them, Petrof Shinsky, immediately turns up dead, the victim of a murder with apparent racial overtones ("'This is the work of a Slovak,'" the women cry; 303). To avoid being caught up in a Balkan "whirlpool" of racial animosity and outrage, Harker must flee the scene with his cohorts, forsaking any immediate prospect of locating his wife's tormentor. The men's response to this setback, phantasmatically effected by their own lingering racism, is to begin "taking Mina again into [their] confidence" (303). Given her telepathic function, this decision is particularly significant because it serves to close the circuit, to complete the connection, between the society of Little England and their vampiric other. At this point, the men finally agree to finish the process of admitting alterity in their midst, to assume the "hazardous" "chance" of racial self-exposure (303). This attitude proves as conducive to their ultimate goal as their blood anxiety has been counterproductive.

With her "man's brain" and "woman's heart," her mixed blood and iconic purity, her undead and yet unvanquished spirit, Mina is not only a hybrid figure but also, through sheer force of overdetermination, a symbolic figure of hybridity; and it is she, tellingly, who puts Little England back on the trail lost in connection with her husband's anti-Semitic lapse. Her determination of the proper route to follow, the river course, merely transposes onto the terrain of action adventure her earlier directions as to the proper ethico-political course to follow. Once again, the narrative and symbolic syntax prompts the discovery that the waterway to finding and defeating Dracula flows inward.

To render this lesson still more forcibly, while keeping the attendant social critique as muted as possible, Stoker contrives to make the final narrative destination, the killing of Dracula, purposively anti- and ante-climactic at the same time. The end of Dracula is anti-climactic because there is no prolonged or gripping death struggle. Dracula seemingly dies at a touch and disappears in the same motion. As Mina records it, "It was like a miracle; but before our very eyes, and almost in the drawing of a breath, the whole body crumbled into dust and passed from our sight" (325). Noting that the collective "butchery" promised by Van Helsing fails to meet expectations, Auerbach and Skal opine that "Dracula's supposed death is riddled with ambiguity" (325). On the contrary, a definite message can be gleaned from the manner in which Dracula's death defies expectations. The body of the vampire does not in the end offer even the minimal resistance necessarily exerted by an independently objectified being. Unsustainable, even as dust, he bears the insubstantiality of a mirage, an internally generated phantom. Mina's phraseology seems chosen to insinuate the imaginary status of Dracula. He vanishes "in the drawing of a breath" because he is a function of breath, metaphorically considered, an emanation of the soul.

In this light, the fate of Quincy Morris may be seen as the terminal and summary instance of the mirroring of vampire and vampire fighters. Received in the very act of slaying Dracula, Morris's death wound serves as a ritual token of Dracula's symbolic value for the members of Little England: it signifies that their effective extermination of the vampire and what he represents can only transpire through the eradication of a blameworthy part of their collective self. That the sacrificial embodiment of this part is an Anglo-American, the ethno-national group inheriting world-imperial domination from the British, suggests that a more broadly colonialist supremacism is at last emerging as the guilty attribute. This brings us to the ante-climactic aspect of Dracula's demise. While the reader might infer that Mina's all-important scar—the mark of her pollution by and subjection to the hibernicized monster—disappears on the instant of Dracula's passing, the spectacle of its disappearance is explicitly paired instead with the end of Morris. Dracula has been gone for some time—indeed, his gypsy allies have since departed—when Morris in his death throes bears witness to the regenerated purity of Mina's visage: "'Look! Look! . . . See! The snow is not more stainless than her forehead! The curse has passed away!'" (326). Timing, as we know by now, is everything in the symbolic economy of *Dracula*. The timing here, the coincidence of Mina's cleansing not with the vampire's destruction but with its *subjective correlative*, indicates that "the curse" consists less in the taint of blood immixture than in the estimation of such immixture as taint. In other words, Mina carries the *stigmata* of her Irish hybridity until the moment, symbolically enacted in Morris's death, when the social *stigma* of that hybridity dissipates.

Jonathan Harker's closing "Note," seven years on, confirms as much on several levels—fact, import, and ethos—all of which converge in the person of the Harkers' first-born child, who signals the renewal of Little England on other terms. The *fact*, first of all, that "the boy's birthday is on the same day as that on which Quincy Morris died" (326) positions him as the redemptive effect of Morris's "gallant" performance as ritual scapegoat in the destruction of the evil doppelgänger. Mina herself draws some such inference in her "secret belief that some of [Morris's] spirit has passed into [her son]," in what amounts to a clear reversal of the vampiric "curse" whose passing is heralded by Morris's death (326). As opposed to Dracula's outright appropriation of the spirit through the lethal ingestion of another's blood, Morris has achieved a *partial* transmission of spirit through the shedding of his own blood. The yoking of the Christian ideal with the politics of hybridity, initiated by Mina, is thus sustained through the coda of the novel.

The *import* of Morris's death is memorialized in the naming of the Harker child. His parents give him a "bundle of names" intended to link the "little band of men together" (326). By this act, he becomes not just the symbolic heir of Little England as a whole but a living emblem of that radical connectivity which proved the ethical correlative of the Little Englanders' triumph, their means of destroying the vampire in themselves. Quincy, the name the boy is called, becomes by extension the master signifier of that connectivity, upon which the first Quincy's death put the seal. In a certain sense, even Dracula himself finds a place in the xenophilic community that young Harker embodies.

As a number of critics have noted, Mina's dark tryst with Dracula means that the blood of the vampire now flows in the veins of her golden child. Some have seen this genetic residuum as an ironic portent of ongoing or recrudescent racial menace, "an element of horror... left over, uncontained," in the words of Daniel Pick.[16] Others see this result as ironic evidence that, as Stephen D. Arata puts it, "the position of vampire and victim have been reversed. Now it is Dracula whose blood is appropriated and transformed to nourish a failing race.... The English race invigorates itself by appropriating those racial qualities needed to reverse its own decline."[17] The former position sees the nightmare of *Dracula* continuing *for* British imperialism; the latter sees the nightmare *of* British imperialism continuing, with Stoker's license. Before we accept this Hobson's choice, however, it is well to remember that insofar as *both* the vampire and Mina Murray Harker are coded Irish in the novel, and undecidably Anglo/Celtic-Irish in either case, this final admixture of blood need not be construed as bearing any significance, as making any objective difference in a *racial* or *ethnic* sense. And this ultimate in-difference is by no means an accident of allegory. To the contrary, Stoker has characteristically reappropriated a well-worn Gothic convention, here the secret ineradicability of vampiric infection, to index what is unconventional about his novel: that it is not finally about blood distinction but blood consciousness. The dominant, seemingly opposed readings of the coda have joined in mistaking the novel's critical object for its ideological objective, a tribute to Stoker's dense, socially motivated cryptology.

The characters themselves, however, do point the way beyond this error by the end of *Dracula*. Arata claims that Harker "unwittingly calls attention" in the closing note to the presence of Dracula's blood in his son and heir.[18] But since Harker clearly neither forgets nor suppresses the incident of his wife's vamping—"Seven years ago we all went through the flames" (326)—his unwittingness can be seen to arise from a comparative unconcern or lack of anxiety about the index of "blood." Indeed, Harker's ease of mind on this score is the political burden of the novel's happy ending. *It is precisely in relinquishing the mania or obsession with blood that the men of Little England have freed themselves from the enthrallment with vampirism, which is but the Gothic literalization of that mania. To accept the influx of Dracula's blood, his racial otherness, is to escape the influence of Dracula's vampirism, his racist obsession with blood as the vehicle of identity.* The vampire fighters have, in Harker's words, gone "through the flames," the Christian symbol of purgation, and it is they who have been purified, not of Dracula's blood, which they only encountered in the process, but of their own liability to blood "hate." In Lacanian terms, the men of Little England have graduated from the Imaginary register, which is defined by an antagonistic struggle for an always elusory self-identity, here presumed to reside in blood; and they have graduated to the Symbolic register, wherein identity is understood to be the aftereffect of a social relationality inscribed in the signifier, here an aptly polyeponymous name capable of linking a group of people together. Projected onto the geopolitical scale, this shift from an Imaginary of blood to a Symbolic of social articulation or interlinkage represents a theoretical model of the shift that Stoker desired and his political hero Gladstone made a Liberal policy goal: from emulous rivalry among the various parties to the Irish Question to coexistence within a multinational state embracing Home Rule for its several constituencies.

Quincy Harker, finally, is the culmination of Mina's role as universal mother, on which basis she has served as the principal exponent of the *ethos* of radical social connectivity celebrated in the novel. Accordingly, the child provides an occasion for punctuating the narrative with a reaffirmation of Mina's preeminence, not just as an iconic presence but as a transformative agency. The task falls to the official spokesman and authority figure of the group, Van Helsing, who holds young Harker, rather like a symbolic prop, upon his knee: "'This boy will some day know what a brave and gallant woman his mother is. Already he knows her sweetness and loving care; later on he will understand how some men so loved her, that they did dare much for her sake'" (327). As he has done before, Van Helsing manages to cast Mina simultaneously as a hyperfeminine ideal, here troped in terms of maternal "sweetness and loving care," and as a gloriously androgynous bearer of masculine virtue, here troped along martial rather than the usual intellectual lines. While the men "did dare so much for her sake," Mina does not occupy the traditional feminine pedestal of treasured object, but proves "brave and gallant" in her own right, a positive force in the struggle against vampirism. One effect of this unconventional gender combination is to suggest that Mina's surpassing courage consists *in* her maternalism itself, in her willingness to acknowledge her imbrication with even the most threatening forms of otherness and to predicate her ethical posture on that radical connectivity. It is in following Mina's hero-

ic lead, in letting go the racialist impetus of their manly ideal, that the men
of Little England become the heroes that they are too readily presumed to
be all along. And it is by following this lead that the "hard men" of young
Harker's generation might have resolved the Irish Question on the principles of domestic cosmopolitanism, first advocated in Stoker's *Address*,
twenty-five years before *Dracula*, instead of resolving the Irish Question
twenty-five years after *Dracula*, on principles of tribal bloodletting worthy of the vampire at his worst.

Notes

Introduction

1. Barbara Belford, *Bram Stoker: A Biography of the Author of Dracula* (New York: Alfred A. Knopf, 1996); Peter Haining and Peter Tremayne, *The Un-Dead: The Legend of Bram Stoker and Dracula* (London: Constable Press, 1997).

2. Stephen D. Arata's "The Occidental Tourist: *Dracula* and the Anxiety of Reverse Colonization," *Victorian Studies* 33.4 (1990): 621–45, was reprinted in *Fictions of Loss in the Victorian Fin de Siècle* (Cambridge: Cambridge University Press, 1996), 107–32; Cannon Schmitt, "Mother Dracula: Orientalism, Degeneration, and Anglo-Irish Subjectivity at the Fin-de-Siècle," *Bucknell Review* 38.1 (1994): 25–43; Chris Morash, "Ever under Some Unnatural Condition," in *Literature and the Supernatural*, ed. Brian Cosgrove (Dublin: Columbia Press, 1995), 95–119; David Glover, "'Dark enough fur any man': Bram Stoker's Sexual Ethnology and Question of Irish Nationalism," in *Late Imperial Culture*, ed. Roman de le Campa, E. Ann Kaplan, and Michael Sprinker (New York: Verso, 1995), 53–71, revised and expanded in David Glover, *Vampires, Mummies, and Liberals: Bram Stoker and the Politics of Popular Fiction* (Durham: Duke University Press, 1996); Seamus Deane, *Strange Country: Modernity and Irish Nationhood in Irish Writing since 1780* (Oxford: Clarendon, 1997), 89–94; Michael Valdez Moses, "The Irish Vampire: *Dracula*, Parnell, and the Troubled Dreams of Nationhood," *Journal X* 2.1 (1997): 66–111. See also H. L. Malchow, *Gothic Images of Race in Nineteeth Century Britain* (Stanford: Stanford University Press, 1996), 126–32. Additional relevant essays include Nicholas Daly, "The Colonial Roots of *Dracula*," in *That Other World: The Supernatural and the Fantastic in Irish Literature and Its Contexts*, ed. Bruce Stewart (London: Colin Smythe, 1998), 2:40–51; and Bruce Stewart, "Bram Stoker's *Dracula*: Possessed by the Spirit of the Nation?" in *That Other World*, 65–83. Daly's argument closely tracks that of Arata in treating *Drac-*

ula as an Irish novel written from an essentially English perspective. Stewart's brief closely tracks that of Moses in its emphasis on the Parnell analogy and the background of Irish agrarian violence.

3. Richards typifies the dubious practice of inferring an Anglocentric basis to Stoker's avowed sympathies for the British imperialist enterprise. See "Gender, Race, and Sexuality in Bram Stoker's Other Novels," in *Gender, Roles, and Sexuality in Victorian Literature,* ed. Christopher Parker (New York: Scholar Press, 1995), 143–71. Glover broaches a much subtler and more satisfying theoretical take on this question: "We see Stoker writing with a dual allegiance to the Ireland of his birth with whose nationalist aspirations he identified, and to the scientific racial theories of his day, many of which accorded the Irish only a degraded and inferior status," though in analytic practice he invariably finds Stoker loyal to the scientific racial discourse. *Vampires, Mummies, and Liberals,* 19.

4. For *Dracula* as urban Gothic, see Kathleen L. Spencer, "Purity and Danger: *Dracula,* the Urban Gothic, and the Late Victorian Degeneracy Crisis," *ELH* 59.1 (1992): 197–225. For *Dracula* as "closet" drama, see Talia Shaffer, "A Wilde Desire Took Me: The Homoerotic History of *Dracula,*" *ELH* 61.2 (1994): 381–425, and Christopher Craft, "'Kiss Me with Those Red Lips': Gender and Inversion in Bram Stoker's *Dracula,*" *Representations* 8 (Fall 1984): 107–33. For *Dracula* as Oedipal myth, see Phyllis A. Roth, "Suddenly Sexual Women in Bram Stoker's *Dracula,*" *Literature and Psychology* 27 (1977): 113–21. For *Dracula* as capitalist allegory, see Franco Moretti, *Signs Taken for Wonders: Essays in the Study of Literary Forms* (New York: Verso, 1988), 90–104. For *Dracula* as reform novel, see L. S. Croley, "The Rhetoric of Reform in Stoker's *Dracula:* Depravity, Decline, and the Fin-de-Siècle Residuum," *Criticism* 37.1 (1995): 85–108. For *Dracula* as degeneration drama, see Daniel Pick, "'Terrors of the Night': *Dracula* and Degeneration in the Late Nineteenth Century," *Critical Quarterly* 30.4 (1988): 77–87.

5. Glover, *Vampires, Mummies, and Liberals,* 41.

6. For treatments of this obsession within a wider European-imperial context, see Ann Laura Stoler, *Race and the Education of Desire* (Durham: Duke University Press, 1995), 31–34, 85; and Daniel Pick, *The Faces of Degeneration: A European Disorder* (Cambridge: Cambridge University Press, 1989).

7. Moses, "The Irish Vampire," 68. Later in this article, Moses adduces "the highly fluid character of Dracula's identity" only to override allegorical readings that depart from his own Parnellite gloss. If his political exegesis of the Count remains stubbornly unilateral, however, his religious or sectarian allegorization of the Count respects his doubleness in precisely the manner that my study essays. See "The Irish Vampire," 93.

8. To clarify the relationship between the terms *Celtic* and *Gaelic:* the term *Celt* took in a much wider cultural/ethnic group than the term *Gael,* but within Ireland they referred to the same group of people. They did come to bear different values or social resonances, but only after the turn of the century, when *Gael* was used

by Irish nationalists as a masculinizing self-designation to counter the imputations of Celtic femininity that had taken hold during the Victorian era. I use *Celt* throughout to refer to the cultural/ethnic group. For more on the Celtic nature of *Dracula*, see chapter 1.

9. For an earlier discussion of the metrocolonial condition, see Joseph Valente, "Between Resistance and Complicity: Metro-colonial Tactics in Joyce's *Dubliners*," *Narrative* 6 (Fall 1998): 215–30. Although I coined the term *metrocolonial*, Declan Kiberd mapped the condition in *Inventing Ireland* (Cambridge, Mass.: Harvard University Press, 1994), 5.

10. For a discussion of the specific misunderstandings of Stoker's origins and their consequences, see chapter 1.

11. George Stocking Jr., *Victorian Anthropology* (New York: Free Press, 1981), 234.

12. Moses, "The Irish Vampire," 68.

13. For the logic of the *vel*, see Jonathan Scott Lee, *Jacques Lacan* (Amherst: University of Massachusetts Press, 1988), 44.

14. Glover, *Vampires, Mummies, and Liberals,* 41. Arata had previously articulated this position as a part of his "reverse colonialism" argument: "Vampires are generated by racial enervation and the decline of empire," a view he cribs, directly and uncritically, from Professor Van Helsing, who is not simply unreliable but, as we shall see, a central doppelgänger of Dracula. See "The Occidental Tourist," 629. Anticipating the political tenor of Arata's argument, John Allen Stephenson formulates the same point in a succinct manner that betrays its problematic nature: "Late nineteenth century Britain, plump with imperial gain, [was] perhaps given to the bad dream that *Dracula* embodies: what if they should try to colonize us." See "A Vampire in the Mirror: The Sexuality of Dracula" *PMLA* 103.2 (1988): 40–48. But *Dracula* is not a *British* (in the sense of English) novel, nor is Stoker, strictly speaking, one of "us," as opposed to the colonized and therefore dangerous "they." In the same vein, Stewart simply asserts that Stoker's phobia about "racial degeneracy" being imported to England is a "well-known fact." See "Bram Stoker's *Dracula*," 71. The basic design of this position does not differ from the dominant "English" line on *Dracula* as advanced by Croley, "The Rhetoric of Reform"; Spencer, "Purity and Danger"; and Pick, "Terrors of the Night." See also Schmitt, "Mother Dracula," 38; and Malchow, *Gothic Images of Race,* 132.

15. Without apparent irony, Glover refers to the protagonists of *Dracula* as Stoker's "heroes." *Vampires, Mummies, and Liberals,* 74. Moses finds the novel's "narrative perspective monopolized by the righteous voices of [Dracula's] victims and enemies." He concedes that those "enemies" commit "a shocking number of improprieties, criminal offences, and political misdeeds," but ultimately attributes all discernible shortcomings of Van Helsing and his confederates to infection by Dracula, "the ultimate source of evil" in the novel and an allegory of the Irish revolutionary forces a heroic Britain must combat. See "The Irish Vampire," 96, 99. See

also Schmitt, "Mother Dracula," 32–33; and Stewart, "Bram Stoker's *Dracula*," 75–76.

16. Glover aligns himself with an anonymous contemporary reviewer of Stoker's work: "It is hard 'to place the novels of Mr. Bram Stoker in the highest class of literary distinction.' His books are 'ingenious,' 'entertaining,' and often thoroughly readable,' but he was no great stylist and in many cases his novels do not cohere fully. . . . One might borrow Henry James's phrase and describe Stoker as, at best, a very superior amateur." Glover goes on to diagnose Stoker as a "transitional figure" caught between Victorian verities and modernist incertitude. See *Vampires, Mummies, and Liberals*, 9. Taking a politically harsher view of Stoker's incoherences, Stewart deems his writing an instance of "Victorian false consciousness." See "Bram Stoker's *Dracula*," 77. Salli Kline goes further in disparaging Stoker's literary skills in the interest of reifying and unmasking his political philosophy: "*Dracula* is a poorly constructed, carelessly written kitsch-romance abounding in unintentional irony . . . an incendiary, demagogic work of literature containing prefascist fantasies of annihilating degenerate human being." See *The Degeneration of Women* (Rheinbach-Merzbach, Germany: CMZ-Verlag, 1992), 271. My reading grows from and seeks to vindicate just the opposite view: that Stoker was the practitioner of a novelistic strategy that answers the complexities of his intervallic time (the fin de siècle) and space (the metropolital colony) with a progressive if less than transparent social vision.

An outstanding exception to this critical tradition is Jennifer Wicke, who has described *Dracula* as the first great modern novel in British literature. Her incisive estimate unfortunately conflates modern and modernist and, more egregiously, repeats the imperialist gesture of subsuming Irish literature within an English cultural tradition. See "Vampiric Typewriting: *Dracula* and Its Media," *ELH* 59.3 (1992): 467.

17. The awareness of authorial distance that I would promote in the racial and colonial registers of *Dracula* studies has been displayed by psychoanalytic critics in the registers of gender and sexuality. See Carol Senf, "The Unseen Face in the Mirror," *Journal of Narrative Technique* 9.3 (1979): 160–70.

18. Glover announces his project in precisely these terms: "I seek to show the local discursive continuities between Stoker's writing and the various 'regimes of truth' on which he draws." The irony is that while this new historicist/cultural studies assumption of continuity between the sociopolitical context and the sociopolitical attitudes of the novel facilitated and even potentiated the development of a robust Irish reading of *Dracula*, it has also functioned to place some regrettable limits on that reading, as I demonstrate below. See *Vampires, Mummies, and Liberals*, 5.

19. Schmitt, "Mother Dracula," 35–39.

20. Moses, "The Irish Vampire," 94. In a bizarre twist, Stewart counterposes his reading against an established "nationalist" reading that does not in fact exist

in the canon of Stoker criticism. Stewart cites Seamus Deane, *Strange Country*, 89–94, and Terry Eagleton, "Form and Ideology in the Anglo-Irish Novel," *Bullan* 1.1 (1994): 17–26, but while each suggests possible allegorical linkages of the vampire to the Ascendancy (to be discussed in chapter 2 of this study), neither offers nor even implies anything like a nationalist interpretation. Stewart props up this phantom straw man by supposing that such exegesis "serves the purposes of Irish nationalism well enough" "but does scant justice to the social and political outlook of its author or the symbolic complexities of the novel," a miscarriage he contrives to repeat and then to extend to the criticism of Stoker's work. See "Bram Stoker's *Dracula*," 65–66, 76–77.

21. Arata, *Fictions of Loss*, 116–20. For substantially the same reading, see Daly, "The Colonial Roots of *Dracula*," 43–46.

22. Glover, *Vampires, Mummies, and Liberals*, 4–5.

23. Ibid., 15.

24. Ibid., 5.

25. Victor Sage, *Horror Fiction of the Protestant Tradition* (Basingstoke, England: Macmillan, 1988).

26. Slavoj Žižek, *The Sublime Object of Ideology* (New York: Verso, 1989), 14–15.

27. Julia Kristeva, *Strangers to Ourselves* (New York: Columbia University Press, 1994).

28. Glover, *Vampires, Mummies, and Liberals*, 29–53; Morash, "Ever under Some Unnatural Condition," 110–16; Bram Stoker, *The Snake's Pass* (Dingle: Brandon, 1990).

29. I find unpersuasive Morash's inference that because Stoker sent a prepublication copy of *The Snake's Pass* to Gladstone that he clearly intended the novel as a serious intervention in the Irish land question. On the one hand, Stoker's passion for the company and approbation of great men is self-evident, and he was more likely to seek those objectives as a topical novelist than as a policy expert. On the other hand, his adherence to the conventions of the metropolitan marriage precluded any feasible recommendation on the thorny questions surrounding Irish land tenure. For one thing, this form tended to detach the land struggle from the colonial problematic by blaming everything on the gombeen man. Focusing as it did on Stoker's representation of this convenient villain, Gladstone's reported appreciation of the novel seems a polite attempt to credit the fantasy with whatever sociological weight it could be finally imagined to bear. Morash, "Ever under Some Unnatural Condition," 112.

30. Dion Boucicault, *Selected Plays of Dion Boucicault*, ed. Andrew Perkin (Washington, D.C.: Catholic University Press, 1987).

31. Ironically, Glover, who does the best job of using *The Snake's Pass*, Stoker's most overtly Irish novel, to read *Dracula*, concedes that the latter "goes farthest in establishing his pedigree as a distinctively Irish writer" who was struggling "ob-

sessively with the cultural meaning of Ireland and Irishness." By Irish pedigree, however, Glover means the Anglo-Irish Gothic tradition from which, in my view, the novel departs ideologically. See *Vampires, Mummies, and Liberals,* 25.

32. *The Snake's Pass,* like *The Shaughraun,* actually adapts a scenario designed to foreground the question of blood for the purpose of evading it. In *The Shaughraun,* the surnames of the English soldier (Molyneux) and his Irish lass (Ffolliott) indicate that both are of Norman descent. The ethnic difference typically to be bridged, between masculine Anglo and feminine Celt, is instead elided. In *The Snake's Pass,* Stoker places the climactic nuptials of Arthur and Norah at Hythe Church, "where the bones of so many brave old Norsemen rest" (247), in order to call attention to the shared Norman ancestry indexed in their surnames, Severn and Joyce, respectively.

Stoker does rather notoriously play with the idea of substantive racial inequality in *The Snake's Pass,* revealing in the process the limits of what I will be calling his domestic cosmopolitanism. Norah's "dark" coloration becomes such a salient clue to her identity and desirability for Arthur that in describing her, he must assure his all-too-Irish interlocutor that "'I don't mean a nigger,'" to which the latter replies, "'a girl can be dark enough for any man widout bein' a naygur'" (101). This exchange has convinced a number of critics that Stoker is imputing a certain racial inferiority to the native Irish Norah, encoded in her skin pigmentation. (See, for example, Glover, *Vampires, Mummies, and Liberals,* 38–40.) But, in fact, as the conversation continues, Arthur clarifies that by "dark," he merely means "a brunette," and elsewhere in the novel, Norah's skin is described as a readily blushing, readily sunburnt "ivory" (233), as befits her northern European blood. Like Boucicault, but with greater, almost parodic self-consciousness, Stoker takes the "marriage" paradigm as an opportunity to *avoid* affirming, contesting, or even fully addressing the question of Anglo/Celtic racial hierarchy.

Chapter 1: Double Born

1. Schmitt, "Mother Dracula," 27; Morash, "Ever under Some Unnatural Condition," 102–3; Glover, *Vampires, Mummies, and Liberals,* 9; Haining and Tremayne, *The Un-Dead,* 41; Belford, *Bram Stoker,* 22–23; Daly, "The Colonial Roots of Dracula,"* 46. Schmitt and Morash mistakenly identify Stoker's ancestry as thoroughly English; Belford and Haining and Tremayne openly and erroneously designate Stoker a member of the Anglo-Ascendancy. Daly treats Stoker's narrative perspective as thoroughly Anglo. Glover adopts the subtlest and so least objectionable position, but definitively links Stoker to the Ascendancy via a certain interpretation of his cultural sympathies and racial attitudes, which allegedly came together in his characteristically Anglo-Irish use of the Gothic form. All these writers recognize Stoker's subject position as being in some way ambiguous, but not as a matter of blood. Working outside of the Irish *Dracula* tradition, Malchow goes furthest in this direc-

tion, commenting on Stoker's compromised class and sectarian status while leaving his ethnic heredity unremarked. See *Gothic Images of Race,* 131.

2. Haining and Tremayne, *The Un-Dead,* 44. For the other Galway Blakes, "La Blacas," see Ida Greehan, *The Dictionary of Irish Family Names* (Dublin: Roberts Rinehart, 1997), 27–28.

3. See Glover, *Vampires, Mummies, and Liberals,* 43, 49; Morash, "Ever under Some Unnatural Condition," 101; and Schmitt, "Mother Dracula," 35–37. For Lord Salisbury on Irish degeneracy, see Pick, *The Faces of Degeneration,* 218.

4. Schmitt, "Mother Dracula," 36–39.

5. Belford, *Bram Stoker,* 16.

6. Ibid., 16, 18; Daniel Farson, *The Man Who Wrote Dracula* (New York: St. Martin's Press, 1975), 13–15; Haining and Tremayne, *The Un-Dead,* 44; Harry Ludlam, *A Biography of Dracula: The Life Story of Bram Stoker* (London: W. Foulsham, 1962), 14. Ludlam describes Charlotte as "so Irish."

7. Stoker evidently came to regard storytelling as a peculiarly Irish talent, which suggests he may have seen it as a means of suturing the ethno-national differences implicit in that designation.

8. Glover treats this sexual ethnology at some length in *Vampires, Mummies, and Liberals,* 22–49. For more concise accounts, see Liz Curtis, *Nothing but the Same Old Story* (London: Information on Ireland, 1983), 54–56; Shaun Cairns and David Richards, *Writing Ireland* (Manchester: Manchester University Press, 1988), 42–57; Joseph Valente, "The Myth of Sovereignty: Gender in the Literature of Irish Nationalism," *ELH* 61.1 (1994): 189–95; Marjorie Howes, *Yeats's Nations* (Cambridge: Cambridge University Press, 1996), 1–42.

9. L. P. Curtis, *Anglo-Saxons and Celts* (Bridgeport, Conn.: University of Bridgeport Press, 1968).

10. Belford, *Bram Stoker,* 137.

11. Gendered taxonomies of the races were the rage in the nineteenth century, and following upon Ernst Renan's influential construction of the Celts as "an essentially feminine race," Matthew Arnold mapped sexual difference onto the racial composition of the British Isles, contrasting the masculinity of the English with the "feminine idiosyncracy" of the Celts. See "The Celtic Element in Literature," in *Lectures and Essays in Criticism,* ed. R. H. Super (Ann Arbor: University of Michigan Press, 1973), 83; and Cairns and Richards, *Writing Ireland,* 42–57. For the proliferation of this gendered distinction in the human sciences, see L. P. Curtis, *Anglo-Saxons and Celts,* 47–89.

12. Greehan, *The Dictionary of Irish Family Names,* 268–69.

13. For popular representations of the metropolitan marriage, see L. P. Curtis, *Apes and Angels: The Irishman in Victorian Caricature* (New York: Smithsonian Institution, 1971).

14. Homi Bhabha, *The Location of Culture* (New York: Routledge, 1994), 66–92.

15. Slavoj Žižek, address given at Mellon Literary Theory Seminar, Tulane University, New Orleans, La., June 1993.

16. The question of gender confusion in *Dracula* was brought to prominence by Craft in "'Kiss Me with Those Red Lips,'" 107–33. It has been a hot topic in the criticism ever since, the most notable subsequent exploration being Marjorie Howes, "The Mediation of the Feminine: Bisexuality, Homoerotic Desire, and Self-Expression in Bram Stoker's *Dracula*," *Texas Studies in Language and Literature* 30.1 (1988): 104–19.

17. For a history of Victorian manliness, see James Eli Adams, *Dandies and Desert Saints: Styles of Victorian Masculinity* (Ithaca: Cornell University Press, 1995). For late Victorian/Edwardian conceptions of masculinity, see J. A. Mangan, "Social Darwinism and Upper Class Education in Late Victorian and Edwardian England," in *Manliness and Morality*, ed. J. A. Mangan and James Walvin (Manchester: Manchester University Press, 1987), 135–59; John M. MacKenzie, "The Imperial Pioneer and Hunter and the British Masculine Stereotype in Late Victorian and Edwardian Times," in *Manliness and Morality*, 176–98; and George Moss, *The Image of Man* (New York: Oxford University Press, 1996), 3–107. For the hardening of the male body image, see Maurizia Boscagli, *Eye on the Flesh: Fashions of Masculinity in the Early Twentieth Century* (Boulder: Westview Press, 1996), 21–54. For the synergetic construction of late Victorian/Edwardian manhood and the imperialist project in Ireland, see Joseph Valente, "Neither Fish nor Flesh," in *Semicolonial Joyce*, ed. Derek Attridge and Marjorie Howes (Cambridge: Cambridge University Press, 2000), 96–127.

18. Robert J. C. Young, *Colonial Desire: Hybridity in Theory, Culture, and Race* (New York: Routledge, 1995), 26.

19. Belford, *Bram Stoker*, 20–21, 29–30, 136–37.

20. Having returned to Dublin in 1885, Charlotte Stoker may well have repeated this performance for Bram Stoker's son Noel in the years of *Dracula*'s gestation, indirectly recharging Bram's memories. See Belford, *Bram Stoker*, 202.

21. Craft's article "'Kiss Me with Those Red Lips'" has helped to make Jonathan Harker's seduction at Castle Dracula a *locus classicus* for queer readings of the novel.

22. Glover, *Vampires, Mummies, and Liberals*, 22–49.

23. Haining and Tremayne, *The Un-Dead*, 54–56.

24. I here disagree with Morash's argument that Stoker shifted his political stance from imperialism to irredentism, along with many of the urban Irish middle class, as the century wore on. See "Ever under Some Unnatural Condition," 111–13. The evidence from Stoker's votes and speeches at the Trinity College Historical Society, as well as from his social contacts, suggests rather that he contrived to entertain both of these positions from the beginning, in keeping with his split ethnonational identification.

25. *Minutes of the College Historical Society* (hereafter *MCHS*), Dec. 13, 1865, May 22, 1872, June 19, 1872.

26. *MCHS*, Apr. 21, 1869 (voted), Dec. 4, 1872 (voted and spoke).

27. *MCHS*, Mar. 3, 1872.

28. Irish Home Rule League, *Proceedings of the Home Rule Conference* (Dublin: n.p., 1874), quoted in H. V. Brasted, "Irish Nationalism in the Late Nineteenth Century," in *Irish Culture and Nationalism*, ed. Oliver MacDonagh (New York: St. Martin's Press, 1983), 83–105.

29. R. F. Foster, *Paddy and Mr. Punch* (New York: Penguin, 1996), 113. Moses thus has it exactly reversed when he writes, in a footnote, "To be sure, it was intellectually possible, if politically difficult, to reconcile the notion of greater Irish autonomy with a more capacious concept of British imperial unity." It was logically inconsistent, and to that extent *intellectually* difficult, to reconcile Home Rule with imperial solidarity, but it was *politically* acceptable in certain quarters, and to that extent "easy" to do so. "The Irish Vampire," 107.

30. For Stoker's vote on India, see *MCHS*, Apr. 10, 1867. For his stance on Stanley and colonial governance, see *Personal Reminiscences of Henry Irving* (New York: Macmillan, 1906), 1:366. Moses properly cites Stoker's response to Stanley as evidence of his abiding affection for empire. See "The Irish Vampire," 83. Moses also recognizes the ongoing tension between Stoker's Irish nationalism and his glorification of imperialism, but seems to regard it as a politically unsustainable anomaly on Stoker's part, rather than as a well-established variant of nineteenth-century political thought in Ireland. See "The Irish Vampire," 103, 107.

31. *MCHS*, Feb. 2, 1869.

32. *MCHS*, Mar. 6, 1872.

33. Glover understands Stoker to espouse a "formal imperialist ideal of citizenship" consonant with high British liberalism. See *Vampires, Mummies, and Liberals*, 34. As the following discussion will show, Stoker's notion of Irish "citizenship," while not discarding that liberal ideal explicitly, complicates it to the point of dissolution.

34. Morash, "Ever under Some Unnatural Condition," 101. It is interesting in this context to note that in Historical Society debates, Stoker once voted against the proposition that morality increased with civilization and once affirmed the proposition that morality declined with civilization. *MCHS*, Jan. 22, 1868, Jan. 4, 1871.

35. On this point I disagree in the strongest possible terms with Morash's reading, which finds in Stoker's *Address* the customary nineteenth-century leap from "individual purity" to "racial purity." See "Ever under Some Unnatural Condition," 101.

36. Glover, *Vampires, Mummies, and Liberals*, 46.

37. Young, *Colonial Desire*, 18.

38. Ibid. In this sense, Schmitt treats Stoker as an advocate, rather than a critic, of the "decomposition thesis." See "Mother Dracula," 35–39.

39. Young, *Colonial Desire*, 87.

40. Roy Porter, *The Eighteenth Century* (New York: Penguin, 1979), 54.

41. Matthew Arnold, *Irish Essays and Others* (London: Smith, Elder, 1891), 1–100.

42. For the program of Thomas Davis and Young Ireland, see Cairns and Richards, *Writing Ireland*, 32–45.

43. Young, *Colonial Desire*, 18. Stoker was one of those for whom, as Foster puts it, "Home Rule did not imply anything to injure the integrity of Empire." See *Paddy and Mr. Punch*, 64. By the time Stoker had begun writing *Dracula*, his political favorite, William Gladstone, was of this school as well: "Instead of denouncing Home Rule as . . . destructive of the unity of the Empire . . . I accepted assurances to the contrary." Further along in the same document he writes, "[Home Rule] aims in the main at restoring, not at altering, the Empire." See W. E. Gladstone, *Special Aspects of the Irish Question* (London: John Murray, 1892), 12, 47. For Stoker's admiration of Gladstone, see *Personal Reminiscences of Henry Irving*, 2:26–36.

44. Arnold quoted in Dillon Johnston, "Cross-Currencies in the Culture Market: Arnold, Yeats, Joyce," *South Atlantic Quarterly* 95.1 (1996): 52.

45. Belford, *Bram Stoker*, 34–35; Haining and Tremayne, *The Un-Dead*, 63.

46. Ibid., 77.

47. Glover, *Vampires, Mummies, and Liberals*, 28.

48. Bram Stoker, *The Primrose Path* (Essex: Desert Island, 1999). Further citations to this work will be given in the text.

49. For this reason, I would dissent from Morash's dismissal of the novel as "an utterly conventional temperance tale." See "Ever under Some Unnatural Condition," 116. Morash's only other comment on the novel is to remark the significance of the name of the temperance advocate, Parnell. But since Charles Stewart Parnell had not yet been elected to Parliament, let alone achieved notoriety, at the time of the story's composition, the use of the name must be seen as a coincidence.

50. James Joyce, *Ulysses* (New York: Random House, 1986), 34.

51. Foster, *Paddy and Mr. Punch*, 281.

52. See, for example, Stoker, *Personal Reminiscences of Henry Irving*, 1:123–24, 350–61, 367–70.

53. Laurence Irving, *Henry Irving: The Actor and His World* (London: Faber and Faber, 1951), 453, see also 315, 448.

54. Ibid., 453.

55. Belford, *Bram Stoker*, 99.

56. Glover, *Vampires, Mummies, and Liberals*, 26.

57. Belford, *Bram Stoker*, 214.

58. Ibid., 227.

59. Ibid., 314.

60. For race as a product of the visual Imaginary, see Bhabha, *The Location of Culture*, 79.

61. Malchow goes so far as to ascribe Stoker's final descent into madness to his

"attempt to construct himself as an outsider in London, without substantial resources in family or personal wealth. The personality that crumbled away in 1912 had a slippery foundation." See *Gothic Images of Race*, 131.

62. Glover, *Vampires, Mummies, and Liberals*, 29. Yeats was sufficiently close to Stoker to inscribe a copy of *The Countess Cathleen* to him in 1892, not long after Stoker began work on *Dracula*. See Foster, *Paddy and Mr. Punch*, 220.

63. Stoker, *Personal Reminiscences of Henry Irving*, 1:366; Nicholas Daly, "The Romance of History in Bram Stoker's *The Snake's Pass*," *Literature and History* 4.3 (1995): 24.

64. Stoker, *Personal Reminiscences of Henry Irving*, 2:31.

65. Ibid., 1:344; for the full text of this piece, see 1:343–44.

66. Both the context and the manner of Stoker's political self-designation support this reading. Encountering Gladstone at the Lyceum in the aftermath of the Parnell Manifesto, which vilified the prime minister, Stoker declared, "For myself, though I was a philosophical Home Ruler, I was surprised and angry at Parnell's attitude" (*Personal Reminiscences of Henry Irving*, 2:31). As any "moderate" Home Ruler would be, without any need to qualify his feelings or underscore their exceptional quality. Stoker's introductory disclaimer, "though," discloses that Stoker found himself breaking with certain principled adherences for good cause. His formulation thus manages to convey a sense of a politics whose "philosophical" basis allows for bilateral or bipartisan critique, of the kind "The Voice of England" broaches. At the same time, it is interesting to consider whether the relationship between Gladstone and Stoker might have been affected by an awareness, on either side, of Stoker's strong facial resemblance to the "immoderate" Parnell.

Glover equates "philosophical" with "moderate" in *Vampires, Mummies, and Liberals*, 28. Moses speaks of Stoker's "theoretical commitment to Home Rule," the term *theoretical* here signifying merely notional or in the abstract. See "The Irish Vampire," 83.

Chapter 2: "The Dualitists"

1. Bram Stoker, "The Dualitists; or, The Death Doom of the Double Born," in *Midnight Tales*, ed. Peter Haining (London: Peter Owen, 1990), 44–58. Futher citations to this work will be given in the text.

2. Jacques Lacan, *Écrits*, trans. Alan Sheridan (New York: Norton, 1977), 1–7.

3. Jacques Lacan, *On Feminine Sexuality: The Limits of Love and Knowledge*, trans. Bruce Fink (New York: Norton, 1998), 1–13, 64–77.

4. Jonathan Dollimore, *Sexual Dissidence* (New York: Oxford University Press, 1991), 14–17. For an application of sexual proximateness to the question of Irish ethnicity, see Joseph Valente, "Thrilled by His Touch: The Aestheticizing of Homosexual Panic in *A Portrait of the Artist as a Young Man*," in *Quare Joyce*, ed. Joseph Valente (Ann Arbor: University of Michigan Press, 1998), 47–54.

5. For Irish hypermasculinity, see Cairns and Richards, *Writing Ireland,* 49–50; and Valente, "The Myth of Sovereignty," 193.

6. Luke Gibbons, *Transformations in Irish Culture* (Notre Dame, Ind.: University of Notre Dame Press, 1996), 156.

7. Ibid.

8. The extreme measure of staking suicides to prevent their undead return was allegedly practiced at an unconsecrated cemetery by Ballybough Bridge, near Stoker's boyhood home. See Haining and Tremayne, *The Un-Dead,* 50.

Chapter 3: The Metrocolonial Vampire

1. Joyce, *Ulysses,* 6.

2. Arata, *Fictions of Loss,* 107–32.

3. Credit for bringing to light the geographical, ethnographical, and sociopolitical parallelism of Transylvania and Ireland goes mainly to Glover. See *Vampires, Mummies, and Liberals,* 32–43.

4. Edmund Spenser, *A View of the Present State of Ireland* (1596), quoted in Peter Stallybrass and Anne Jones, "Dismantling Irena," in *Nationalisms and Sexualities,* ed. Andrew Parker, Mary Russo, Dorris Sommer, and Patricia Yeager (New York: Routledge, 1992), 166.

5. Lady Wilde ("Speranza"), *Ancient Legends, Mystic Charms, and Superstitions of Ireland* (London: Ward and Downey, 1888), 37–39, 100–107.

6. Moses, "The Irish Vampire," 80.

7. Glover, *Vampires, Mummies, and Liberals,* 41.

8. Leonard Wolf reports that Stoker's main historical source, *The Land beyond the Forest* by Emily Gerard, puts the number of Transylvanian nationalities at just three and Transylvanian ethnicities at six, *not* counting subdivisions (*ED* 31). To extend Stoker's constrained symmetry, the United Kingdom comprised four nationalities and, as we shall see, the relation between ethnicity and nationality is crucial to the metrocolonial problematic addressed in *Dracula.*

9. Joyce, *Ulysses,* 21.

10. T. P. O'Connor, *Memoirs of an Old Parliamentarian* (London: Ernest Benn, 1929), 1:188.

11. Isaac Butt, *Irish Federalism: Its Meanings, Its Objects, and Its Hopes* (Dublin: John Falconer, 1870), 22.

12. J. L. Hammond, *Gladstone and the Irish Nation* (London: Longmans Green, 1938), 384–90.

13. F. S. L. Lyons, *Ireland since the Famine* (London: Weidenfeld and Nicholson, 1971), 251. Arthur Griffith, the architect and leader of a Sinn Fein movement explicitly modeled on the Hungarian scheme, openly acknowledged that his strategy had been anticipated by Parnell in the 1880s. See R. F. Foster, *Modern Ireland, 1600–1972* (New York: Viking, 1988), 491. Parnell himself had been anticipated

not only by Isaac Butt but also by the celebrated Fenian revenant John O'Leary. See Liz Curtis, *The Cause of Ireland* (Belfast: Beyond the Pale, 1994), 92.

14. Bram Stoker, "Working Notes for *Dracula*," Rosenbach Library and Museum, Philadelphia, Pa.

15. It should be noted, pace Moses, that Dracula does not have the allegiance of the peasantry a la Parnell, but merely of the Szgany, whom the text not only distinguishes from the peasants but also describes in terms that recall another, more marginal fixture of the Irish landscape, the Tinkers: "They are gipsies . . . peculiar to that part of the world, though allied to gipsies the world over . . . [and] are almost outside of all laws" (*D* 42). See also Moses, "The Irish Vampire," 68.

16. Deane, *Strange Country*, 89–94; Terry Eagleton, *Heathcliff and the Great Hunger* (London: Verso, 1995), 215–16.

17. For Shelley, see Liz Curtis, *The Cause of Ireland*, 25. For Parnell and Davitt, see Foster, *Modern Ireland, 1600–1972*, 351. For O'Brien, see Liz Curtis, *The Cause of Ireland*, 148. Davitt was an acquaintance of Stoker, and O'Brien, a literary colleague.

18. Joep Loerrsen, *Remembrance and Imagination: Patterns in the Historical and Literary Representation of Ireland in the Nineteenth Century* (Cork: Cork University Press, 1996), 223.

19. For the importance of the Celtic myth of sovereignty to modern Irish nationalism, see Valente, "The Myth of Sovereignty," 189–210.

20. Thomas Davis, *The Poems of Thomas Davis* (New York: Haverty, 1860), 177–78.

21. Liz Curtis, *The Cause of Ireland*, 73.

22. "The modern literature of Ireland, and indeed all that stir of thought which prepared for the Anglo-Irish wars, began when Parnell fell from power in 1891. A disillusioned and embittered Ireland turned from parliamentary politics; an event was conceived; and the race began, as I think, to be troubled by that event's long gestation." W. B. Yeats, *Autobiographies* (London: Macmillan, 1955), 559.

23. W. B. Yeats, *Cathleen Ni Houlihan*, in *Eleven Plays by W. B. Yeats*, ed. A. Norman Jeffares (New York: Collier, 1984), 227.

24. Bram Stoker, "Working Notes for *Dracula*," Rosenbach Library and Museum.

25. For the complexities of the Draculas' Balkan alliances, see Moses, "The Irish Vampire," 78.

26. L. P. Curtis, *Apes and Angels*, 77–79.

27. Joyce, *Ulysses*, 26.

28. Deane, *Strange Country*, 81.

29. Lord Salisbury, "Disintegration," in *Lord Salisbury on Politics: A Selection from His Articles in the Quarterly Review, 1860–1883*, ed. Paul Smith (Cambridge: Cambridge University Press, 1977), 343. The main depot of this contagion was supposed to be London's East End, the haunts of Dracula and the hovel of many

an underclass Irish émigré. See Judith Walkowitz, *City of Dreadful Delight: Narratives of Sexual Danger in Late-Victorian London* (Chicago: University of Chicago Press, 1992), 26–30.

30. See L. P. Curtis, *Anglo-Saxons and Celts*, 11–19, 38–89.

31. Robert Twiss, *A Tour of Ireland*, quoted in Liz Curtis, *Nothing but the Same Old Story*, 38; see also L. P. Curtis, *Anglo-Saxons and Celts*, 53–57.

32. Not coincidentally, all the workers transporting Dracula's boxes around London educe drink as their ruling passion. One group in particular, who requests "a stiff glass of grog, or rather more of the same," works for a company in the "Orange Master's Yard" (D 143), a coded reference to the predominantly Anglo-Protestant owners of the Irish means of industrial production. For a brief history of Irish immigration to England and a partial list of the resulting stereotypes, including items 2, 3, and 5 above, see Fergus D'Arcy, "Saint Patrick's Other Island: The Irish Invasion of Britain," *Eire Ireland* 28 (Summer 1993): 7–17.

33. See, for example, David Lloyd, *Anomalous States: Irish Writing and the Post-Colonial Moment* (Durham: Duke University Press, 1993), 119.

34. Arata, *Fictions of Loss*, 107–32.

35. L. P. Curtis, *Anglo-Saxons and Celts*, 69–73.

36. Glover sees the novel as a qualified enactment of this fantasy. See *Vampires, Mummies, and Liberals*, 32–70.

37. Salisbury, "Disintegration," 343; Young, *Colonial Desire*, 22–26; Stoler, *Race and the Education of Desire*, 32–50; Nancy Stepan, "Biology and Degeneration: Race and Proper Places," in *Degeneration: The Darker Side of Progress*, ed. J. Edward Chamberlain and Sander L. Gilman (New York: Columbia University Press, 1985), 97–120.

38. Pick, *Faces of Degeneration*, 11–27, 222–40; Robert Nye, "The Irony of Progress," in *Degeneration*, 49–71.

39. See, for example, Stoker, *Personal Reminiscences of Henry Irving*, 1:362–70.

40. Bhabha, *The Location of Culture*, 125–33.

41. For reproductions of "The Irish Vampire," see L. P. Curtis, *Apes and Angels*, 81; and Roy Douglas, Liam Harte, and Jim O'Hara, *Drawing Conclusions: A Cartoon History of Anglo-Irish Relations, 1798–1998* (Belfast: Blackstaff, 1998), 105. An illustration can also be found in Moses, "The Irish Vampire," 66. For Moses's reading of the cartoon and Stoker's use thereof as a commentary on Parnell, see "The Irish Vampire," 74–75.

42. A reproduction of this cartoon can be found in Douglas, Harte, and O'Hara, *Drawing Conclusions*, 106. For a brief analysis of the cartoon, see L. P. Curtis, *Apes and Angels*, 81.

43. This has been done not only by Moses, who draws the title of his essay from the Tenniel cartoon, but also by Malchow in *Gothic Images of Race*, 127–28.

44. W. J. McCormack, "Irish Gothic and After," in *The Field Day Anthology of Irish Writing*, ed. Seamus Deane (Derry: Field Day, 1991), 2:841–45.

45. Greehan, *The Dictionary of Irish Family Names*, 268–69.

46. Bram Stoker, "The Great White Fair in Dublin," *World's Work* (London) 9 (May 1907): 574–75. See also Glover, *Vampires, Mummies, and Liberals*, 13.

47. Donal P. McCracken, "Fenians and Dutch Carpetbaggers: Irish and Afrikaner Nationalisms, 1877–1930," *Eire Ireland* 29 (Fall 1994): 109–25.

48. Gladstone, *Special Aspects of the Irish Question*, 72–73. For the Irish and Jewish settlements in London, see Gareth Steadman Jones, *Outcast London* (New York: Pantheon, 1971), 99–151.

49. Jules Zwanger, "A Sympathetic Vibration: Dracula and the Jews," *English Literature in Transition* 34.1 (1991): 33–44. The quoted material is from Malchow, *Gothic Images of Race*, 154–55.

50. Malchow, *Gothic Images of Race*, 155.

51. For an elaboration of "cross-dwelling," see Charles Spinoza and H. L. Dreyfus, "Two Kinds of Anti-Essentialism and Their Consequences," *Critical Inquiry* 22.4 (1996): 735–63.

52. Franz Fanon, "On National Culture," in *Colonial Discourse and Post-Colonial Theory*, ed. Patrick Williams and Laura Chrisman (New York: Columbia University Press, 1994), 38.

53. D. George Boyce, "The Marginal Britons: The Irish," in *Englishness: Politics and Culture, 1880–1920*, ed. Richard Colls and Phillip Dodd (London: Croak Helm, 1986), 230–53.

54. Stephenson, "A Vampire in the Mirror," 40–48.

55. For a much different but not unrelated construction of Dracula as a political nightmare, see Moses, "The Irish Vampire."

56. Arata, *Fictions of Loss*, 124.

57. "The Irish . . . actually looked like the English to the point of undecidability." Kiberd, *Inventing Ireland*, 11.

58. Liz Curtis, *The Cause of Ireland*, 117.

59. Boyce, "The Marginal Britons," 230.

60. Ibid., 240.

61. Sheridan Gilley, "English Attitudes toward the Irish in England, 1780–1960," in *Immigrants and Minorities in British Society*, ed. Colin Holmes (London: Allen and Unwin, 1978), 81–110.

62. L. P. Curtis, *Anglo-Saxons and Celts*, 102–3.

63. George Bernard Shaw, *John Bull's Other Island* (New York: Brentano's, 1913).

64. The metaphor echoes the rubric devised by Stoker's political hero, Gladstone, for English *support* of Home Rule, "The Union of Hearts" suggesting how the customary personification of the nation-state encouraged a biologistic terminology consistent with the romantic assumption that the nation expressed a racial essence.

65. Boyce, "The Marginal Britons," 234.

66. Arnold's "decomposition theory" of hybridity, in which Irishness would be assimilated within Englishness, represented an attempt to square this metrocolonial circle on racial grounds alone.

67. Kiberd, *Inventing Ireland*, 29.

68. Stephanie Foote, "Impossible Persons," ms. I am greatly indebted to Foote's work and her conversation for insights into the parvenu condition that have informed my sense of Stoker's social concerns. With its systematic and theoretically sophisticated understanding of social membership and the arriviste, *Impossible Persons* is destined to become a landmark critical text.

69. For Gladstone's position, see Boyce, "The Marginal Britons," 234.

70. Richards, "Gender, Race, and Sexuality," 162.

71. In this regard, race consciousness would seem to participate in what Slavoj Žižek calls "the fundamental paradox of fantasy." See "'I Hear You with My Eyes'; or, The Invisible Master," in *The Gaze and Voice as Love Objects*, ed. Renata Saleci and Slavoj Žižek (Durham: Duke University Press, 1996), 119.

72. Phillip Dodd, "Englishness and National Culture," in *Englishness*, 2.

73. For the distinctively Irish nature of this combination, see Kiberd's brilliant analysis of *The Real Charlotte* by Edith Somerville and Martin Ross in *Inventing Ireland*, 77.

74. Foster, *Paddy and Mr. Punch*, 193.

75. Wicke persuasively argues that Dracula is "a partner in imperialism." See "Vampiric Typewriting," 487.

Chapter 4: Double Agents

1. Stoker, "Working Notes for *Dracula*," quoted in Christopher Frayling, "Bram Stoker's Working Notes for *Dracula*," in *D* 342. In this version of the text Stoker almost certainly alludes to a line from Oscar Wilde's *The Picture of Dorian Gray*: "Every portrait that is painted with feeling is a portrait of the artist," an aphorism that, taken in context, likewise refers to the transferential articulation of illicit desire. Oscar Wilde, *The Picture of Dorian Gray* (New York: Norton, 1988), 10.

2. Lacan himself holds the function of "the Thing" to be imaged in the subject's unconscious as the obscene father, whose lethal attractiveness/repulsiveness lies in his violent appropriation of a *droit de seigneur* to unbounded and therefore illicit enjoyment. He enjoys in our place everything forbidden to us. Dracula's pronouncement upon confronting the men of Little England, "'Your girls that you all love are mine already'" (*D* 267), would fit with this mythic profile, particularly in its derivation from Freud's father of the "primal horde" in *Totem and Taboo* (New York: Norton, 1950). So too would Dracula's implicit role as a dark paternal surrogate, a negative authority figure, for a group distinguished by the absence (Jonathan, Mina) or the present loss (Lucy, Arthur) of parents.

But as we have observed, in the political register of the novel, Dracula figures as the *other* who enjoys in our place, the baleful stranger/sharer upon whom we project the necessarily unrecognized pleasure that we have in the anxiety that he induces. This mythic role is less paternal than fraternal (hence the doppelgänger motif), involving the subject more intimately and reciprocally in the libidinal cathexes that he conjures. Hence instead of proclaiming his exclusive title to the women of Little England, Dracula's words may yield a more modest and yet more chilling claim: such is your unadmitted fellowship with me, such the consubstantiality of your enjoyment with my own, that I have possessed "your girls" in and through the kind of love you bear them, not in contradiction to it. The sequel promised by Dracula—"'and through them you and others shall be . . . my creatures, to do my bidding'" (267)—signals, in turn, what I would call his recursive dualitism, that is, his figuration of the real and domineering effects of the projective fantasy that he embodies upon those who dream it.

3. See Tim Dean, "Two Kinds of Otherness," *Critical Inquiry* 23.4 (1997): 910–20.

4. Parveen Adams, *The Emptiness of the Image* (New York: Routledge, 1996), 127.

5. Slavoj Žižek, *The Plague of Fantasies* (New York: Verso, 1997), 75–77.

6. One colonial reading that takes the doppelgänger relation of Harker and Dracula seriously is Arata, *Fictions of Loss*, 124–25. Arata does not, however, take the implications of dualitism to the point where they disturb the binary logic of self and other, metropole and colony, us and them. His conceit of reverse colonialism ultimately functions to stabilize the geopolitical oppositions at play in Stoker's text.

7. When Seward declares, upon meeting Harker, that he had not expected to find such a "quiet business-like gentleman" (199), his words chime ironically with Harker's sudden and unexpected rise to bourgeois status.

8. Arata is the exception. See *Fictions of Loss*, 124–25.

9. Mary Louise Pratt, *Imperial Eyes* (New York: Routledge, 1992), 5–7.

10. Wicke, "Vampiric Typewriting," 472.

11. Dinah M. Copelmen, *London's Women Teachers: Gender, Class, and Feminism, 1870–1930* (New York: Routledge, 1999), xiii–xix, 3–30.

12. Carol Senf, "*Dracula:* Stoker's Response to the New Woman," *Victorian Studies* 26.1 (1982): 33–49; Kline, *The Degeneration of Women.*

13. Bram Stoker, *Dracula* (New York: Random House, 1899).

14. Moses, "The Irish Vampire," 86.

15. Ibid.

16. Ibid.; Arata, *Fictions of Loss*, 128–29.

17. See, for example, Stoker, *Personal Reminiscences of Henry Irving*, 1:323, 362–70.

18. Wicke elaborates the connection between the speech patterns of Dracula and Van Helsing. See "Vampiric Typewriting," 488–89. For a very different take, see Franco Moretti, "A Capital Dracula," in *D* 437.

19. Peter Stallybrass and Allon White, *The Politics and Poetics of Transgression* (Ithaca: Cornell University Press, 1986), 149–69.

20. For fine discussions of the gender implications of Mina's exclusion, see Geoffrey Wall, "'Different from Writing': *Dracula* in 1897," *Literature and History* 10.1 (Spring 1984): 18–19; and Marjorie Howes, "The Mediation of the Feminine," 113–15.

21. For the text's implicit contradiction of Stoker's official gender politics, see Howes, "The Mediation of the Feminine," 115.

22. This is not unlike Heathcliff's function in Charlotte Brontë's *Wuthering Heights*. See Geoffrey Galt Harpham, *On the Grotesque* (Princeton: Princeton University Press, 1983), 95–96.

23. Richards, "Gender, Race, and Sexuality," 167.

24. As Richards points out, heroic Viking associations crop up regularly in Stoker's novels as a badge of racial nobility for his protagonists and an index of his own weakness for northern European supremacism. That the Viking associations of the Little England men and their pride therein are tainted by the vampire's similar identification with the figure of Thor is a small but very telling clue to the distinctive position Dracula holds in Stoker's corpus. Its metrocolonial agenda, to pose a challenge to Anglocratic blood consciousness within the British Isles, redounds directly against the imperialist agenda and Eurocratic ideology that Stoker sometimes advances in his later fiction. See Richards, "Gender, Race, and Sexuality," 167.

25. Moses, "The Irish Vampire," 94.

Chapter 5: Beyond Blood

1. Janet Oppenheim, *"Shattered Nerves"* (New York: Oxford University Press, 1991), 141–80.

2. For a discussion of this traditional identification, see Joan Copjec, *Read My Desire* (Boston: MIT Press, 1994), 128–29.

3. As in contemporary slasher films, the heroine (Mina) actually exceeds stereotyped gender expectations in ways that the female victims (Lucy and her mother) do not. See Carol J. Clover, "Her Body, Himself: Gender in the Slasher Film," *Representations* 20 (Spring 1987): 187–228.

4. Wolf takes her "whole argument" to be "dictated from afar by Dracula." See *ED* 367 n. 17.

5. See Oliver MacDonagh, *States of Mind* (London: Allen and Unwin, 1983), 34–51.

6. In Stoker's time, there was a Roman Catholic church called Mary, Star of the Sea, off Leahy's Terrace in suburban Dublin. See Don Gifford, *Ulysses Annotated* (Berkeley: University of California Press, 1988), 384.

7. The phrase *sweeter counsels* recalls another prominent appellation of Mary, "Our Mother of Good Counsel."

8. Moses, "The Irish Vampire," 87.

9. For a detailed anatomy of the role of religion in *Dracula,* see Moses, "The Irish Vampire," 89–96.

10. Tom Garvin, *Nationalist Revolutionaries in Ireland* (Oxford: Clarendon, 1987), 157.

11. Lyons, *Ireland since the Famine,* 188–94. In every other edition of *Dracula,* the *Plan of Campaign* is capitalized, so the Norton's lowercase rendering is surely an error.

12. Liz Curtis, *The Cause of Ireland,* 152.

13. Ibid., 152–53.

14. Ibid., 153.

15. Ibid., 153–54.

16. Pick, "'Terrors of the Night,'" 77.

17. Arata, *Fictions of Loss,* 129.

18. Ibid.

Index

Act of Union, 3, 62, 72
Adams, Parveen, 57
Aisling poetry, 65
American imperialism, 99
Anamorphosis, 87, 97, 110
Ancient Legends in Ireland ("Speranza"), 52
Anglo-Celts, 4, 15, 18, 41, 150n
Anglocentrism, 12, 52, 77, 146n
Anglo-Irish, the, 16, 27, 35, 38, 66; ascendancy of, 8, 59–62, 137; espionage of, 73; likened to vampires, 56; literature of, 53; political relations of, 72, 75–76, 137–38; Protestants, 3, 4, 15, 22, 24, 158n; racial relations of, 70, 92, 141; social relations of, 2, 39–40, 44; Stoker's relation to, 15, 27, 150n; subjectivity of, 8. *See also* Irish, the
Anglo-Saxons, 2, 15, 24–26, 75, 77; standard of beauty for, 96
Anthropology, 1, 61–62
Anti-Semitism, 110; Irish tradition of, 69
Anxiety: class, 7–11; gender, 19–20; racial, 5–8, 11, 74, 79, 81; reverse logic of, 19, 79–81
Arata, Stephen, 1, 8, 52, 62, 73, 99, 141, 147n, 161n
Arnold, Matthew, 18; connection to vampirism, 27, 82; "decomposition thesis" of, 26, 82, 160n; ethnology of Britain, 25, 26, 151n; on racial incorporation, 27
Auerbach, Nina, 54, 139
Austin, Lewis F., 38
Austro-Hungarian Empire, 54

Balkans, 5, 65, 138, 152n
Banshee, 16
Beddoes, James, 61–62
Belford, Barbara, 1, 38
Bentham, Jeremy, 73
Bhabha, Homi, 18, 39, 64
Blackstone, William, 26
Blake, Kathleen, 59
Blood, 2, 114, 118, 138, 142; blood consciousness vs., 11, 69, 112, 141; bloodletting, 87, 140, 143; degeneration of, 61–63; as ethnic marker, 7, 27, 79; feast of, 58, 93; hierarchy of, 118, 119; manhood and, 20; sucking, 95; thematics of, 5, 70; vampiric conversion and, 81–82, 133
Blood consciousness, 11, 50, 80–83, 114, 129; critique of, by Stoker, 39–40, 60, 67, 80, 83, 102; critique of, in *Dracula*, 5, 8, 11, 21, 27, 60, 67, 69, 80, 83, 103–5, 111, 112, 141, 142

Blood sacrifice, 56–58, 136
Boucicault, Dion, 12–13, 42
Boyne, Battle of, 66, 135
Breuer, Josef, 85
British colonialism, 2–4, 65, 73, 77, 99;
    decline of, 7, 62, 139; domestic, 41;
    in Ireland, 8, 26, 36, 45–46, 51, 68,
    71–72; Irish participation in, 23, 75;
    vampirism and, 62–63
British liberalism, 45–46, 99, 134, 137
British Liberal party, 72
Britishness. See English, the
British Secret Service, 73
"British Vampire, The," 65
Bubb, Ephraim (in "The Dualitists"),
    43–44, 49
Bubb, Sophonisba (in "The Dualitists"),
    43–44, 49
Bubb, Zachariah (in "The Dualitists"),
    44, 47–49
Bubb, Zerubbabel (in "The Dualitists"),
    44, 47–49
Butt, Isaac, 22–23, 54

Captain Moonlight (in Dracula), 45, 59
Carlyle, Thomas, 18, 61
Castle Dracula, 19, 53, 86, 95
Cathleen Ni Houlihan, 57; vampiric
    associations of, 58
Catholic emancipation, 72
Celticism, 12, 26, 110
Celts, Celtic-Irish, the, 3–4, 38, 52–53,
    59; assimilation of, 26, 42, 75; as bar-
    barous race, 16, 23–25, 62; Catholics,
    2, 28, 62, 66, 101, 135; fringe groups,
    18, 38; Gaels, Gaelic vs., 146–47n;
    and sovereignty myth, 56, 58, 135.
    See also Irish, the
Charcot, J. M., 85
Cholera epidemic (1832), 16, 55
Church of Ireland, 72
Clerkenwell Prison, 137
Colleen Bawn, The (Stoker), 12–13
Colonial hybridity, 19, 25; decomposi-
    tion thesis of, 26; incorporation mod-
    el of, 27, 40–41, 91–92, 132; metro-
    colonial immixture vs., 18; mutual
    incorporation model of, 26–27, 39–
    40, 77; proximity thesis of, 27. See
    also Arnold, Matthew; Young, Robert
    J. C.

Colonialism: impacted, 72, 75; reverse,
    1, 8, 52, 72, 147n; reverse vs. impact-
    ed, 52, 62, 72, 75, 161n; and vampir-
    ism, 62–63
Colonial literature, 39
Colonial mimicry, 64, 74
Colonial subaltern, 8
Conrad, Joseph, 6
Conybeare, Charles, 137
Corsican Brothers, The (Boucicault),
    12, 42
Counterrepresentivity, 68, 70–71
Countess Cathleen, The (Yeats), 155n
Crimes Bill (1897), 46
Croley, Laura, 59
Cultural studies, 7, 9, 10, 68, 70, 148n

Dalby, Richard, 32
Daly, Nicholas, 39, 150n
Darwinism, 114
Davis, Thomas, 26, 57, 67
Davitt, Michael, 56
Deane, Seamus, 1, 55, 60
Decomposition thesis, 26
Dedalus, Stephen (in Ulysses), 6, 52
Dilke, Sir Charles, 61
Domestic cosmopolitanism, 22, 39, 40–
    41, 46, 143; in Dracula, 41, 69, 125;
    of Stoker, 23–25, 39–41, 46, 69
Doppelgänger, 18, 36; Dracula as, 18,
    45, 50, 81–82, 85, 161n. See also Du-
    alitism
Dowell, John, 6
Dracula, 49–51, 94, 128, 136, 157n; as
    ascendancy landlord, 55, 56, 59, 60,
    62, 71; blood sacrifice and, 56, 58;
    colonial mimicry of, 54, 74, 90, 134;
    conflicting Irish associations of, 2, 3,
    54–62, 64, 65, 69, 71, 81, 82, 120;
    connection to Stoker, 38–39, 60, 62,
    64, 67, 75; contempt for peasantry of,
    64, 90, 103; as criminal type, 61, 102,
    108; defiance of ethnological classifi-
    cation, 69; as degenerate bogey, 50,
    76, 80–81, 83, 141; as doppelgänger,
    18, 45, 50, 81–82, 85, 161n; as em-
    blem of metrocolonial subjectivity, 71,
    81–82; erotics of blood and, 81–82,
    84, 85, 91; as ethnic parvenu in Lon-
    don, 74–75, 89; as exponent of racial-
    ism, 50, 69, 80–82, 112, 120, 132; as

Fenian nationalist, 56, 58–59, 112; as imperialist, 63–64, 89, 90, 112; Irish fairies and, 52; Irishness of, 18, 45, 52, 59, 64, 67, 71, 75–76, 80, 120, 129; as Irish residuum in London, 57, 60, 61–62, 64, 71; Irish stereotypes and, 59–61; Jewish associations of, 68; Matthew Arnold and, 27; as metrocolonial agent, 62, 73–75, 88, 89; mixed ethnic and class status of, 55, 60–61, 67; as obscene father, 113, 160–61n; as projection of racialist attitudes, 70, 80, 83, 86, 88–89, 97–98, 131, 134, 141; self-defeating tactics of, 133; as sovereignty deity, 58; unconscious desire and, 81–82, 88, 90, 97–98, 107, 110–11. *See also* Dualitism

Dracula, 75, 107, 137; American edition of, 96–97; anti-essentialism of, 13, 24, 41, 60, 67, 69; anti-imperialism in, 11, 63; Christian rhetoric in, 129, 131, 140, 142; conversion narrative in, 131, 133–34; counterrepresentivity of, 70–71; critique of degeneration theory in, 81, 83; critique of identity politics in, 27, 41, 115, 119–20; critique of misogyny in, 21, 110–11; critique of racialism in, 5, 8, 11, 21, 27, 60, 67, 69, 80, 83, 103–5, 111, 112, 141, 142; "crypt," secret of, 80, 141; domestic cosmopolitanism in, 41, 69, 125; doppelgänger in, 18, 45, 50, 72, 81–82, 84, 85, 161n; English school of reading, 2, 3, 5, 147n; geopolitics of vampirism in, 101; heroism in, 20–21, 90, 132, 143, 147n; homoeroticism in, 87–88; impacted colonialism in, 72, 75; Irish allegory in, 1, 2, 4, 51–56, 66, 133; Irish fantasy construct of, 6, 10, 11, 64, 70, 74, 120; Irishness of, 3, 4, 12; Irish references in, 1–2, 4, 5, 9, 51–55, 64–65, 72, 73, 136–37; Irish school of reading, 1–5, 7–9, 11, 42, 52, 150n; Irish-Transylvanian parallel in, 11, 51–53, 62, 64, 156n; ironic viewpoint of, 5, 21, 53, 109, 123, 138; metrocolonial problematic in, 156n, 161n; political ambivalence of, 8, 9; precise arrangement of, 5, 11, 89, 95–98, 113, 121–23, 131, 136, 138–39, 140; proto-modernism of, 6, 70; psychoanalytic influence on, 85; racial politics of, 3, 5, 11, 13, 70, 82, 110, 120; recursive moral/political logic of, 12, 37, 50, 69–70, 82, 96, 102–3, 109, 114, 120, 124–25, 131–32, 134, 136, 138, 141; sexual politics of, 21, 110, 160–61n; stereotypes of Ireland in, 52–53; turning points in, 87, 120, 125, 127–28, 131, 133, 134; vampiric seduction in, 81–83. *See also* Dracula; Dualitism; Harker, Mina Murray; Little England; Westenra, Lucy

Dream. *See* Fantasy

Drink, 29–32, 34

Dualitism, 82; Dracula and Holmwood, 112; Dracula and Jonathan Harker, 86–90, 93, 97, 107, 110, 126; Dracula and Little England, 82, 98, 109–12, 119, 125, 129, 134, 139, 160–61n; Dracula and Lucy, 84; Dracula and Mina Harker, 84, 132; Dracula and Morris, 98, 100; Dracula and Van Helsing, 84, 103–11, 132, 147n; Renfield and Little England, 118, 119; Renfield and Seward, 113–15

"The Dualitists" (Stoker), 12–13, 155n; as anticipation of *Dracula,* 49, 87, 88, 130; anti-essentialism in, 46–47; critique of lineal distinction in, 46, 48; Gothic structure of, 47; homoeroticism in, 43, 87; mandate of self-identity in, 46; as metrocolonial allegory, 42, 46, 49, 78; proximateness in, 44; recursive moral and political logic in, 46, 50

Duality, 44; schismatic, 46–48, 78, 130; symbolic, 46–48, 64, 71, 78

Dublin, 24, 52

Dublin Castle, 16, 22

Dublin Evening Mail, 22, 28

Eagleton, Terry, 55

Easter 1916, 58

Eastern Question, 51, 54; Irish Question and, 51, 54–55

Emmett, Robert, 56, 57

England, 22, 30, 41, 62, 73, 88, 98, 110. *See also* Great Britain

English, the, 26, 37, 72–74; anxiety over

being, 74, 76; hybridization of, 40, 73, 74, 76, 77
English law, 40, 77
Ethics of alterity, 124; coded Irish, 130–31
Ethnic differences, 25–26, 35, 39, 76–77, 82, 102; antagonism and, 34, 40–42, 44–45
Ethnicity. See Blood
Ethnography, 35, 62
Evolutionary theory, 61
Extimacy, 85

Famine, Great (Ireland), 16, 45
Fanon, Franz, 71
Fantasy, 40, 51, 111; allegory vs., 10, 32; Anglo-Celtic, 41; Anglo-Irish, 8–9, 41; class, 7; context vs. form, 11, 32–33, 51; degeneration, 9, 80, 83; metrocolonial, 64, 70, 120; popular, 8, 10; racial, 7–8, 98, 131, 138
Feminine persona of Ireland: Blessed Virgin Mary as, 130, 135; Cathleen Ni Houlihan as, 57, 58, 130; Erin as, 13, 26, 130, 135; Hibernia as, 130, 135; Mother Ireland as, 58, 130; Poor Old Woman as, 58; Shan Von Vocht as, 13; Speirbhean as, 130
Femininity, norms of, 21, 108, 124, 125; domestic cosmopolitanism and, 125; ethics of alterity and, 124–25; maternal ideal and, 124–25, 142; social connectivity and, 125
Fenianism, 40, 77, 79, 135; agrarian, 45, 59; blood sacrifice and, 56–58, 136; Dracula and, 56–59; Fenian Risings and, 26, 73
Foote, Stephanie, 76, 160n
Foster, R. F., 23, 33, 82
Freud, Sigmund, 8, 51, 85, 107, 160n
Froude, J. A., 61

Gaelic Athletic Association, 57
Gaels, Gaelic, the. See Celts, Celtic-Irish, the
Gender typologies, 19, 21, 111, 116, 125
Gibbons, Luke, 46
Gilley, Sheridan, 75
Gladstone, William, 46, 54, 68, 72, 159n; multinationalism of, 77, 142

Glorious Revolution, 101
Glover, David, 1, 2, 8, 10, 21, 28, 53, 146n, 147n, 148n, 149n, 150n
Gothic, the, 8, 11, 17, 54, 70, 74, 137; as allegory, 31, 55, 103, 111, 123, 128; Anglo-Protestant, 9, 150n; conventions of, 6, 9, 35, 47, 55, 106, 107, 111, 132; metrocolonialism and, 116; political uses of, 112–13; Stoker's use of conventions of, 6, 9, 35, 47, 71, 74, 80, 84–85, 98, 111–13, 119, 124, 132, 134, 141; urban, 2
Government of Ireland Act (1886), 46
Great Britain, 3, 8, 25, 41, 77. See also England; Ireland; United Kingdom
"Great White Fair, The" (Stoker), 67
Grinnell (in The Primrose Path), 31–32, 36

Haining, Peter, 1, 150n
Harker, Jonathan (in Dracula), 7, 58, 75, 107, 128; anti-Semitism of, 138–39; doppelgänger motif and, 84, 86–94, 97, 107, 109, 110, 126; erotics of blood and, 91; as ethnologist/tourist, 53, 68, 92; as imperialist, 89–90, 92, 97; likeness to Stoker, 89; orientalism of, 52, 65–66, 90, 96, 103, 129; parvenu status of, 89; as physiognomist, 102; sexual ambivalence of, 20; vamped by Dracula, 97; as vampire, 94–96
Harker, Mina Murray (in Dracula), 6, 17, 58–59, 87, 160n; acceptance of vampiric taint, 129–31; blood consciousness of, 128–29; blood sacrifice of, 136; bond with Renfield, 117, 121–23; constructive androgyny of, 94, 108, 139, 142; as criminologist, 102; dual Irish associations of, 66, 92, 130; as Erin, 66, 92; ethics of alterity and, 27–29, 131, 133, 142; feminine norm and, 120, 124; as figure of hybridity, 121, 139; as figure of social connectivity, 125, 130, 132, 142; isolation of, 106–9, 121; likeness to Job, 128; maternal ideal and, 125–27, 133, 142; as Mother Ireland, 130; as New Woman, 93, 124; psychic telepathy of, 132–34, 136, 138; purification

of, 140; redemptive agency of, 125, 127–29, 131–33, 138, 142; symbiotic duality and, 130

Harker, Quincy (in *Dracula*), 140–42

Hawkins, Mr. (in *Dracula*), 89

Hildesheim, Immanuel (in *Dracula*), 138

Historicist scholarship, 2

Holmwood, Arthur (Lord Godalming; in *Dracula*), 20–21, 104–6, 117–18, 126–27; doppelgänger motif and, 111–12; as imperialist adventurer, 99–100

Hughes, Thomas, 18

Hungarian devolution, 54

Hunt, James, 62

Hybridity. *See* Colonial hybridity

Hyperfemininity, 17

Hypermasculinity, 45, 123

Imaginary register, 44, 142

Imperialism, 89–90, 139; correspondence with vampirism, 101; homosocial romance of, 101; masculinism of, 108, 127. *See also* British colonialism

Ireland, 1, 4, 30–31, 44, 73; ambiguous class formation in, 60; ethnological profile of, 24–25, 52–53; otherness to itself, 51, 53

Irigaray, Luce, 10

Irish, the, 3, 11, 12, 21, 26, 79, 135, 137; analogy to the Jews, 68; as immigrants to London, 60–62, 66, 103; martyrology and, 56–57; mixed identity formation among, 13, 25–27, 70; peasantry, 42, 136; self-alterity of, 44, 67; self-otherness of, 4, 71; symbiotic duality in, 48, 130. *See also* Anglo-Celts; Anglo-Irish, the; Celts; Celtic-Irish, the; Irish stereotypes

Irish Home Rule, 38, 46, 75, 77, 159n; Hungarian model for, 54–55; and imperialism, 23, 72, 153n; morality and, 45, 46; movement for, 22, 23, 65; nationalism and, 2, 7, 22, 45, 47, 55, 57, 58, 73, 147n; Parliament and, 54; and racialism, 68; Stoker's support for, 22, 27, 40, 54–55, 138, 143, 150n, 152n, 155n

Irish Question, 42, 46, 79; as analogy to

Eastern Question, 51, 54–55; domestic cosmopolitanism and, 22, 26, 142–43

Irish Republican Brotherhood, 57

Irish stereotypes: connection to vampire kind, 68; as criminal types, 61; as degenerative, 61–62, 68, 134; as dirty, 61; as drunkards, 29, 31, 34–35, 61; as feminine, 13, 15, 17, 45, 130, 133, 157n; as hysterical, 114; Paddy, 76, 114; as primitives or savages, 15, 23, 60–61, 62, 66, 75, 120; as simians, 61; as superstitious, 68, 135; as violent, 114. *See also* Celts, Celtic-Irish, the

"Irish Vampire, The" (Tenniel), 65

Irving, Henry, 12, 37–38, 40, 41, 76, 79

Irving, Laurence, 37–38

James II, 66, 101

Jews, the, 137; analogy to the Irish, 68; connection to vampire kind, 68; racial typology of, 68; sexual ethnology of, 68

John Bull, 17, 26, 75

Jouissance, 43, 79, 85

Joyce, James, 6, 54

Kingsley, Charles, 18, 61

Kline, Salli, 148n

Knox, Robert, 61

Kristeva, Julia, 10

Lacan, Jacques, 4, 42–43, 85–86, 142, 160n

Lady of the Shroud, The (Stoker), 77

Land Acts (1881, 1885), 45, 72

Land League, 45, 65

Land War (1879–82), 45

Lansbury, George, 137

Lecky, W. H., 16

Le Fanu, Sheridan, 9

Little England (in *Dracula*), 52, 74, 85, 121, 124, 126; blood consciousness of, 80, 82, 111–12, 114, 120, 125, 129, 132; collective anamorphosis of, 87; dualitism with Dracula, 82, 98, 109–12, 119, 125, 129, 134, 139, 160–61n; dualitism with Renfield, 118, 119; judgments of Dracula by,

58, 61, 133; manichean logic of, 115, 117, 121; self-defeating tactics of, 100, 105–10, 115, 118, 120, 125, 131–32; social connectivity achieved by, 140–43; turning Irish, 134–38; unconscious affiliation with Dracula by, 64, 82, 98, 100–101, 107–8, 111–12, 114–15, 117, 120, 130–31
Loerrsen, Joep, 56
Lombroso, Cesare, 61, 102
Loveday, H. J., 38
Lyceum Theatre, 38, 42, 77, 80, 117

Macintosh, Daniel, 61
MacManus, Terence Bellow, 57
MacNall, J. G. Smith, 22
MacSwiney, Terence, 136
Malchow, H. L., 69, 147n, 150–51n
Manchester Martyrs, 57
Manhood, ideal of, 17–18, 43, 45, 123, 142; Irish cultivation of, 57; prominence in Dracula of, 20–21; vampiric structure of, 124, 132–33; xenophobic structure of, 123–24, 133, 143
Mariolatry, 135, 161n
Masculine gender identity, 43, 45, 123
Master-slave dialectic, 113–14
Mephistopheles (Mons; in The Primrose Path), 31, 34, 36
Merford, Harry (in "The Dualitists"), 42–44, 47–49, 87, 130
Metrocolonialism, 3–4, 64, 66, 74, 119, 147n; allegorized, 45–46; in Dracula, 156n, 161n; duality and, 78, 112–13; social connectivity and, 130; Stoker and, 3–4, 7, 9–10, 18, 70, 72, 76
Metrocolonial subjectivity, 13, 42, 72; ambivalence of, 46, 48, 71, 75–78, 81, 136; colonial hybridity vs., 18; gendered, 18, 21; immixture of, 19, 22, 40–41, 46, 48, 73, 81, 119, 140, 141; likeness to vampiric condition, 18; metrocolonial unconscious and, 119; proximateness and, 76; psychoanalysis and, 48, 85
Metropolitan marriage, 12–13; the Harkers' marriage and, 93–94; Matthew Arnold's Celticism and, 26; in The Snake's Pass, 12–13, 42, 150n; Stoker's ancestry and, 17; vamping of Mina and, 92

Metropolitan society, 7, 9, 33–34, 38, 72–73; as degenerative, 63
Morash, Chris, 1, 24, 149n, 150n, 152n, 153n, 154n
Morgan, Matthew, 61
Morris, Quincy (in Dracula), 20, 100, 104, 118, 127; dualitism with Dracula, 98, 100; fate of, 139–40; as imperialist adventurer, 99–100
Moses, Michael Valdez, 1, 24, 149n, 150n, 152n, 153n, 154n
Mother Ireland, 58
Muldoon, Mr. (in The Primrose Path), 29

Nationality, 75–76; and race, 76
National League, 65
"Necessity for Political Honesty, The" (Stoker), 12, 23–27, 153n; anti-essentialism in, 24–27, 67; critique of racialism in, 26–27; domestic cosmopolitanism in, 26–27, 143
New Departure (1882), 45
New Woman, 93, 124
Nietzsche, Friedrich, 63
Nightmare. See Fantasy
Nordau, Max, 63

O'Brien, William, 39, 46, 56
O'Connell, Daniel, 22
O'Connor, T. P., 54
O'Grady, Standish, 22
Orange Order: in Dracula, 158n
Orientalism: of Jonathan Harker, 52, 65–66, 90, 96, 103, 129; occidentalism vs., 52
O'Sullivan, Jerry (in The Primrose Path), 24; ethnic parvenu status of, 32; immigration to London by, 30–35; Irish stereotypes and, 36; likeness to Stoker, 33
O'Sullivan, Katey (in The Primrose Path), 29–30, 32
Other, the, 86

Pale, the, 51–52, 72
Panopticon, the, 73
Parnell, Charles Stewart, 2, 54–55, 57, 65, 73, 156–57n
Parnell, Fanny, 56
Parnell, Mr. (in The Primrose Path), 29–31, 35

Parvenu, 72, 76, 160n

Patriarchy, 47, 107–8, 124

Personal Reminiscences of Henry Irving (Stoker), 12, 40, 77

Phallic signifier, 19, 43–46

Phantom, The (Boucicault), 12

Phoenix Park murders, 57, 73

Pick, Daniel, 141

Picture of Dorian Gray, The (Wilde), 160n

Plan of Campaign, the, 46, 136–38

Political cartoons, 61, 65

Popular fiction, 6, 8

Postcolonial theory, 1, 85

Pratt, Mary Louise, 92

Primrose Path, The (Stoker), 12–13, 27–37, 154n; autobiographical germ of, 33–34; critique of blood consciousness in, 35, 37, 69; doppelgänger motif in, 36; as emigration parable, 29, 35–36; ethnic antagonism in, 34; fantasy construction of, 33; Gothic devices in, 30–31, 36; recursive moral/political logic in, 37; as temperance tract, 29–30, 35–36, 154n

Proximateness, 44–45; metrocolonialism and, 70, 72, 76, 81

Proximity thesis, 27

Psychoanalysis, 8, 10–11; conventional views of, 78–79, 107; vampiric analogies in, 18, 44

Psychobiographical approach, 8, 10, 33

Race. *See* Blood

Racial atavism, 5, 15–16, 46, 62, 67

Racial degeneration, 1–2, 5, 8–10, 59, 134; as imperialist contagion, 62–63; reverse colonialism and, 62–63, 67, 147n; vampirism and, 62–63

Racial essentialism, 47, 53; as neurotic pathology, 78

Racialism. *See* Blood consciousness

Racial typologies, 63, 79–80; English, 96, 111; Jewish, 68. *See also* Anglo-Saxons; English, the; Irish stereotypes; Sexual ethnologies

Renfield, R. N., 52, 55, 84, 102; bond to Mina Harker, 117, 121–22; connection to Stoker, 117; death of, 122; dual allegiance of, 116–17, 119–20; dualitism with Little England, 118,
119; dualitism with Seward, 113–15; respectability of, 118

Richards, Jeffrey, 2

Sage, Victor, 9

Salisbury, Lord, 16, 54, 60, 75, 151n, 157–58n

Santon, Tommy (in "The Dualitists"), 42–44, 47–49, 87, 130

Schmitt, Cannon, 1, 8, 15, 148n, 150n

Scotch-Irish Protestants, 66

Seward, John (in *Dracula*), 6–7, 20, 107, 113, 161n; affiliation with Dracula, 115–17; dualitism with Seward, 113–15; as imperialist adventurer, 99–100, 110; Plan of Campaign and, 136; self-defeating tactics of, 118–19, 121–22

Sexual ethnologies, 151n; of Anglo-Saxons, 17, 19, 21, 26, 42; of Celts, 17, 19, 21, 26, 42, 45; of the English, 13, 130; of the Irish, 13, 15, 17, 45, 130, 133, 157n; of the Jews, 68

Shaughran, The (Boucicault), 12–13, 150n

Shaw, George Bernard, 75

Skal, David, 54, 139

Snake's Pass, The (Stoker), 12–13, 29, 42, 149–50n

Social connectivity, 115, 124; of Little England, 140–43; Mina Harker and, 125, 130, 132, 142

Spencer, Herbert, 61

Spenser, Edmund, 52

Stallybrass, Peter, 103

Stanley, Henry, 23

Stephenson, John Allen, 147n

Stewart, Bruce, 8, 147n, 148n, 149n

Stocking, George, 4

Stoker, Abraham (father), 16, 27

Stoker, Bram: ambiguous class status of, 9–10, 15, 27–28; ambitiousness of, 33–34, 37; ancestral narratives of, 16–17; Anglicanism and, 15; Anglo identifications of, 16, 19, 21–22, 27, 71, 102, 146n; anti-essentialist strategies of, 25, 67, 69, 80, 106, 143, 150n; attitude toward Henry Irving, 38, 80; awareness of Hungarian devolutionary model, 54; Celtic identifications of, 16, 19, 21, 146n; critical misconceptions of, 7, 15, 24, 150n; critique of British imperialism, 63, 68, 152–53n; critique of degeneration theory, 67, 80, 83; critique of identity politics, 40–41; critique of Matthew Arnold, 26; critique of racialism, 39–40, 60, 67, 80, 83, 102; domestic cosmopolitanism of, 23–25, 39–41, 46, 69; emigration anxiety of, 34, 37; ethnic parvenu status of, 33–34, 37–39, 64, 67, 69, 72–73, 76, 80, 87, 117; ethno-national ambivalence of, 9, 16–17, 22–23, 28, 39, 70, 76, 80, 82, 101, 133, 146n, 152n; gender anxiety of, 19; immigration to London, 13, 15, 28, 34, 39, 67, 72–73; immixed (Anglo-Celtic) ethnic heritage of, 9, 13, 15–17, 21–22, 27, 45–46, 67, 69, 71, 76–77, 101, 133; influence of gender ideals on, 17, 19; innovative use of Gothic conventions, 6, 9, 35, 47, 71, 74, 80, 84–85, 98, 111–13, 119, 124, 132, 134, 141; Irish brogue of, 38–39, 67; Irishness of, 2, 4, 15, 23–26, 133; literary methods of, 6, 12, 25, 35, 37, 47, 94, 98, 105, 109, 138; member of Irish Literary Society, 39; metrocolonial subject position of, 3–4, 7, 9–10, 18, 70, 72, 76; openness to psychoanalytic conceptions of, 86; parents' emigration, 28; parvenu strategy of critique, 80, 101–2, 105, 129–30, 139, 141; proximity thesis of, 27; racial politics of, 2, 9–10, 12, 25, 39–40, 60, 67, 80, 83, 102, 148n, 150n, 162n; response to ethnic stereotypes by, 38–39; sexual ambivalence of, 19, 21; status anxiety of, 11, 27–28, 72; strategy of political disavowal, 22–23, 39–40; support for British imperialism, 22, 63, 67–68, 101, 153n; support for Irish Home Rule, 22, 27, 40, 54–55, 138, 143, 150n, 152n, 155n; as target of ethnic resentment, 37–38, 77, 79–80; use of recursive logic, 12, 37, 50. See also Dracula; "The Dualitists"; "Necessity for Political Honesty, The"; The Primrose Path; "The Voice of England"

Stoker, Charlotte (mother), 16, 55, 152n
Stoker, Florence (wife), 38
Stoker, Noel (son), 152n
Sullivan, T. D., 137
Symbolic register, 44, 48, 142
Szekeles, the, 51, 112
Szgany, the, 157n

Tenniel, Sir John, 65, 157n
Thing, the: vampire as, 85, 128
Thor, 112, 162n
Tone, Wolfe, 56
"Tone's Grave" (Davis), 57
Toryism, 45–46, 60
Transylvania, 60, 65, 129; as dreamscape, 109, 136; ethnological profile of, 52–53; parallel to Ireland, 11, 51–53, 65
Tremayne, Peter, 1, 150n
Trinity College (Dublin), 24, 26–27, 40, 54; Historical Society, 22–23, 152–53n; Philosophical Society, 22

Ulysses (Joyce), 52
Unconscious, the, 107–8, 110; and the undead, 18
Unionism, 27–28, 60, 75
Union of Hearts, 137
United Kingdom, 3, 30, 41, 44, 62, 72, 76–77. See also Great Britain

Vampire hunters. See Little England
Vampires: blood sacrifice and, 58; breastfeeding and, 112, 124–27; emasculation and, 123; Irish folklore and, 52–53, 156n; jouissance of, 91–92; lore of, 85–86, 98, 105–6; racial incorporation and, 91–93; reproduction of, 82, 91–92, 97, 103
Van Helsing, Professor (in Dracula), 7, 21, 94, 113, 147n; as allusion to William of Orange, 101; blood sacrifice and, 136; collectivist ethos of, 108; complicity with Dracula, 105–6, 108, 111, 147n; as criminologist, 102; dualitism with Dracula, 103–11; erotics of blood and, 110; his contempt for servants, 104, 129; hysteria of, 21; occult authority of, 61, 86, 133–34; as patriarchal lawgiver, 107–

8; racialism of, 104–5; Roman Catholicism of, 101, 130, 135; unreliability of, 147n

Vel, 4, 147n

"Voice of England, The" (Stoker), 12–13, 77, 79; anti-essentialism in, 78; critique of identity politics in, 41, 77–78; domestic cosmopolitanism in, 40–41, 69; ethnic antagonism in, 40–42; as personal allegory, 78; recursive moral and political logic in, 103; support for Irish Home Rule in, 40–41, 138

Westenra, Lucy (in *Dracula*), 21, 104, 120, 125, 160n; doppelgänger motif and, 84; dual Irish associations of, 65–66; as Erin, 66; rape of, 110–13; as Thing, 111; vamping of, 49, 56, 59, 128; as vampire, 105–6

White, Allon, 103

Wicke, Jennifer, 148n

Wilde, Lady Jane (pseud. "Speranza"), 39, 53, 57

Wilde, Oscar, 39, 160n

William of Orange, 66, 101, 135

Wolf, Leonard, 95, 98, 109, 156

Yeats, W. B., 39, 53, 57, 155n, 157n

Young, Robert J. C., 19, 25–27

Young Ireland, 26, 57, 67, 154n

Žižek, Slavoj, 11, 18, 152, 160n

Zwanger, Jules, 69, 15

JOSEPH VALENTE is the author of *James Joyce and the Problem of Justice: Negotiating Sexual and Colonial Difference.* He is also the editor of *Quare Joyce* and the coeditor of *Disciplinarity at the Fin de Siècle.* He is currently finishing a book entitled "Contested Territory: Race and Manhood in Modern Irish Literature." His essays have appeared in numerous academic journals, including *Critical Inquiry, ELH, Narrative, Modern Fiction Studies, Novel,* and *College Literature.*

Composed in 10/13 Sabon
with Sabon display
by Celia Shapland
for the University of Illinois Press
Designed by Dennis Roberts
Manufactured by Thomson-Shore, Inc.

University of Illinois Press
1325 South Oak Street
Champaign, IL 61820-6903
www.press.uillinois.edu

DATE DUE

Spring 2004 Reserve	
Fall 2005	Reserve
Reserve	Fall 2007